LEFT OF LONDON

LEFT OF LONDON

L. ELYSE KINYOUN

DEDICATION

To my husband who read his first romance novel reading this.
Calm down. I didn't kill off the cat.

To my sister who won't read this until it's an audio book.
I'm sorry I didn't kill off the cat.

Prologue

These stones haven't always been this jagged.

The ascent up to Mam Tor's summit took the three of us twice as long as the internet claimed it would. Two of us are panting like dogs, and "I told you so" might earn me a shove to the bottom. Climbing down these steps isn't making my thighs scream the way they did on the way up, but it's requiring a level of focus I've never had.

This hike isn't really a hike. It's a one kilometer trail of steep stairs leading up to a breathtaking peak. It's said to be a half hour round trip, but it took that long just to reach the top. I can't say it wasn't worth it.

The view across the ridge and green hills is otherworldly. I'd climb twice as high to see half as much. It attracts travelers from all over. We're lucky we missed the mass of social media influencers that flock here for the sunrise. Five in the afternoon has been lovely, save for the fierce wind and blinding sun.

We managed to haul a bottle of cheap wine and a bag of crisps to the top. Sitting cross-legged on the thick grass, we bantered about bridesmaids dresses and the best deodorants. If the afterlife is like this, I'd be glad to die now.

I peer behind me at the two women I could never navigate life without. The one at the back has been my dearest friend since primary school. The one between us, the one we're sandwiching with protection, is the force of nature that raised me. Her seventy year-old body is strong by most standards, but her balance is making me paranoid. She insisted on doing this again. I think we last came when I was fifteen. I'll admit she's been as steady today as she was then - so far, at least.

Lana finished nursing programme a year ago. I'm confident she could clean up a tumble if needed. It's nice to have a human first aid kit these days, but I would've made sure she spent the weekend in the Peak District with us anyway. The fact that she's so accomplished while I'm still a dish washer doesn't piss me off the way it used to.

"You alright?" I shout after them both. "You won't need to exercise for weeks after this!"

"My calves will be chiseled to perfection!" Lana laughs and shouts over to me. She can't pretend this is challenging for her in the slightest. She's an athlete to her core.

I notice our fearless matriarch in the middle is starting to get wobbly in the knees. She looks up at me with concern, but has a determined smile that says she isn't slowing down. This woman is indestructible. I'd love to think it's genetic, but no one's more fragile than I am.

"I've got her," Lana assures me. I'm certain she does.

I turn back toward the climb down and flatten against the left hand rail as another walker squeezes past. I'm starting to feel dizzy. The wind's picking up at my back, and some cruel force in my brain is pulling me close to the edge. I grip the rail until my knuckles turn from brown to white. I continue down one step at a time.

1, 2, 3, 4...

I realize the rail ends for a portion of the walk, and I'm not sure I can stay upright until it starts again. There's a steep drop on both sides. Each slab I set foot on feels like it's tilted downward, not level enough to keep me vertical. I pause and hear a soothing voice just behind me.

"Easy, my Mira. Trust yourself. You trotted down this same slope like a pony years ago."

An eternity passes while I hold my breath and clench my hands to my chest for the seven steps it takes to reach the next hand rail.

1, 2, 3, 4, 5, 6, 7...

I'm relieved enough to throw a tantrum. "I think I'm going to be sick. The website said this was the easy walk! This is pathetic. We're lying in the dirt by the car for twenty minutes when we get to the bottom. I'm never -"

I hear gravel slide, and a faint crack. A walker far behind us gasps, and my head spins backwards.

All I register next is an empty bottle of Chardonnay rolling over the edge, and a pool of crimson seeping from a crown of curls.

One

February

OLLIE

I'm not sure when the car wash became my Friday evening therapy of choice. My mind quiets down, muscle memory kicks in, and I can pull out of the parking lot feeling like the inside of my SUV isn't as much of a mess as my brain is. It doesn't hurt that it kills time when I'm not in meetings or reading emails until my eyes bleed. I've almost gotten good enough at scrubbing coffee splashes off the steering wheel without ruining my nails. I'd be happy if I never got a manicure again, but it'd be unheard of for Olivia Kincade to show up to the office with gel polish missing from three fingers. I refuse to trade my open coffee mug for a travel cup, so the cycle continues.

I never imagined I'd be trying to come up with ways to fill up my evenings. Ten years ago, I was rushing back home from a business trip in time to shuttle a twelve-year-old to Jiu Jitsu - or whatever my ex's fixation was at the time. I savored those car rides with Judah. I lived for the moments when we'd sit in silence until he shocked me with a philosophical question, or a new word he learned on the school bus. I lived for it, because I was his safe space and he was mine. Now, I'm pulling out of the car wash parking lot wishing I'd found old fries under the passenger seat because it'd mean he was here. I need to stop calling him so much if I want him to keep coming home to Chicago from Indianapolis every month. He's the only thing my mind migrates to when it's quiet.

I peek into my mirror to make sure the sneaky tears in my eyes dried up only to be caught off-guard by the gray bags hanging under them. When will I get used to this person? Since moving to the city from the suburbs a few years ago, I'm down a few sizes, which feels good. I'm starting to see the legs I had in high school again. I've formed a bad habit of trying new hair products, so my dark auburn head has more shine to it these days. Still, my face looks like it's aged a decade.

"See ya, Ollie!" shouts the attendant at the exit.

I roll down my window to make sure he sees my genuine smile. "Have a good night, Darius!"

I don't think he remembers that Judah played lacrosse with his older brother in high school. That kid comes from a tough home, but he's pure sunshine. It felt right to introduce myself with the name that people outside of work have always called me. Olivia has never felt like a real person, even if her name is etched in plaques.

I've spent eighteen years in Public Relations, all at the same firm. It'd be a dream job for a lot of people, and I constantly remind myself of that. It funds a comfortable life - the kind I never thought was in the cards.

When I got pregnant with Judah right after high school in Kentucky, Nathan and I did everything in our power to support ourselves. I can't imagine what I'd be doing right now if we'd followed the biggest dreams we had at the time instead of becoming parents at eighteen. I wanted to be a cosmetologist or an English teacher. Nate didn't have a plan beyond playing basketball at UK.

Nathan was a preacher's kid – a PK in every stereotypical sense. My parents decided to join a church in my sophomore year, right after 9/11. At Wednesday youth group, Nate and I hit it off instantly. We went to different high schools, but both got a summer job at the local plant nursery after graduating. We found an excuse to be together every day that summer.

They never said it out loud, but I know his parents thought of me as a short-lived rebellious streak. I didn't fit their criteria. I wasn't born blonde and obedient. Perhaps they hated the purple dye I had in my hair. Maybe it was because I needed help reconciling an invasion on Iraq with the Ten Commandments.

The embarrassment my pregnancy caused our families was crystal clear. Nathan Kincade, the golden first-born of four, gave up his scholarship and any hope of a relationship with his dad. My mother hinted at terminating the pregnancy before the news made its way around. Of course, she wanted a say in every decision after I insisted on keeping it. It's funny how we often don't know our parents until we're parents.

Nonetheless, our moms threw an extravagant baby shower in the church basement. It felt more like a funeral. A procession of housewives smelling of coconut lime verbena hugged me like I was terminally ill. My best friend, Paige, cut the tension with inappropriate jokes. She's the only reason we got through that day. She's the only reason I get through a lot of things. Nate and I left with baby gear we couldn't possibly have afforded ourselves and a shared motivation to move as far away as we could.

I make a sharp right turn, and my empty coffee mug from this morning tips on my clean passenger seat. It wasn't empty.

At nine months pregnant and living with Nate's Aunt Kathy, we got married in a Kentucky courthouse. We had Judah at the local hospital, and both worked grueling hours while Aunt Kathy took care of him. By Judah's first birthday, we had a way out of that town. Birthday cards and twice-a-year phone calls stopped years ago. We build whatever we have - whatever we *had* - on our own.

Nathan landed an entry level job with a luxury landscape design company in the Chicago suburbs and quickly moved up the ranks. I earned an online degree while keeping Judah at home. We were in a rough part of town then. I applied to every full-time job I saw and took an administrative role with the first one that called, Finch & Associates.

I whip into the drive-thru at my usual coffee spot and order an iced latte with one pump of hazelnut. I forgot to order decaf. I'll regret it later.

After begging for two years, I became a junior consultant and found myself getting assigned to more high-profile accounts. I became a person that felt like an alter ego. I traded a bright wardrobe for tailored neutrals. I swapped cheap makeup for good skincare. I learned to make eye contact and smile when I passed people in the hall. I learned to speak in short sentences, even when my brain is spinning at 2X speed. I stopped cursing aloud and started cursing more in my head, which is a surprisingly good composure tactic. When someone does something impressive, I make sure they know it. I remember how important validation was to me once.

When Fortune 500 executives didn't question my advice, I questioned if they knew how much of a train-wreck I feel like half the time. It took time for me to accept that people don't experience me the way I experience myself. Olivia Kincade has a reputation for being steady; confident. I'm not sure I'd describe Ollie that way.

"We're out of hazelnut. Sorry!" My favorite barista apologizes at the window. "Vanilla?"

I've got to cut back on sugar. "You can skip the syrup. Thanks!"

At 41, I'm the firm's top consultant and I don't question if I'm good at my job anymore. I don't think much about how I'm perceived at all. I've gotten less excited about landing big clients. When I'm not frustrated with the stories I help people tell, I guess the job is a healthy outlet. I'm not sure how to feel gratitude and jaded at once.

What I do question is if this is all there is until I retire, have even more time to fill, then die with a clean car and an outstanding collection of Pilates socks. I'd volunteer at the senior center again if they didn't guilt-trip me for missing weeks when I'm on the road. Maybe the food bank makes sense. It's minimal people interaction. I could start looking for a good hand-knotted rug for under the dining table no one sits at. How does one host a dinner party when their only friend lives over a thousand miles away?

Judah's call rings through the car. He rarely calls first. Something's broken or he's broke.

"Hey, kid."

"Mom, do oil changes cost $130?"

"Who's telling you $130?"

"This place in Indy. I'm not coming home next weekend, so I need to do it here."

"Why the heck aren't you co — . never mind. That's more than you'd pay at the place your dad likes, but normal for that car."

"K. Can you send me $130? Maybe $200?"

"Judah"

"I'm doing better, Mom. This one crept up on me. The light just came on. I'll pay you back." Hilarious.

"Pay me back by coming home the weekend after next."

"Yeah. Love you, Mama."

"Love you most."

I can't pretend my recent transaction history with Judah pisses me off. Cutting the cord is what a good mom would do. It also means I'd be picking him up on the side of the road in another state when he blows his paychecks on food delivery instead of getting an oil change.

I pull over to send him $200, tell myself its self-preservation, and pull back onto the highway.

Why the hell is Nathan calling?

"Hey"

"Does the car you bought Judah take $130 oil? He just text me."

"I took care of it. He must have called me when you didn't reply."

"Oh. Ok, great. You know I would have taken this one."

I finish the last sip of my iced latte. "Don't worry about it. You paid enough for repairs on the hatchback before it bit the dust."

"He said he's really liking the internship you got him, but uh, the company doesn't sound super stable."

"Stable-ish."

"What does that mean?"

"They aren't hitting their sales targets but are in better shape than other startups I work with."

"The latest article I read said they were experiencing unprecedented growth".

"They are. They hadn't seen any before last quarter."

"Right, so, unprecedented is the word you handed them because they went from zero to something - or negative to net zero."

"Mm."

If I start talking about how excruciating that engagement was, I'll spiral.

He chuckles. "Classic. I've never liked how good you are at this stuff."

"Me neither. Anyway, it's good for him to be there right now. He can come back home if it goes south. My apartment's got space, and—

"

"OR… he could look for a better opportunity in Indianapolis and figure it out."

"We're not rehashing this. We would have killed for help when we were that age."

"We proved we didn't need it, so maybe less coddling would — "

"Nate."

"Sorry."

Silence.

"Did you guys have a good time a few weeks ago? He said he isn't coming home next weekend."

"Yeah, did he, uh, tell you about it?"

"'bout what?"

"I've been seeing someone."

That light is red. Damn it. I slam on my brakes. My gym bag flies into the floor.

He clears his throat and continues, "I've been seeing her...for a while. The three of us went to dinner at Murphy's."

It's been two years. It's been two years. This is fine. This is fine.

My voice ticks up to a sweet octave he knows is fake. "Do I know her?"

"No, no, I met her through Jared at work. His sister-in-law. She's a chiropractor."

Say nice things. Say nice things.

"Nice! What's her name?"

"Natalie."

"Cute."

"Smart-ass." I detect his blue eyes rolling the way they always do when he says that.

"No, no, it is cute. You're Nate and Nat."

"OK, stop." I can hear his smile through the phone.

"Love that for you." I know he can hear mine.

My voice lowers to my usual tone. "Seriously."

"Thank you."

"I'm parking. I've gotta go. I'm sure I'll get to meet her at some point. I actually have this weird pinch in my neck, and maybe she..."

"Bye, Ol." Still smiling.

"Bye."

I tap End Call on the touch screen too aggressively and blow out a breath.

I didn't have a chance at a good night's rest anyway. I remember the box of Cinnamon Toast Crunch in the pantry and thank myself before hauling my work bag, gym bag, water bottle, coffee mug, and empty latte cup inside.

Two

February

"We're under contract with Sparkline" James Finch announces as the team settles around the conference table five minutes late, as usual. I've always called him Jim. He's a short and stout character with a thick gray mustache. He's got a head of curly hair that a lot of men his age would kill for.

"Mark and Olivia played a huge part in winning this client."

The team interjects with obligatory claps. Mark's beaming. I'm glad Mark's getting recognized. He's still new to the company and took a while to get comfortable.

I'm aware that Jim has no idea what it took to secure this account. His admin, Martha, knows this business inside and out and feeds him all he needs to know to say the right things in front of a room. She could do all our jobs with her eyes closed but probably makes the same amount of money per month that Jim drops on one of his watches. It's funny when you consider he still needs her to tell him what time it is. I know I've been her favorite ever since I trained her on my former role. I feel like she's watched me grow up.

Candice and Sharon sit to my left. I've always liked Candace. She's more strategic than she realizes and doesn't put up with Davis' cockiness. She has twin daughters and great porcelain veneers. I'd probably have lunch with her if she asked, but I'd never ask first. That's not my thing. I've learned I get annoyed with people too quickly. I suddenly stop being available, and it bruises their egos. The kind to do is avoiding it altogether.

Sharon's between Candice and Davis. She acts like more of a ditz than she is when she's in meetings with Davis - married Davis. She slaps him on the arm when he makes a joke, and her hand lingers a little long.

Someone, please slap her.

I'm already thinking about what to pack for Detroit to help get the Sparkline account off the ground. I should find a Pilates studio there this time. I hope Mark isn't sent with me again. He's a genuinely nice guy, and objectively attractive - about six feet tall and salt-and-pepper hair. He's probably ten years older than I am. I'd never date a colleague, but my track record says I'd run in the opposite direction even if he wasn't.

Mark catches me staring blankly in his direction. I look away. I think the slate blue shirt he's wearing is new.

Eight months after I moved out of the house and into my apartment in Logan Square, I'd been putting all my energy into furnishing and decorating the new place. It did turn out pretty amazing. Paige was visiting from Salt Lake City where she's built somewhat of an interior design empire. She pressured me to create an account on a dating app, which is the most terrifying thing I've ever done.

I'd never been on an adult date, at least not as an unmarried person. In one month, I endured five first dates. Three were horrific, mostly because I was horrifically awkward. One was mediocre. One was good enough that I continued seeing him for several weeks.

Bryce wasn't perfect, but he was a catch. He opened doors for people. He stopped to pet dogs. He took his work as a podiatrist seriously, but not himself. I liked that. I couldn't get past the weird music he listened to and how picky an eater he was. I also hated how often I checked my phone for his texts, even though he'd usually respond within minutes. I wasn't convinced he was into me anyway. Part of me still feels bad for ghosting him. He probably moved on quickly.

Paige claims I looked for reasons that Bryce and I wouldn't work just as I was starting to feel something. She thinks I was protecting myself. I think it was more about not wasting his time. I was starting to feel myself liking him less and didn't want to drag things out. Maybe what I disliked was how he pulled my focus. It was like giving someone else control over my emotional thermostat. Work and Judah require enough regulation. I'm not sure romance is worth giving that power to a third thing. It's easier for me to feel something when it's on my terms. It was all too soon after the separation anyway. Thank God Judah never knew.

I'm zoning out. What did he say?

"... so, Mark will stand up the Sparkline account in Detroit. He's capable of handling his first solo job at this point." Jim explains as he pats Mark on the back too hard.

Why did Mark get that account? Jim senses I'm checking out. He thinks I'm disengaged. That's probably what he wants to meet about this afternoon.

The day after Nate brought home the papers for me to sign two years ago, Jim knew something had happened. He was more supportive than I could have asked for, forcing me to take time off to manage the move. It's been too long to use the split as an excuse. I'll have to let him call me out. It's annoying, but I'm not rattled like I would have been years ago.

The meeting adjourns and the team starts to pack up.

Martha slides over in her rolling chair with her sleek gray bob, loafers, and laptop. "Jim needs to move your three o'clock with him up to eleven. Can you meet now?"

Here we go.

"Can he do 11:05? I drank way too much coffee this morning and I need a bio break."

"I'll plug you in at 11:15". She smirks. "... so, you have time to make another cup. I don't think the chat with him will take long."

Because telling me to get my shit together doesn't take long.

"You're a treasure, Martha."

"Oh, shut up." She mumbles and winks. She's my favorite, too.

* * *

I walk through the second floor of the office. Jim let me convince him to remodel it last year. It's modern, but warm. He took my advice to tone down Finch & Associates' signature bright orange to a burnt orange color. It pairs well with the wood-grain cabinets and matte black lighting. I wish he would have opted to replace the floors. Maybe that would have dipped into quarterly bonuses.

At the latte machine, Mark's stirring a packet of honey into his cappuccino. I put my coffee mug from home under the dispenser and press the decaf option, then the strong setting.

"Back to Detroit you go. Congrats!" I smile at him. Jeez, that shade of blue is his color.

"Yeah! Thanks! My first stop will probably be that sandwich place at the airport."

"Jealous. Order a French dip for me. I still dream about it."

There was no way to gracefully eat a sandwich dipped in au jus in front of that man, but it was divine.

"I've got you." He laughs a real laugh. "I uh... would love your advice on some things for when I get out there."

"My afternoon just freed up. Wanna meet? Davis might have some good pointers to share, too."

"I was wondering if we could grab dinner, actually. Like, maybe tomorrow night before I head out Wednesday. Just... casual."

I glance at his face and can't tell if he truly thinks of this as casual. My coffee is done dispensing, and I grab a few pods of half & half.

"Kincade, you ready?" Jim calls into the break area.

I turn back to Mark. "I'll check my calendar, yeah. I have a thing tomorrow night, so we might need to catch up later." The thing is doing laundry and watching *House Hunters*.

The defeat in his face. The dimples. He probably did just want some advice and nothing else. I adjust my brown wool blazer and walk into Jim's office with my mug and self-loathing in tow.

* * *

"How was your weekend?"

"Good! Caught up on some to-dos. Planned a little getaway with a friend. Nothing outrageous."

I sit in the chair on the left facing his desk.

"You're doing alright, Olivia?" The air turns a bit thicker.

"I am, I think. Things feel... routine."

"Judah's good?"

"Judah's good." Ish.

"Glad to hear it." I can tell he's sincere.

"Did you want to talk to me about why I didn't get the Sparkline account?"

"I do."

Pause. He closes a manila folder he has in front of him, and studies my face just before I break the silence.

"I'm sorry. I haven't been as focused as I usually am. I probably need someone to train. Or a new kind of project. Maybe Candace needs a partner in Phoenix."

"I think you need a new challenge. I agree."

Long pause.

"Mark's going to do a fine job in Detroit, but he couldn't have landed that account without you there. I heard the Sparkline team pushed for us to send you specifically last month."

Thanks, Martha.

"Maybe. Mark was the one that won them over."

"I know." he continues, "There's a larger client we just got - one I've been working with directly. I want you on it. It'd be a long project, but big."

"The one in Portland?"

"No, a bit longer of a flight." He smirks and waves at someone passing by the glass door behind me.

"OneDer is launching a new feature in their app - something really innovative."

"OneDer, like the travel booking platform? That's huge."

"Exactly. This new feature they want to release is the only of it's kind from what I know. How we help them position it will be critical – not just for them, for us."

"I can take it."

"Olivia, their office is in London. I'd want you there for a while. Probably six months - maybe nine."

Hard swallow. There's no way.

I'd have to sublet my apartment. Where would I keep my car?

I'm supposed to be going to Spain with Paige.

Judah.

"The UK." It's more of a statement than a question.

"Yes. We'd obviously set you up with a nice place to stay. You wouldn't need a car, but we could get you one if you happened to need it. We'd give your other accounts to some of these new consultants so you could focus."

"OK, right. I do need some... time. I think an old client we had works for them now, Theo Bryant. It might be nice to work with him again."

"Sure, but I'd expect you do need some time to consider. I'll send you their file. Look it over. Let me know by the end of this week, if you can. I want someone there in a month, and I'd rather not send Davis."

I stand up from my chair and my knee pops. Lovely. I'm getting too old for this circus.

"Olivia", he makes sure he has my attention. "I think this would be good for you."

"Thanks. Thanks for thinking of me. This is big for us."

"It is."

I pour out the lukewarm coffee I never touched, and don't remember the drive home.

Three

February

"London?!" Paige shouts through the phone. I have her video chat propped up on the glass coffee table while I sort laundry, just like every Monday night.

"It'd be impossible. It's a nice thought, I guess. I just can't take off for a year with everything I have going on."

"You mean like your weekly manicure? Or the boyfriend you don't have?"

"Ouch. No, it just feels nuts. I have a routine I like. Judah isn't adulting super well yet."

"You don't like your routine."

"I do like my routine."

"You like the predictability of it, sure. You're bored."

"I'm content."

"You're numb, and Judah's fine. Nate could get to him just as fast as you can if something came up."

"True." I sometimes almost hate her. She knows me better than I know me, I think.

Paige has been my best friend since we were twelve. In the seventh grade, we both tried out for the role of Glinda in *The Wizard of Oz*. She got the part because she looked the part. I was cast as an apple tree and ultimately dropped out of the whole thing. Redemption came later when I married the boy we both had a crush on in high school. It clearly turned out well...

I'm getting dizzy watching her walk with her phone. "You know, only psychos take video calls while they're grocery shopping." She bends over to check yogurt labels, and I notice her blonde hair is shorter than she usually goes when she gets a trim.

"Then I'm proud to be Exhibit A. One year isn't that long, Ollie. You did talk about wanting to go back to London after the last time we went. You could visit that food market we didn't get to see like a hundred times."

"Borough Market. I could eat chocolate drenched strawberries every day until I'm sick.

"Exactly."

"I wouldn't even know how to find someone to rent this place until I'm back. I'm not giving it up. I don't know if that's allowed."

"Don't let a stranger set foot in that gorgeous apartment. Have Judah check on it when he's in town."

"If he doesn't decide to stop coming home altogether, sure. He's perfectly comfortable when I can send him money from anywhere."

I'm half joking, half venting.

"Stop. You know that's not true. He's obsessed with you. He'd be over the moon about visiting you in London, as would I."

How is she managing to make me consider this? If anyone gets why I wouldn't want to shake things up, it's Paige. It took me months to stop running on adrenaline when I first moved to the city. I went into a deep spiral, making sure every corner of my apartment was perfectly organized and perfectly decorated. I spent countless hours on Pinterest and countless dollars online shopping.

It was Paige that pulled me out of my toxic distraction-seeking and helped me get comfortable with my new normal. She made sure I was leaving the house when I wasn't working. She made sure I wasn't forgetting to eat. She gently nudged me to stop saying "we" by accident when I should have been using "I". She's always been the one to push me toward what needed to be next for me, and maybe she's doing that now.

"You wouldn't be bummed that Spain is off the table?"

"Find me a Spanish man in London before I get there, and I'll be fine. Someone who speaks English is a plus, but not necessary. Gracias in advance."

I've told her that her Bad Bunny playlist won't prepare her for Barcelona.

"I can't believe you're talking me into this."

"You deserve more than you let yourself have, Ol – and I'm not talking about more leggings that cost a Benjamin."

"Don't knock it until you try it. They're life-changing."

"Then maybe you do need more." She laughs at herself. "Just promise me one thing."

"Not likely". Probably likely.

"Tell Jim tomorrow. If you wait until Friday, you'll chicken out."

"I'll see what I can do."

"Ice-cream's melting. Gotta check out. Text me tomorrow."

* * *

What am I doing? The TV is on, but there's no way I can scroll through shows I've already seen and decide on something to distract me. I can shuffle through seven streaming apps for hours without deciding, even on days when I'm not considering abandoning my life to escape across the globe for six months.

Is that what the thought of London feels like? An escape? Does it feel like a trap? Is where I am a trap that I made for myself – a peaceful, millennial-beige trap?

I look up at the pinch-pleat drapes I had custom made to fit the floor-to-ceiling windows. This unit is the only one in the building with towering windows like this. The white walls can feel sterile if the overhead lights are turned on, but through trial and error I've become the world's best at styling cozy lamps and overpriced soy candles.

The first new piece of furniture I bought was this linen sectional Nate was so opposed to us having before. It took three months to come in and had to be completely disassembled to make it up the stairwell. It got put together just in time for me to cry myself to sleep on it when Judah decided to go to Florida for spring break instead of coming home. He slept on it for two nights when he got the flu after graduating with his software engineering degree last fall. He has a perfectly good bed in the second bedroom. I assume he wanted to be closer to my bedroom but would never admit it.

I think about the hours it took me to put together the cane-back counter stools that look like they belong in a French cafe. Paige sat in one while I showed off the amateur latte art I'd taught myself to do with my fancy espresso machine. The world's most gorgeous set of matching white coffee mugs sit on an olive-wood board right next to it. They're dishwasher safe, which reminds me of how much I love this dishwasher.

I pick myself up off the couch and make my way to the bedroom.

Nate offered to let me bring our old California king-sized bed here when I left. Even if the bed-frame was still my style, the mattress never would have made it around the entryway corner. That meant I could splurge on the iron canopy bed I'd been eyeing, and Egyptian cotton sheets he would have found ridiculous. I crawl under the fluffy duvet and wonder what it'd cost to ship my memory foam pillows to London. I could pack my silk pillowcase.

I switch off the lamp.

I made this place for me. I think it's the only thing I've ever done just for me. Piece by piece, I created the way it feels, and the way it calms my mind.

I wove the net that caught me when life turned sideways, even if I had seen it coming for years, even if I couldn't have done it without selling my soul to Finch & Associates. It doesn't get more safe, more comfortable than this.

Is comfort the thing I crave anymore?

I'm not sure I crave anything.

* * *

"Are you a sushi kind of gal, or do you eat French dip sandwiches at every meal?" Mark takes a bite that was a tad too big. "No judgment, just curious."

I decided that if he truly did need some advice before taking off for Detroit, I should be available for him. I remember how alone I felt when I'd just started.

"I like the occasional California roll. I'm quite cultured in that way."

He chuckles. "So you're not really into sushi? We didn't have to come here, we could've –"

"No, I know. I wanted to come. Not for the sushi. I want to help. This is a big deal, this account. I'm excited for you."

He's quiet for a few moments, probably realizing he added too much wasabi to that last bite.

"Yeah, I appreciate that." He takes a sip of water. "I also think we work well together, you know? We make a good team."

"Hm, yeah you might be right. Sparkline thought so"

"I think we have fun working together, right?"

He has the same look on his face he had at the coffee machine earlier when he asked to meet - hopeful.

I've worked with more than one new consultant throughout the years that cozied up to me with a self-serving agenda. Usually, it's because they think I can help them get ahead. I don't know if people think I'm feeding Jim names of who should get the high-profile projects. They don't realize what a force of nature Martha is behind the scenes.

I'm genuinely happy to spend time with people when they're up-front about wanting advice. I'm less enthused about giving them my time when they want ride my coattails and disguise it as friendship. I wouldn't know what to do with friendship if I had it – other than Paige, of course.

Mark clearly wants help. He asked me for it. That's straight-forward enough. He doesn't need to sell me on some notion that we're work buddies, though he seems to be a stand-up guy.

"I do think we have fun working together." I divert the conversation. "In this case, you're a one-man show, so let's set you up for success."

We go on to talk through how Mark might go about building relationships at Sparkline that serve Finch well long-term. We discuss which initiatives he might recommend they prioritize first. At first, he listens intently and asks a few great questions about navigating team dynamics. His interest tapers off after ten minutes or so.

We split the check and walk outside into the sharp Chicago cold. Why the hell did I decide to walk here?

"Maybe we can do this again when I'm back. Maybe... talk less about work. No sushi next time!"

That eager face again. I pull my hood up over my head and snap the buttons at my neck, not breaking eye contact.

When I don't reply, he continues "Did you walk here? Can I walk you home - maybe call an Uber?"

"No, I'm alright."

This isn't going to be the thing I think he wants it to be.

"I'm close by. Safe travels, Mark! You're going to crush it."

"Yeah, thanks. Get home safe."

I walk directly into the freezing wind for what seems like the entire way to my building and wish I'd prioritized the laundry over this.

Four

March

OLLIE

The elevator in this building is tiny, but I knew better than to try to lug two massive suitcases up the stairs after the fiasco with the revolving door. I'll have a nice bruise on my shin for a week or two. I don't think I packed any sunless tanner to disguise it.

226. 226. 226.

I unlock apartment number 226. The second-floor studio sits on the third level of the building. I was quickly reminded of how that works here when I got off on the second level.

The space is bright but dated. The carpet needs replacing. The bed looks comfortable and the appliances in the kitchenette look new. The bathroom is bigger than I would have expected for this building. They probably had to expand the door-frame to install the deep vanity. The tile shower doesn't seem to have been remodeled when the rest was, but it's clean.

My phone goes off with a video call.

"How was the flight?" Paige's energy exceeds mine by far, but that's not new.

"I can't ever sleep in those lie-flat seats."

"Poor thing. Your life is hard."

I make a face at her.

"Are you in the apartment?"

"I just got here. It's not bad. The grocery store on the corner looks OK, and there's a cute restaurant across the street that I don't remember seeing when I looked up the map a few days ago. It must be new."

"When do you go to the office?"

"Tomorrow morning, if I can find it. It's supposed to be walkable from here. I might leave early enough to see if that gym nearby looks sketchy."

"I don't think you're in a sketchy part of town."

"Sketchy comes in all income brackets."

"Ha! You know that best." She does, too.

Paige stayed in Kentucky after Nate, Judah, and I left. She had every intention of finishing an online degree in Interior Design until she didn't. She took off to Denver, which seemed to be a radically uncalculated move. For a long time, she made ends meet as a waitress and an assistant to a local designer. In some turn of events that happened too fast for me to recall, she started her own Interior Design business.

She struggled for the past fifteen years, then business boomed out of nowhere. She eventually moved her home base from Denver to Salt Lake City, which makes sense being that her reputation took root in the LDS community. She spends her days designing interiors for wealthy housewives and loves every second of it. I love every second of the stories she tells.

"Text me later. It's way before my wake-up time."

"Will do. I'm going to find food."

My appetite is beating out my exhaustion. I drag myself to the nearest sandwich shop.

I walk around with a tomato and mozzarella baguette in my left hand and my phone in my right. It's probably a good idea to find

OneDer's office ahead of time to make sure I'm not late in the morning. I have no idea what time zone my body thinks it's in.

I stroll along the side of Hyde Park. It's late March, so plenty of families are meandering and pushing strollers - pushchairs. Professionals with an array of accents walk quickly, talking to each other or to their phones. I forgot how vibrant this place is.

I walk on the right sidewalk – pavement, toward the dot on the map I'm being routed to and realize it's on the opposite side of the street. I keep walking to make my way to the next crosswalk, then backtrack to OneDer's main entrance. It's Monday, so there's plenty of foot traffic at lunch hour. There's no use trying to go in. I won't have badge access until tomorrow, and I'm in a frumpy sweatshirt. At least now I know how not to be the lost American chick in the morning, which is a good start.

I turn back toward the way I came to see a group walking in my direction. I think one of them is Lynn Miller, the VP Jim had been working with. We had one video call before I flew out, so she hopefully won't recognize me in my sweats and hat if I keep my head - "

"Olivia!"

Damn it. Theo looks wildly different. He wore locs and about thirty more pounds the last time I saw him. He reaches for a quick hug.

"Hi, Olivia! Pleased to meet you in person. You're early." Lynn is just as warm as she was on screen. Her ebony skin is gorgeous against her butter yellow scarf.

"I just landed. I'm sorry for..." I gesture to my outfit. "I wanted to make sure I knew where I was going tomorrow morning."

"Mission accomplished!" Theo grins. "Glad you're here. I told them you're the best there is." He nods toward two others in the group who are deep in conversation and headed past me.

One is an insanely tall red-headed man. He's wearing a wool quarter-zip, and his shoes cost more than my rent. I'm pretty sure he's CMO Craig Hill.

The younger man with him is wearing all black with olive skin and thick, dark hair. He's the level of attractive that's almost inhuman, and he probably knows it. That type always does.

I turn back to Theo and Lynn, "I appreciate that. I'm looking forward to working with you. Your team has already laid good groundwork from what I hear."

Lynn seemed to like that response. "We'll let you get back to your stroll. The team's eager to meet you tomorrow."

"Enjoy your afternoon." When they turn away, I knock the baguette crumbs I just noticed off my chest, not that I have much of a shelf for them to land on.

* * *

I take a slight detour on the way back to my apartment - my flat, to scope out the gym I saw online. There's no Pilates studio within short enough walking distance, but this gym has a lap pool. I packed a swimsuit in high hopes this place wouldn't give me weird vibes. I don't think I've worn it in years. Here's to hoping it fits, or that the pool isn't well-lit.

I'm able to find the gym easily and instantly feel under-dressed when the female attendant offers to give me a tour. The entrance smells like sandalwood and has a water feature and live greenery. High-tech cardio equipment is lined up to face outside toward a green space. White free weights are stored in chic shelves. There are enough benches and racks for anyone that likes to lift heavy and private functional areas for floor work and stretching. The locker room and showers are nicer than the spa I like to visit back home. The sauna is a nice touch. The lap pool is massive, but more brightly lit than I'd hoped.

I guess swimsuit shopping is on the list. I won't charge it to Jim, but will definitely be expensing this monthly membership. Gym access was part of my short list of conditions, which he happily accommodated.

I'm led to the desk to complete the sign-up process and I'm barely awake enough to type my name into the tablet, much less to read the waiver they have me e-sign. She walks me through downloading the app I can use to book classes and order from the smoothie counter.

"You'll access the door during unstaffed hours with the QR code in the app." She explains.

I might remember five percent of everything she just said.

"Thanks!"

"Right then."

I turn away wondering how she keeps her sneakers – trainers so clean.

I head back to the apartment building just a few blocks away. I fumble my way into the door only to remember I haven't unpacked. I have clothes to steam for tomorrow morning, and I can't be trusted with hot gadgets right now. Instead, I fish out the oldest and softest t-shirt I own, a green baseball jersey with "Judah's Mom" printed on the back, and a partially torn pair of ducky pajama shorts.

I set my alarm for seven in the morning. and I'm out cold by three in the afternoon.

* * *

At four in the morning. I'm wide awake. I woke up once and counted sheep, literally, until I was out again. This is a bit excruciating, but at least it gives me a chance to review OneDer's file one more time and steam my outfit.

I'm sure Judah's still up, but I refrain from calling. Maybe a text would be OK? No. Stop, Ollie.

I boot up my laptop and start to search for OneDer's file by typing in *o-n*, and instead see photos from what I realize was our last trip as a family of three in Ontario. It was just a short weekend getaway, but we squeezed in the time to see a hockey game in Toronto and to visit Niagara Falls.. Nate and Judah loved the hockey game. I think my face was sore just from wincing in reaction to it all. I'd probably still sit through a sporting event like that one before a football game, or God forbid, a golf tournament.

I click through photos and land on one where we stand in front of a bridge together at Niagara Falls. The plummeting water behind us roared so loud. I'd been taking photos of the falls and of Judah with my phone. A kind woman and girl with accents that were probably German asked if we wanted a family photo, which didn't make sense to deny.

I remember the drive back to Toronto being eerily quiet. The sun was shining that day. I was only slightly carsick, but something else felt off. I think this was one of the many moments that made up the slow burn leading up to the separation. Something was dying, but not in a traumatic way. It was subtle; gentle. Maybe it wasn't ever alive to begin with. The fall was more of a float down than a plummet, which we never tried to stop.

I take a deep breath and return to the search bar to pull up OneDer's file.

Five

March

RAMI

Theo's pulling up the deck and can't manage to connect to the conference room monitor. It's no surprise he needs to call his admin over to set it up, five minutes after we were meant to get started, no less. I've always been curious what kind of hypnosis he put Lynn under to land a role here. I don't think I can ask without sounding petty. These things often solve themselves.

"Well, then." Lynn fills the silence.

"While Theo prepares, we can start with some introductions." She nods toward the lady sitting next to her at the mahogany table where twelve of us are sat. "Olivia Kincade joins us from Finch & Associates, a top PR firm based in the US. She came highly recommended by an old colleague. She's here to help us with our marketing and communications strategies."

Lynn continues explaining the subprojects she'll be supporting. I'm not sure why she's doing the talking as VP of Digital Innovation when VP of Brand & Marketing, Arthur, is in the room. Arthur isn't a bad boss. He's always given me a lot of autonomy, but his contributions are virtually zero lately.

She moves around the table with rapid-fire explanations of our roles, "Theo, as you know, is Director of Digital Innovation and has played a significant role in leading development on the tech side. Arthur Morris oversees Brand & Marketing as VP."

The consultant, Olivia, sits leaned back slightly in her chair with her hands crossed in her lap. She looks like a stock photo that would come up if I searched PR Professional. She's in a navy suit with her guest badge clipped to the lapel. She's approachable but doesn't seem like she's here for small talk. She looks in my direction.

"And this is Rami Hadid" Lynn continues. "He'll be your primary contact as Director of Brand & Marketing."

I give her a slight smile and nod as Lynn side-glances to check on Theo's progress. She continues introductions around the other side of the table.

I can see Olivia's eyes scanning the room. She's assessing power dynamics. She's reading body language and likely picking up on how badly Theo wants to impress Lynn, how Lynn loathes Arthur, how often Arthur taps his Smartwatch, and how the software developers to my left would rather be anywhere other than this room.

She can probably see I was at the bar until half two. I sit up straighter and adjust my collar.

Theo's admin finishes and takes a seat in the corner.

"Right! Olivia, let's brief you on the new feature, shall we?" Lynn defers to Theo.

"OneDer, as you're aware, is a travel booking platform. Current state, the app functions consistently with similar products in the market." He continues. "Some of our competitors aren't just catching up to us. They're moving quickly with enhancements we're still struggling to get right. They're winning more of our consumers, which Rami could share more about from our customer insights data."

Her eyes shift back to me. I meet them and quickly look away.

Theo transitions slides. "Instead of pouring resources into trying to stay a step ahead with our flagship product, we've developed a new one – something that will help us retain our customer base and attract new users."

He pulls up two screenshots. One of them shows a list of names and profile photos and the other of a map with purple dots.

"TwoRist is a new menu option inside the OneDer app. It allows travelers who've booked through the OneDer platform to find each other and connect using location services. It's going to be a game changer for solo travelers, or for larger groups."

She squints at the screen and crosses her arms, still smiling politely but not ready to speak.

Theo goes on, "TwoRist uses booking data from OneDer to give the user access to a list of travelers who are, or will be, in the area at the same time."

She's still processing, or she's choosing her words wisely.

"Being seen on this list is optional, of course." He continues. "If someone who has an account with OneDer chooses to activate TwoRist, their profiles can be found on the list. They can then browse other activated travelers. They can filter by interests, review profiles, even chat with other travelers before requesting to connect. Connecting is what enables visibility into the other's pinpoint on the map. The pinpoint shows a relative location, not exact. We're taking safety seriously."

I'm not sure I agree on that front.

The consultant speaks for the first time. "A dating app and a location tracker inside a travel booking app."

"Could be a dating app!" His enthusiasm exceeds hers. "Or just a way for groups to find other groups. That's also a function."

She raises her eyebrows and leans forward slightly.

"I get it. 'TwoRist', like *tourist*, because it helps one traveler become two." She's amused enough. "TwoRist. OneDer. They make sense together. Have you done any research on why someone would choose to book through OneDer just so that they can access TwoRist?"

She's not an amateur.

Theo's confused. "Why wouldn't they?"

"It'd limit them to using just one travel booking platform. If I already have a booking app and a meetup app on my phone, what's the benefit to me if I started using OneDer and TwoRist instead?" The room tenses. "It's my job to play devil's advocate. It'll help us get ahead of any critics."

I interject. "Incentives."

The room's attention shifts to the far end of the table where I sit at the back.

"Travelers who connect unlock perks to share: hotel discounts, restaurants deals, ride-share vouchers. Travelers who connect with others over multiple trips earn badges that can translate to status with our affiliate brands. It's more than a customer retention play. It's an avenue for new partnerships."

She nods slightly, then studies the slide again.

"Mm. Can you talk about your privacy and security measures?" She turns toward Theo.

She's inching closer to what he likes to sweep under the rug.

"What specifically? Booking data? That's all on the back-end. Encrypted."

"I'm thinking about how a teen might interact with the app. All they'd need is a booking confirmation number, right?"

There it is.

He always laughs when he's defensive. "We've considered that. It doesn't seem like a kid would go through the trouble of swiping a confirmation number from a parent if they could connect with strangers through social media anyway."

"Maybe not. The big social media apps do have parental controls these days. Are you looking into that?" She questions more gently.

"We've got some things in testing. I'm not sure what will be ready by our release date." He nervously shuffles from one leg to the other, looking at the developer team to avoid looking at her. "Parents can always block kids from downloading social apps, or not give them a phone at all."

"Fair. OneDer isn't a social app, though. It's categorized as an e-commerce platform. Is that right? It might not be on their radar."

"Is this a liability conversation or an ethics conversation?" Lynn chimes in.

"Pretty sure it should be a marketing conversation". Theo jabs.

Olivia's expression isn't readable. "Ethics conversations are yours to have." She continues. "My aim is to help you see risk and circumvent it. I'm not sure how much time you've spent with your legal team, but I'd recommend - "

"We don't consider any of this a high risk." Theo interrupts her.

The conversation feels more American every second.

"Understood. Your current customer base, which I'd bet is 35-44, might see child safety as a risk. I know my son was clever enough to figure things like this out when he was a teenager."

An adult son. She can't be much older than 35.

Olivia realizes she's been assertive enough to capture Arthur's attention, and she goes on more softly. "It seems like it'd be wise to have a position on the topic, maybe some canned responses ready."

The air is thick. I try my best to cut through it.

"That's your job, Mrs. Kincade."

Heads whip toward me. Bloody hell. That did not come out appropriately. Lynn looks gobsmacked.

"It's our job" I recover. "Pardon me. You see why your expertise is needed." I loosen my posture and smile broadly to cut the tension. "We know it's important that we frame the value proposition well. It's clearly there."

"It is." Her tone is kind, but her jaw is clenched. "I'm confident I can help get it right." She doesn't break gaze. "... and it's Ms. Kincade, thanks. Olivia is better."

"Brilliant!" Lynn transitions us to close twenty minutes early instead of aligning on next steps. Her EQ has always been the highest in the room.

"I trust we've got a productive week ahead. Rami, I believe you and Olivia have time later this afternoon to start getting more tactical."

Olivia and I both speak at once. "Sure Thing." "We do".

I offer her a forced half smile as everyone moves toward the door.

* * *

After a long day of going over ideas for advertising, media engagements, and risk mitigation, I'm optimistic Olivia knows what she's doing. She is quite transactional about it. She probably thinks we're negligent in terms of risk management. I'm more concerned about what Lynn shared with Craig after this morning's meeting. I acted daft, as did Theo. Arthur seemed unbothered about it over lunch, but to be fair he practically slept through most of the session. Craig would have sent me a note if it'd made its way to him.

I glance at my email from my phone before walking through the courtyard gate toward the maisonette I bought a few years back. More space has been nice. We needed it. I was glad for higher ceilings, being six foot two last time I checked. It's closer to the pubs and bars I frequent, as well as the gym I overpay for. Moving was a hassle for the three of us, but I don't regret it.

This life wasn't in the cards for me. I grew up skint near Edgeware Road and applied for bursaries and scholarships. I took a degree in Computer Science sixteen years ago and bounced around small tech companies for years after. I paid my dues in call centers, then in sales, which eventually brought me to OneDer where I managed accounts with hospitality brands.

This company has been good to me - too good. When family matters took a turn for the worst, Craig encouraged me to slow down; to take care of myself. He kept it all private, which I appreciated. There was no rule book for how to manage during times like that, so I found coping mechanisms that somewhat help – most days. Drowning myself in work may be one of them.

When Arthur moved into a VP position, they bumped me up into his Director role. I've spent most of the past year working with Theo on the TwoRist project. As much as he does my head in, I'm prouder of this work than I've been of much else lately. It's also been a well-timed distraction. This project might be my best ticket to a VP promotion. The release has to go smoothly.

I fumble my keys in one hand with a bag of takeaway in the other, ready to block Hercules from darting out in an orange flash. I've been picking up takeaway nearly every evening since Ramadan ended. I reckon it won't get eaten, as usual.

Hercules weaves between my feet as I close the door behind me. I set the food on the black quartz counter top, and I can smell a lavender candle burning in the sitting room.

I ignore how much I hate it and go change into my gym kit.

Six

March

OLLIE

I've been up since four in the morning. My body has no idea what day it is. It's clear my mind doesn't either after today's meetings. They'll ship me back any day now. I came on too strong too early, but I wasn't wrong. I think Rami knows it but might be focused on the wrong things. Theo doesn't get it. I don't remember him being this touchy. I think Arthur is the one who'd have to make the call to Jim if they want to cut ties. I have no clue where I stand with Lynn.

The gym isn't where my last ounce of energy should be tonight, but an incline walk seemed like what my brain needed. The temperature outside was too low for my liking, even if I am a Chicagoan. I've got fifteen minutes left. I feel my cheeks getting hot. I hate how red they get when I do cardio.

The front door buzzes as someone scans themselves in.

This is not what my brain needed. Rami Hadid takes the treadmill three down from mine, and nods at me.

Thirteen minutes.

He puts an earbud in and starts the machine. I turn the incline up a degree. A chunk of stray hair is stuck to my forehead. I skip to the next song playing in my earbuds.

Am I breathing loudly? Does he have both earbuds in?

He's worked up to a full sprint. He looks tense. He's probably here to blow off Olivia-induced steam. Sorry for doing what you're paying me to do, Hadid.

Six minutes.

I listen to two more songs, tap the cool down button on the screen and start to catch my breath. I grab my water bottle and phone and walk behind him as he continues to sprint.

His gray shirt is sticking to him already. He must do something other than run, because the muscles down his back are giving Brad Pitt in Fight Club.

I head to the locker room, splash some cool water on my face, and grab my bag. I time my exit just as Rami's stepping off his machine and removing his one earbud.

His voice is deep; commanding, but not abrasive. "You alright?"

"Yeah, thanks." I remember being caught off guard the first time a Brit greeted me that way. "This place isn't bad."

"Not hardly, no. Good equipment. Convenient."

"A pool", I add.

He glanced down at my legs. I try to move them around in a way that looks natural so he doesn't see that I haven't shaved in a week.

"What happened there?"

Why the hell did I wear shorts?

"A minor travel accident. A fender-bender."

"You were in a car accident?!" He's still catching his breath and apparently concerned.

"No, no, it was me. I was the accident." He still looks concerned. "I tripped. I fell walking through a revolving door. It was when my little section wasn't inside or outside."

"You were pinned inside."

"On the ground, yes. The doorman couldn't get to me. He kind of just watched in amazement."

"Damn! Sorry." He's trying not to laugh. "Do you have a plaster? Looks like you could use it."

Bleeding again.

"No. I haven't... I didn't think I needed one."

"There's a supermarket around the corner. I'm headed that direction."

"It's across from where I'm staying. I'll stop in. I need a few things."

We both walk in toward the door. The cool air is jarring.

"Pretty good area you're staying in here. There are some buildings a few blocks down where our vendors usually stay. Closer to the office, but I reckon it's not as comfortable."

"I'm happy with it, yeah. Finch usually negotiates a good setup for me. I've been with them a long time."

"Doing the same work the whole time?"

"Most of it. Every job's so different. Some are fun. Some are... really crazy. "

"I suppose you wouldn't be saying that if ours was in the really crazy category?"

"Nowhere near it. Not yet, at least."

He laughs and runs a hand through hair that's starting to curl around his ears. I didn't notice the silver around his temples before. "Stay tuned." He jokes in a dramatic tone.

"Would you put OneDer in a crazy category?" If he would, he wouldn't say so.

"I might have to be outside that category myself to know if OneDer belongs in it."

"I don't think any of us could make that judgment, then."

"Maybe not." He hands me a basket when we step inside and walks me to the aisle where the bandages – plasters are. Is he really going to tag along until I grab all I need? I don't love the idea of buying deodorant with a client.

"This is it! Thanks."

"Yeah, sure. I've gotta grab some things, too." He steps away. "Nine tomorrow?"

"Yep." We both grab our things and awkwardly intersect again at the checkout counter.

"Have a good night." I grab my shopping bag and almost forget my water bottle by the cash register.

He picks it up and hands it to me.

* * *

My phone vibrates just as I'm drying off from my shower and reaching for the box of bandages.

"Hey, bud"

"Mom, what's the code to your apartment? I forgot." He's not supposed to be checking on things until Friday.

"What? Are you there?"

"My internship ended. Budget cuts, I don't know."

"It's 020404. They gave you no notice?"

"Yours and Dad's anniversary? Really?" It was my code to everything when I first set it up. I hear the buttons beep. He goes on. "There were rumors, but I wasn't worried. I thought they'd hold out until July."

"And you found this out when?"

"Yesterday. I didn't want to sit around in Indy, so I just came here. Your plant looks like it needs watering."

"Put an ice cube in it, not water."

"An ice cube is water." He laughs at himself. That boy was in braces for almost three years.

"You know what I mean." I miss him. "Do you think you'll want to stay in Indianapolis? Find something else?"

"Probably not. My apartment building is still the dump it was when you saw it. My hot water goes out all the time." I hear him close the pantry door too hard, as usual. "There's no food in here."

"Why would there be? I'm four thousand miles away. Order from that wing place, just don't eat it on the couch."

"Is it good?"

"The wing place? Yeah, we had it when Paige was here, remember?"

"No, London."Nice of him to ask. Also, weird.

"Yeah, it's good. I banged up my leg a little, but other than that, it's alright."

"Nice. These clients aren't idiots?"

"Not idiots. Misguided, maybe. I don't think I'll be here past September. I'll send you money for the wings."

"No, I've got it. It might be the last time I can buy my own dinner for a while - thanks, though."

He'd be letting me pay if that were true. "You'll figure it out, Jude. I'll call you tomorrow about the apartment stuff. You could probably negotiate the fine for breaking the lease..."

"Dad's helping... and I know someone I could probably sign it over to."

"K. Make sure the door is locked before you go to bed."

"Oh my God. Bye."

It twists my stomach in such a weird way when he's hurt. He seems to be handling this one OK. Nate won't love him moving back to Chicago, but it solves the problem of my rent money being wasted. It'd be smart of me to have him cover the utilities if he can find something else quickly. God, I hope he finds something else quickly.

I'll thank myself in the morning if I take the time to lather on some night cream and use a whitening strip on my teeth. I'll pass out in less than thirty minutes, so the latter might not be wise.

Mornings are probably when I should prioritize the gym. I'm not sure my first impressions with OneDer can afford another evening run-in like tonight's.

He's good. Rami knows good messaging. He knows how to leverage relationships. People listen when he speaks. He gets what his consumers want and anticipates what won't work. He has a long-range view, just a few blind spots he chooses to ignore. It didn't take long to pick up on that from one painful thirty-minute meeting and a two-hour working session.

I set my alarm for six o'clock. and hope I sleep 'til then.

* * *

By the end of lunch hour the next day, my body still isn't sure what time it is. I didn't sleep well last night. Coming here was a wild idea. I miss my pillows and my candles. I miss my big TV and my bathtub. I'm not sure I miss having a car to drive. Walking to the office is nice, even with the chill in the air. Taking the tube anywhere else I need to go isn't ideal. I haven't had to do it yet.

Theo walks through the marketing floor where I'm sitting at a large table in a common area. I don't think he saw me before walking right past.

"Theo" he stops. "How's your day going?"

He gives me a slight wave and walks over. "It's all good. How you settling in?"

"OK, I think. I'm still finding my bearings with this city. It'll probably take even longer to find them with this project."

He lets out one quick laugh. "Yeah, it's an interesting one - probably different from anything else you've worked on."

"It's similar to others I've supported. It is innovative." I offer some positivity to offset my obvious skepticism.

"It is. Rami and I have been nose-deep in this for over a year. We've thought through it all from the inside out."

"I can tell." I can't tell if he's trying to tell me to stay in my lane.

He looks away and shuffles from one foot to the other before looking back at me.

"I think you're gonna add a lot of value here. I do. I also think you'll be even more valuable if you focus on the PR stuff – the commercials, the ads, the scripts for the higher-ups."

I study him, but don't respond.

"...you know, worry about the face of the product. Leave the brains of it to others - to me. I've got it."

This is rich. "I understand."

"Do you?" Condescending clown.

"OneDer pays me to be thorough. I won't deliver bargain work at a premium rate, not when crisis management is in my scope."

He seems to be deciding whether to respond but walks away instead.

My phone goes off with a text.

Mark – Finch & Assoc: *Back in Chicago. I hear you're across the pond. When do you wrap up?*

I don't reply.

Seven

April

OLLIE

The launch date is in five weeks. So far, we've finished production on one commercial and approved proofs for billboards and tube advertising. Craig presented in a shareholder meeting along with Lynn's boss, CTO Catherine Neely. Rami and I set them up well, I think. They dodged a few questions I would have liked to see them address head-on with the language we gave them. I'm still pleased with how it went.

OneDer's UK headquarters isn't a bad place to spend three days a week. The building is old, like everything here, but their royal purple branding livens it up. The team is usually only in the office Tuesdays through Thursdays, leaving me time to explore, or sleep, or stare at a wall.

I've spruced up my flat with a few candles and fresh flowers. This week I went with white tulips. I've been at the gym in the mornings but haven't braved the pool yet.

I'm not bored. Long sessions with Rami's team have been a drain on my mental energy, but not in a way that's frustrating - so far. He does tend to question himself when we're brainstorming one on one. He projects confidently, so his indecisiveness can be surprising. He clearly wants to keep climbing the ladder here. He's probably one of those people that don't know who they are outside of work.

It takes one to know one.

The break area is buzzing at two o'clock, and I drop a bag of earl grey into my cup of hot water. I should shop for a mug this weekend. I'd have to wash it by hand at my flat, which I have all the time for but no patience for. I drop a third sugar cube in as Rami walks over.

"Ever have milk in it?"

"Milk? No, it's taking me the last week to figure out the exact amount of water and sugar I like."

He reaches toward the cooler for a carton. "Try a splash. I usually -
"

"No, I'm good. I'm... particular." I'm controlling.

"Fair enough". He closes the cooler door and playfully puts his hands up in surrender. "You don't like enjoyable beverages."

"I find my beverage enjoyable enough, thanks." I laugh and blow on the steam. "Didn't the queen have her tea with no milk?"

"She didn't take sugar. Milk was her non-negotiable."

"Well, sugar's mine."

"Rami!" Theo interjects. "I can't join in for birthday pints after work. So sorry."

"You told me this morning you could make it, mate. Craig had to pull out, too."

"I know, sorry. My boys set up a tennis match."

He's annoyed. "Out of order, bruv." He still smiles "Best of luck."

Theo walks away, giving him a thumbs up over his head.

"Your birthday?" I sip my unorthodox tea.

"Guilty." He grabs a banana from the bowl on the break room island, peels it, and takes a bite. "Can I interest you in another enjoyable beverage?"

* * *

This isn't appropriate.

I also don't think it's inappropriate. I go out with clients all the time. This is strictly professional. The sun's still up. I don't intend to get hammered. He doesn't wear a ring.

"If you order an espresso martini, we're renegotiating your contract."

We sit on leather stools at the polished wood bar. This pub, The Victoria, is a time machine. Deep wood walls and ceilings are embellished with ornate mill-work. Heavy burgundy drapes and old books are highlighted by glowing low lighting. Gold framed paintings hang above fireplaces in each of the many sprawling rooms.

I did want an espresso martini.

"We can't have that happening now, can we?" He knows my sarcasm by now. "Unless you're saying you'd do it so you can pay Finch more for me."

"You're worth it." He realizes how it sounded and clears his throat.

The bartender lays two napkins in front of us.

"Pint of mild. Cheers."

"Old fashioned"

"You could've ordered an espresso martini."

"With how intimidating you were about it? I'm playing it safe, sir."

"With something harder?"

We sat in silence for several seconds. The bartender puts down both glasses, and I take a generous sip.

"Don't be shy, Ollie."

I do a double take.

He catches it. "What?"

"My friends call me that. My friend."

"Ah, yeah? You seem like you'd be an Ollie"

"Hm... Explain."

"I don't think I can."

I give him a suspicious side-glance.

He got a haircut. I think the curls behind his ear suited him better. Mine is in a high ponytail. I'm in a cream sleeveless vest today with silver buttons down the front. If I'd ordered the drink I wanted, I'd probably ruin this top.

"What were you doing on your last birthday?" The question surprises him.

"Maybe watching a match? I don't know. I've had a lot of these - 38 now. I don't recall." He takes a sip and continues. "Ah, I do, actually. My sister came into town. Had a nice dinner. Went out for a few pints after - alone. Exciting."

"You're close to your sister?"

"Not really - not lately. She's in Oxford. Close enough that I should see her more often, but you know..." His eyes turn down toward where he holds his glass with both hands. "You?"

"My last birthday? No clue. I've had a few more than you have." He didn't need to know that.

He exaggerates his shock on purpose. "You're joking. How many more?"

I can't hold in my laugh. I shake my head.

"What? Inappropriate?" He asks, knowing it is.

"Yes." I'm grinning at him.

"Sorry. Still don't believe you, but I'm sorry. When is yours?"

"You're forgiven - and it's in February."

"Ah. Aquarius?"

"Pisces." This sounds too much like a cheesy first date.

"May I ask about your son? You mentioned you had one in our first meeting - the one where I was a jerk."

"Which one?"

"Was I a jerk in more than one meeting?"

I laugh. "Kidding. No, you've never been." I need to slow down on my drink. "I do have a son. Just the one. Judah."

"Judah."

"Mhm. He's 22 - almost 23. He's finding his way. It's not easy help-ing him navigate from a different continent."

"Is that what parenting is when they're that age? You're a satnav?"

"More like AAA. That's probably not a thing here. Do you have kids?

"We do have it here. It's just AA, and yes. I have one child. Small."

"Like, primary school?"

"Too busy for that. Licking his paws and strutting around all day, you know."

He's pleased with himself. I can't hold back my smile. "His name?"

"Hercules. He's a massively difficult cat. We never agree on any-thing."

Everything about his face says he adores him.

"Then you and I can relate." I stir my straw around the ice in my glass.

"But we're their whole worlds, am I right? Hercules makes me feel like a king when I get home. I'd bet you're Judah's hero." His expres-sion is sincere.

I finish off my drink. His has been gone for a while."Another? My treat, obviously."

We each have one more, too much for me, and decide to order food. We stay for another hour after, and the conversation seamlessly dances from our childhood pets to the rise of AI and the return of mustaches. He went into passionate detail about his collection of clas-sic fiction and his least favorite authors.

When we leave, we reach a gate to what must be his terraced apart-ment since he's slowing down.

"You didn't have cake. That's important."

"It's alright. I might ask that you still sing. It's the right thing to do." He wouldn't be asking if he knew I had the vocal range of a frog.

"Singing is not in my contract, which has not changed given my drink selection."

He throws his head back at the night sky with one big laugh.

"You can, however, tell Hercules that I think his dad is a jolly good fellow." Stupid. Stupid. Stupid. I'm swearing an oath of sobriety.

"I can be happy with that" He walks through the gate and up the walkway. "Don't forget - half past eight tomorrow morning. We need to firm up everything we worked on today before meeting with Arthur at nine."

Sober now. "I'll finish up the deck tonight."

He waves.

I walk a few blocks down and turn into my building. The elevator isn't working again. These stairs will be the death of me. I wind around and up until I'm on the third level, and crash onto the bed.

I pull my hair-tie out to free my ponytail, and nothing has ever felt more wonderful. Maybe the strain on my brain is why I acted like an imbecile after dinner.

I did enjoy myself. I don't think I've laughed like that in ages. I also think it's been ages since I've had a conversation that wasn't related to work, parenting, or Paige.

Rami seems to be too well-rounded to be as successful as he is. There has to be a catch somewhere - a major flaw, but it's none of my business. I can't help but feel more human around him. I'm not sure that's a good thing.

My phone goes off with a text:

Rami Hadid – OneDer: *I realize I should have walked you to your flat. I'm sorry. Let me know when you've made it.*

I reply: *It wasn't far. I'm safe and sound. Thanks for checking in.*

He's typing again. He stops. Typing again.

Rami Hadid – OneDer: *Night, Ollie*

Eight

April

OLLIE

Saturday afternoon might not have been the best time to finally explore the market I've been wanting to see. It's chaotic,
but absolute bliss. Borough Market is massive. The structures are made
up of green wrought iron, glass, and brick. String lights and greenery
are strung across the ceilings, covering countless stalls selling fresh
produce and prepared foods.

The spices are intoxicating. Paella is served from an enormous pan,
feeding a mile-long line of customers. I see someone walk by with a
plate of steaming dumplings that look incredible. I've already bought
blackberries and a few ounces of gouda. I'm eyeing the doughnut
booth I've heard about and refuse to leave without one of the crème
brûlée flavored ones - or two.

It's warm today, so I've opted for a beige mini-dress and white
sneakers. With a lavender lemonade in my left hand and a straw tote
bag over my right shoulder, I wander to find the item at the top of my
priority list. I find the tables with rows and rows of cups filled with
deep red strawberries and silky chocolate drizzle. I find a place to set

my lemonade and dive in carefully. It's pure perfection, but there's no way I'll finish it all.

The rest of this week has felt off at the office. I've tried to keep conversations more focused on the work. There's enough of it. My temper is getting shorter when it comes to how OneDer wants to sell this whole thing. The world has enough ways to find people to party with, and enough ways for creeps to target people. Maybe I'm an old recluse and should be buying into it. Maybe I'm reaching the end of my rope with this career. Maybe I miss home more than I'm admitting to myself.

I toss the last half of my chocolate strawberries in a bin and head back toward the exit.

I think it annoyed Rami at first when I kept diverting the conversation back to the project tracker Wednesday morning after our meeting with Arthur. It was tough to keep myself from bantering with him when he was being cheeky. I'd think it was flirting if I wasn't wise enough to know better. By Thursday he was strictly business.

I can't let things slip like I did that night. It felt too casual; too unfiltered. I'll be back in Chicago in five months, and this client is too big to screw up. It's easy to slip with him, and I'm annoyed with myself for it.

I've been browsing weekend getaway ideas. I've got to get my mind in a better place. Judah called yesterday and isn't having any luck finding a job that interests him. He's working at a packing and shipping store and delivering groceries for extra cash. He's down. I wish he'd call the therapist he saw a few times after the separation.

I pass a middle eastern stall on my way out and tell my mind to stop drifting.

* * *

"Where are you gonna go?"

Paige is on speaker while I try on my old swimsuit to see if my first dip in the pool is an option tonight. I probably gained five pounds at the market, so it could work.

"I don't know, the countryside. The Cotswolds, maybe. One of those thatched roof houses, like that Christmas movie where the women swap houses."

"Will it come with a wavy-haired British man with sexy spectacles?"

"There will be zero men anywhere in sight."

"And you're sure you haven't met anyone yet that you fancy? No good-looking British men at this company?"

It's impossible for me to say nothing when she does this.

"There are some semi-attractive men, yes."

"You met someone. You did. Spill the earl grey." She turns away to shout into a drive-thru speaker. "I'll have a number one with a diet coke and two ranch."

"OK, he's not... no. He's a client, and I don't do that. He is British, but some kind of Mediterranean descent."

This ugly floral one piece is still fine on the bottom half but sagging around the top. Why did I ever go through a floral phase?

"And you're keeping things professional? Is he a jerk? How attractive is he?"

"Yes-ish, no, and probably an eleven out of ten"

"Ollie! First, explain what 'yes-ish' means then we'll get to the eleven thing."

"His friends bailed on him for his birthday a few days ago, so I went to a pub with him after work. It was fun... and I won't be doing it again."

"Yes, you will, Olivia Kincade. Carpe diem. You won't be there long."

"I'll wear my W.W.P.D. bracelet." Sometimes I think she's still twelve. "This little weekend getaway is adventurous enough at the moment."

"Whatever. How do you plan to get there?"

I hadn't thought that through. "I'll rent a car, maybe."

"Have you driven on that side of the road before?"

"Yeah, I mean… I watched Nate do it years ago. The worst part was the roundabouts."

"The roundabouts! I heard those are a death trap." She isn't wrong. "Take it slow and pray for the best."

"I think the last time I prayed was when Judah had RSV 20 years ago. You know I haven't set foot in a church since the baby shower from hell."

"The egg salad sandwiches were fire, though." She's eating while driving, probably dripping sauce on the steering wheel.

"Who says fire?

"I think we're supposed to now. Here, I'm sending you a link to a place. It looks cute – like, 400 years old. A row house. Adorable blue kitchen."

"Is it fire?"

"Tell me if it is when you get there. How's the swimsuit?"

"I think I'm just going to wear it. I had two too many doughnuts for a treadmill today."

"One for each of your lovely thighs – perfect."

* * *

The echo in here is soothing. Each splash rings off the wall with every stroke from one end to the other. The place is empty, so I know the sounds are all mine. Evening light pierces through the skylight.

My arms fatigue midway over the deep end, and I wade toward the wall to catch my breath. My heart rate slows slightly as I dip beneath the water.

Silence. Pressure.

I see how long I can stay under until my chest burns.

I kick my way to the surface and lie flat on my back. I surrender to the water's support, starting with my feet and moving up to my head until my ears submerge. I float for several minutes with my eyes closed, drifting, turning.

What an odd feeling it is to be held.

Nate was never particularly affectionate. To be fair, I wasn't either. Of course, we acted like teenagers when we were teenagers. When we had no choice but to become self-sufficient, we shifted into survival mode. We stayed each other's biggest supporters and peacefully shared the logistical load of the life we built together. We've always been genuine friends, We loved each other's company, just maybe not each other's connection.

Little things did compound over the years, which is normal, I suppose. He hated the way I parked in the garage. I hated the way he scooped cream cheese out of the container. He wanted to join a church, and I was entirely uninterested. I wanted to invest more money, and he wanted to take more vacations. He couldn't understand the degree to which planes and hotel rooms had lost their appeal.

I do sometimes wonder if we truly were too far gone by the time we decided we'd run our course. I wonder if neither of us tried to keep what we had alive because we were too busy, or if we'd become less compatible with age. I worry it had something to do with a fear we both had of getting vulnerable. That seems like a problem someone would take with them when they leave.

I hear sandals scuffing on the floor and bolt upright.

Two women walk to the far corner of the room and pick up a towel one of them must have left behind. False alarm. They exit again. When I pull myself out of the lukewarm water, I tug my loose swimsuit into place and dry off.

As I wrap my towel around my torso; the door creaks open again.

The alarm wasn't false this time.

"No weekends off?" He asks playfully. His body language is tense as he walks near me to toss his bag on the bench. His gray t-shirt and swimsuit suggest he's not here for small talk."

"Nothing too crazy. It clears my head." I bet I have mascara running down my face.

"You've got a little, uh…" he gestures to his eyes.

I wipe at them too hard, making it worse, I'm sure. "Thanks." I pull my towel tighter around me.

"You've got a busy head? Something happen?" He sounds distant, but genuinely curious.

"You don't? My head's always busy." I turn away to grab my water bottle. "Not sprinting like an Olympian today?" I turn back toward the pool as he's walking toward the steps.

Jesus, I did not expect this man's shirt to come off.

We don't objectify, Ollie.

"Sore shins. Overdid it this week." He works his way down into the shallow end.

I don't look at him directly. "You could have taken a rest day instead of swimming. Even the pros do, Hadid."

He chuckles and slips under the water and back up again. He still seems reserved, but he's breathtaking. His toned chest is broad, stretching as he strokes toward the center. "I don't know. Busy head." He makes eye contact with me for the briefest second.

Must. Leave. Now.

"Enjoy your swim. I'm planning to be remote Monday if you're good with that. Is this Monday and Friday remote work standard a real thing? I think you go into the office every day."

"I prefer it. It helps me focus. Do you prefer working from your place?"

"I'll be wherever you need me to be." I'm not sure if that's Olivia or Ollie talking.

"Noted, Kincade." He starts to stroke toward the deep-end, and I finally reach the door. He calls out "If I need you to be at the launch party next month, would you be there? It's supposed to be a whole cocktail attire thing…"

I don't think I received a formal invite. "If you need me to be." Definitely Ollie talking.

He smiles. His brown shoulders finally relax, and he takes off again toward the deep end.

Nine

May

RAMI

I don't let anyone use my car. I hardly use it myself. She was going to have to hire one on her own. It doesn't make sense that her firm would have covered it for leisure, anyway. I suppose she could have used public transport, but it did mean I got the chance to show her how to drive on the left side of the road before she hopped into a hire car and smashed it.

I'm not positive where she's going, but she could use the break. She mentioned she was headed to the countryside and wanted to take a few meetings from there. The car wasn't difficult to offer up. I haven't got to be an appointment chauffeur this week. This is the first Friday I've opted to work at home for months.

Olivia keeps up with me. We might disagree even more than Hercules and I do, but it's working for this project. We're so close to the finish line. In a few week's time, I'll be breathing easier. This release will be one of the most unique innovations the industry has seen.

I don't think everyone gets it. I don't think people understand the value of bringing individuals together from a million separate places, just hungry for connection. It breeds possibilities. My parents could never have made the frightening move from Lebanon to London if strangers hadn't lent a hand. OneDer, and TwoRist, will make the world feel smaller and bigger all at once. I hope the gravity of it comes through in how we're marketing it, even if it doesn't come through to Ollie – Olivia.

I open my computer and settle at the small wood desk near the window. Hercules curls up behind the screen against the wall.

"Morning", "Hiya", "Morning" rings through the speakers as the team joins the call.

Lynn looks like she's had a long week. Her voice disguises her exhaustion, and we get started.

Olivia's sat at what might be a dining table with a set of double doors behind her framing bright green bushes. The light shining toward the camera from behind her head obscures her face.

The call is silent. Damn it, I'm the one leading this.

I clear my throat. "We got the commercial slots we wanted on three of the four broadcast networks we're working with. The fourth network attracts the smallest percentage of our target market. I feel there's cause to celebrate the shape we're in."

Smiles on the screen are accompanied with clapping hand emojis. "Theo, what's the status of the privacy concern you mentioned last week? The security team was researching a fix."

"Yes – yep. It looks good. We're squared away for the launch."

"OK." He'd usually have more to say. "So, the encryption issue was fixed?"

"It is."

Piss poor mood he's in. "Brilliant. Let's move on to the agency that will be distributing our print materials. Olivia, you've got an update there?"

"I do." Her connection is poor wherever she is. "They're supposed to receive the shipment first thing next week and will overnight it all where it needs to go. I'm not worried about timing. They'll get any extra supply back to us in a few weeks."

"Right on. Great progress there."

Theo interjects, "Olivia, have you thought to reach out to someone about storage for it all? We've got piles of old computers in the supply closets, so it'd be smart to find a different place to throw your marketing assets."

She's either fumbling to unmute or letting the silence get uncomfortable on purpose.

"You seem to have solved all the IT obstacles you've been focused on. You think you'll have a few extra minutes next week to find someone to clear the closet on the Marketing floor?"

Her connection was clear as a bell that time around.

Theo hesitates to respond, "I'm sure there's an admin that will have time in a month or two." Lazy.

"I'm going to ask that you have the old IT equipment moved off my floor within two weeks." I'm unapologetic. His attitude is repulsive. "Olivia, would you look through your calendar later and let him know the date you need it gone?"

"Happy to." She seems surprised at my directive toward Theo.

We move through the rest of the agenda, and Lynn chimes in only a few times to offer input and praise where warranted. The team begins to drop off the call one by one until just three of us remain: myself, Olivia, and Lynn.

Lynn smirks into the camera, and her call disconnects.

"How's the Range Rover?"

"It's nice! A little large for the narrow roads in this area, but I've managed to make the squeeze without scratching her. I hope."

She picks up her laptop and walks into another room, her camera still on. The ceilings are low and I can see wood beams reaching across.

"Good! If there's something minor, I'll consider only mild consequences."

"May I have that in writing?" She teases. "Thanks for backing me up. I'm not sure what's gotten into him lately. I think he likes having your full attention. I've reminded him my days are numbered..."

"Probably numbered low if you're not planning to come back from where you are. It looks like a quaint little escape."

"I'm, uh..." she seems like she'll say she's not pleased.

"Hate it?" I try to finish her sentence.

"No...no, It's incredible. It's peaceful. I went for a fancy afternoon tea all on my own yesterday. Scones, jam, all of it. I walked to the supermarket here and got some eggs and rashers for breakfast. I don't know how to use this ridiculous stove."

"Is it an AGA?"

"Yes! It's beautiful, and terrifying. I'm not supposed to turn it off. This morning when I walked into the kitchen it was like a sauna, but not in a suffocating way."

"It's supposed to heat the place, yeah. I've always wanted to cook with one of those. They cost a fortune, you know."

"You do not cook, Rami Hadid."

I laugh aloud at her disbelief." Not every day, but I do. Why does it look like you aren't buying it?"

"Because you live at OneDer's office where there isn't an oven or stove in sight. There's a toaster..."

"I'm not there today, am I? Does this look like the office? Not a speck of purple." I gesture around me toward the shelves filled with old trinkets and rows of worn books. Treasure Island is the only one I've picked up in years.

"Fair." She looks entirely relaxed, but somehow frustrated about it.

"I want you to take the rest of the day off, Ollie. Soak up some sun."

"You're comfortable with my daily rate covering just this one meeting?"

"You're worth it." My gaze does not falter this time – even if it is through a hazy screen.

"Ok" it's almost a whisper.

* * *

I head out the door with a tennis racket and electrolyte beverage after making sure all's settled at home. Tennis isn't my sport, not that anything is apart from watching Arsenal. Craig hasn't been able to make Thursday pints for some weeks now, so I agreed to suffer through this for him.

"Agh!" He grunts as he dives toward where the ball nearly lands outside the line – again. "He's got a lot on his mind, mate." He makes excuses when I blow off steam about Theo's lack of professionalism.

"Who doesn't? When your husband was sick last year, you didn't give Catherine Neely hell at work just because you were drained from caring for him. You were steady." I swing at the ball again, slightly more in bounds this time. "You were still a decent teammate to her, even if things do look different in the C-suite."

"They do look different..." He pummels the neon ball back toward me, and I miss. Point. "... and I was decent, yeah. I tried, at least. How's the consultant Lynn brought on working out? Is she decent?"

He's trying to throw off my game. I told him she took his place when he flaked on my birthday. I never should've mentioned it.

"She's good, yeah. She's made me think differently about our angle."

We rally for about a minute before he takes the game point.

"Keep focused, Hadid. You've got a big future here." I can't decipher if that was an encouragement or a warning. He continues when I don't reply, "...and things you still need to process at home, maybe?"

I reach to shake Craig's hand over the net with a smile and he returns it, but with concern on his face. I dry my face off with a towel and chug my beverage while I walk out of the recreation center and into the warm sun – the same sun I insisted that Olivia soak up today.

What is this woman doing to my mind? Why am I annoyed with Craig who's handed me most of the success I have. I'd usually fall in line at his request. He isn't wrong. Her contract will be up soon enough, and she'll be back to Chicago. It's harmless.

Is it harmless?

She's in my thoughts more than she should be. I'm not making much of an effort to stop it. She's reliable and entirely unexpected at the same time. It's like there are two versions of her. The one I spoke with today was the same one at the pub – Ollie, not Olivia. Ollie's playful and optimistic. Olivia is laser-focused and a tad cynical.

Sometimes Ollie makes an accidental appearance, twirling a loose hair in a meeting or with subtle bruises on her incredible legs – no doubt from tripping or bumping into something. It's my favorite thing about her. As soon as she can see that I see it, Olivia locks Ollie away again. The fact that it drives me mad drives me mad.

I reach the same pub that set me into this frenzy and take a seat. A shower would have been a smarter idea.

Two pints and two whiskeys later, I make my way back to the ones that need me. The only ones that actually need me these days.

* * *

I've got to start tackling some of these projects at home on my weekends instead of reading industry news.

I made a quick breakfast, which was a good start. Usually I'd serve up jam and toast, but I added in some soft-scrambled eggs and tomatoes this time. Tomatoes are barely in season, but standards aren't high here these days.

I wander to the garage to take inventory of the planters and soil I have left from last year. I could opt for faux greenery on the front stoop this season. I don't have the patience for anything requiring daily maintenance. I'm at my quota there.

My phones goes off with a text:

Mira: *I know you're still avoiding that closet. You should look at it today.*

That's not on my list of possibilities today. Not even close.

Mira: *I can come help. There might be some bits and bobs in there that belong to me. I never grabbed it all.*

I stack the planters I'd taken down back up and migrate inside. I make my way to one of the extra bedrooms upstairs and stand in front of the small closet. I know it's full to the brim, and the most over-whelming thing in my world right now.
I open the bi-fold doors and sit on the edge of the bed. There are years of memories stacked to the ceiling, and not neatly. If I pull one of them out, the rest will tumble out of control.

I reply: *No time today. Thanks for the nudge. You should come grab what's yours. It'd be nice to see my little sis.*

I close the closet door, the bedroom door, and that corner of my mind.

Ten

May

OLLIE

I wasn't going to argue with Rami about a free afternoon. I'm calmer than I've been in months – years, even. Unfinished work is nagging at me a bit, but I'm trying my best to push it out of my mind as I push the old shop door open.

Tables of polished silver and copper are overflowing just inside the entrance of the antiques store around the corner. I never see treasures like this back home, unless they're brought over from a market in France or a hidden gem like this. I could get lost in places like this for hours.

Heavy wooden trunks with iron fasteners are tucked in corners, filled with handmade lace. Oil paintings framed with ornate wood are hung floor to ceiling in the staircase leading to the second floor. Arranged on large provincial dining tables are crystal vases and brass candlesticks scattered about.

This place has a hidden history no one could ever know. I can hear the old lights making low buzzing sounds, and the wood floors creaking as the shopkeeper wanders from room to room. Being at the center of a row of shops, there isn't much natural light. Rays peek through a slim display window at the front, and a few small windows at the back.

The scent in here is weirdly satisfying - like mahogany, dried herbs, and age. I flip through stacks of old leather-bound books and boxes of art prints. Sketches of birds and animals look like they were copied from an old science book. I like how much the English seem to decorate with comforting creatures: squirrels, rabbits, ducks, deer. My grandmother used to do the same.

I walk back toward the ground floor and run my hand over a ginormous wall tapestry that has to be hundreds of years old. Deep shades of green are woven with a lighter shade of sage creating a grass landscape for a towering beige castle, two horses, and bushes blooming with white roses. It's flanked by two enormous armoires with intricate carvings. They both are locked with tarnished brass keys embellished with yellow tassels.

I turn a corner and run right into a very old standing globe, nearly knocking it all the way over. It's scratched lightly in some places with a small tear at the base near the axis. I hope my graceful crash isn't what did that.

If Judah were here, he could tell me exactly how old it is based on the nations and borders. It's kind of incredible. I twirl it until I land on England, then twirl it further slowly while I run my finger between London and Chicago.

I text Judah a picture of it.

He's been applying to internships again. It seems like he's really trying to pull himself out of this tough spot he's in. I've been reminding him that it can take years to get in a good place after graduating. I don't know if he's taking it to heart. I'm glad he's taking initiative – finally.

My phone goes off.

Judah: *Nice. It looks like the one we saw at that store in Boston*

I loved that trip. We followed a few nights in Boston with a drive up the coast of Maine, and it was pure Heaven.

He texts again.

Judah: *I applied to something in Boston. It's a long shot.*

I reply: *What's the sports quote? The one about missing one hundred percent of the shots you don't take?*

Judah: *Wayne Gretzky*

I reply: *Wise philosopher*

I approach the small room used as an office area, where it seems I'll check out. I chose a sketch of three sheep, which will probably end up in a desk drawer. I had no reason to buy it other than being drawn to it. It's a simple piece of joy. I don't stumble upon much of that, so I felt like I needed to grab it while I could.

The old man inside has a large brown dog at his feet. He has a red collar and looks up at me with wide caramel eyes but doesn't budge.

"All set?"

"I am" He sees me peering at the dog, subtly trying to get a reaction out of him.

"Charlie's a spoiled one. Plenty happy to be a doormat all day."

"He's a handsome doormat."

"And he knows it! Don't mention it too loud, or he'll be getting a big head." He looks for a pen, moving stacks of papers and receipts around the old desk. "He can hardly hear now, so it's probably all right."

He slowly writes a receipt, carefully capturing each word and number. He tears off the first page and tucks the second into the bag with my sketch.

He must enjoy such a leisurely pace of life. I can't imagine what could possibly rattle him, or Charlie - maybe a broken glass or aggressive negotiator. I'd imagine he's living off very little, but that might be easy to do if you're happy with very little.

The secret might be wanting less. I don't know what that means for how much I want my memory foam mattress back home or my drive-thru iced coffee with one pump of hazelnut. I don't know how to want my silk pajamas or favorite perfume any less.

Maybe it's not about wanting less. Maybe it's about savoring more. It's about finding deeper pleasure in fewer things, which perhaps aren't things at all. Maybe it's moments. I wouldn't know how to begin to get good at that, but strolling through an antiques store in Stow-on-the-Wold on a sunny day might be a strong start.

* * *

My roasted potatoes came out much better this morning than they did yesterday. I think the rosemary and twenty extra minutes did the trick, but chances are they'll never turn out this great again. I never perfected the rashers but managed to eat three times more than I planned.

Part of me wanted to crawl back into the soft, squeaky bed and stay there until I didn't feel stuffed anymore. I've got less than 24 hours left in this little town, so the idea of fresh air and a walk won me over.

It's overcast today. It somehow makes this place even more beautiful; haunting even. I wander down winding cobblestone streets and tilt my head up toward birds chirping on the rooftops. It's early and eerily quiet.

I stumble slightly over one uneven stone and start paying more attention to where my feet are landing. The last thing I want to do is drive a borrowed Range Rover back to London tomorrow with a sprained ankle.

It's unreal to think of how many centuries of people have walked these same alleys. I wonder if their thoughts were like mine. I wonder what they'd think of me stressing about my son's employment, my client's reputation, or my weight being up by five pounds. They'd be too busy worrying over a plague, damaged crops, or a child that might not make it through winter.

We let such small things consume us. It's blinding, and kind of devastating.

I pass through an open gate into a shady courtyard next to a church with a towering steeple. There are headstones all around, many crumbled so much that the markings aren't legible.

Everything feels frozen in time. The breeze stops and the leaves and branches are still. I walk around a winding path and get the odd feeling that I'm welcome, as long as I'm silent.

I stop in front of a massive arched wooden door nestled between two ancient trees, and I'm stunned. Above the door are stained glass windows and an iron lantern. It has a dark and whimsical feel to it, like elves and hobbits could emerge any moment. I can't avoid a strong sense of reverence and wonder at once.

Faint voices grow a bit louder as an elderly couple turns the corner toward where I'm sitting. I think the man is the same one from the antiques store yesterday.

"It's lovely, isn't it?" The woman says in passing. It takes me a moment to realize she's talking to me.

"It is. It's beautiful." She nods and they continue on to exit through the other side of the courtyard.

I imagine that they've been each other's person for decades. There's an ease about them that says they're entirely comfortable not just with each other, but with themselves. It might have taken years to achieve or might have existed right from the start. Perhaps they met as teenagers and have spent seventy years becoming what they are. Perhaps they met at 41 and still had forty years to adore each other.

Would she have seemed just as content if she had walked through that gate alone? Would she have noticed and marveled at the building and the nature around it if she didn't have a partner to ground her? I think she would have. You can tell when someone knows themselves so well that they can move around the world without reservations. I'd bet she knows herself and loves herself. It probably makes it even easier for him to love her, which makes her even more confident.

Maybe it's not just about learning to love yourself. Maybe it's also about learning how to be loved.

My phone rings loudly and snaps me out of my sappy thoughts. It feels like it's a major offense to someone. I'm not sure if it's to the dead or God, but I quickly shuffle out of the courtyard toward the town square and answer it.

"Martha, why are you up at three in the morning?"

"You know I don't sleep! I figured I'd check in on you. It's been a few weeks. Things are going well!"

"They're going. Launch date for their new app is on schedule. Marketing campaigns haven't been too much of a nightmare. Feedback from testing has been positive, but there are still some security things I'm not confident about. I'm hoping to be back home soon."

"Are you though?"

Fair question.

"I think so. I am... not technically in London right now. I snuck away to the countryside for the weekend, but I'm headed back tomorrow."

Lavender wisteria cascades above the windows and doors of limestone buildings. Every inch of this village is like a fairy tale. My eyes scan across the storefronts where doors are opening and lights are turning on. The sun's starting to peer through the clouds, and town square is waking up.

"I'm glad you're taking some time away! You don't take enough time off." She's said that a thousand times. "How has this team been to work with? Typical Brits? I hear Lynn runs the place - even Craig and Catherine."

I chuckle. She isn't wrong. "Lynn's great. She's a strong leader, but not overly authoritative. People want to follow her. She leads technology, but has a pretty balanced perspective on the business."

"Rare praise from you. What about the guy she has you working with? Hadid? He's well-liked over there."

I get him out of my head for twenty full minutes, and she goes and ruins it.

"He's been alright. We've been spending a lot of hours together. I'm probably driving him up a wall, but he seems to like the challenge. He's... different."

"Good different?"

"I think so."

"Well, I did look him up online. There's got to be a few perks to being stuck in a room with him for hours..."

"Martha! I don't think that way."

"The rest of the world does, darling." She laughs at herself. "What have you got planned for the rest of the day?"

"There's an Inn for sale in town here, apparently. I'm going to go make a bid on it so you can quit your job and become the cutest Innkeeper in England."

"Ha! Doug would never go for that. We couldn't move our dogs across the world. You go ahead and follow that dream yourself, sweetheart."

"You mean it?"

"Hell no. I'm holding you hostage at Finch until one of us dies."

I laugh so hard I have tears in my eyes. I miss her.

"Are you doing OK? Still feeling like a chaos conductor every day?"

"That's what I do best. Mark might be getting that promotion soon. Jim's become a fan of his, following him around like a little dog - probably because you're not around. It keeps him out of my hair, so I'm just fine with it."

Damn it. I never replied to Mark. I'm sure he's recovered.

"Good for him. He deserves it." I mean it. "I'm going to walk to the supermarket and grab some things. I might have a little picnic somewhere if the rain holds off."

"That sounds wonderful, and totally out of character for you. You should!"

"Get some sleep. I'll keep you posted."

I'm not sure when a picnic became out of character for me, but I'm starting to question a lot more than the weather forecast. I enter the co-op on a mission to find flour, yeast, and milk.

The one thing on my to-do list today is making enough bread and butter to convince myself I could stay here forever, though I know I never would.

Eleven

May

"Was it everything you dreamed it would be?" Paige questions through the car speakers as I drive back to London.

"It was, actually. I miss it already. It was so quiet and slow, Paige. There were birds, lots of them. There are sheep everywhere." I won't miss these roundabouts. I can't get a good look at the sheep and drive on these narrow roads at the same time.

"Does it smell like sheep?"

"It smells like Heaven. I'm so relaxed. I don't think I've felt this light in ages, even though I've probably gained ten pounds. I made bread yesterday."

"Bread? You baked something?"

"It wasn't good. It wasn't even edible, but I did it."

"You couldn't eat any of it?"

"I guess I could have. It didn't turn out as bad as the butter did."

"You tried to make butter? Who are you?"

"I could have been successful if I had more upper body strength - or a machine."

"Or just a package of delicious butter from the store that's already been made."

"That's boring. If I invested in some dumbbells or a standing mixer, I could make it happen. Nothing tastes better than accomplishment."

"OK, now you're starting to sound like you, but not exactly. What did you do with her?"

I laugh and grip the steering wheel a little more tightly when a semi truck passes by in the right lane.

"I think I might look into a long-term rental thing for the rest of my time here, just for the weekends. Maybe even Thursday through Monday. I feel like I'm coming back to London a better person."

"Wouldn't that cost a fortune?"

"The client's still covering my apartment here and Judah's helping with the rent in Chicago. I think I could swing it."

"The same place?"

"Maybe. I really like it. The stove and I are becoming acquainted. The house next door is a rental unit, too. It's got to be just as adorable inside as this one was."

"That would be incredible. You have to do it. Are you going to look into it tonight - see if it can be a long-term rental thing?"

"I have to find a cocktail dress tonight. The client wants me to go to this launch party. I think it's an internal company thing because I never got a formal invite, but he asked me to be there, so..."

"Whoa. The one that's an eleven out of ten?"

"That's the one."

"Ol."

She's reading too much into this. "Stop."

"OK, so it's possible this could be strictly a professional ask he's making of you, but you better be planning to look hot. I'm going to need photo evidence that you made a point to look hot. When is it?"

"Next weekend."

"Will there be a lot of people there? Will you see him there?"

I debate mentioning the next thing that comes out of my mouth, "I'll see him in about an hour, actually."

"You have a work thing on a Sunday?"

"He told me to drive his car to the Cotswolds. I've got to drop it back off at his place."

"Olivia Anne Kincade, what the hell? You're driving his car?!"

"He didn't want me to have to rent one. He barely uses his. It made economic sense for both of us."

"And romantic sense."

"There's nothing romantic about this." I'm angry at myself for the huge smile across my face.

"Confirm that for me after next weekend. You have to text me dress pictures before you buy one. Promise me."

"I promise."

* * *

I'm deeply regretting the amount of water I drank on the way here as I turn onto Rami's tree-lined street. It's a miracle that I could parallel park in this massive thing and an even bigger miracle that I made it back without a scratch. After he sees the crumbs in the passenger's seat he may never let me borrow it again, but I can't say I'd accept it again if he offered. Trains and buses might be a less nerve-wracking option - if I do go back. I hope I do.

I grab my duffle bag from the back seat, and notice him standing right inside the gate with his hands in his pockets. His hair is a little tousled and he's wearing a white t-shirt and worn jeans.

Neither of us say a word until I make it to the outside of his iron gate and reach through to hand him his key.

"You look well."

"Do I?" He must be a fan of old sweatshirts and denim shorts.

He nods with a smile that deepens the dimple in his left cheek.

"I feel well. Thanks for letting me borrow the car. I think I brought her home in one piece."

"You brought both of you back in one piece. Well done, Kincade."

"I do have a slight problem. I drank too much water on the way here, and I'm afraid I won't make it back walking to my place..." His face goes blank. "I could stop somewhere else on the way. I just thought..."

"No, no, of course. Come in. You can use mine." He opens the gate to guide me through.

"I'm really sorry for imposing. I shouldn't have asked."

"It's alright." He opens the front door and blocks the most fluffy orange cat from darting past.

"Hercules!" I step inside and bend down to scratch him behind his ears. "I'm so glad to meet you."

I notice shoes lined up next to the door and decide to take off my own. Rami walks me down the main hallway and points to a door to the left just before the kitchen. I use the restroom and can't help but think about how tense he became in a split second. I shouldn't have asked to come in. I wasn't thinking. It wasn't a big deal in my mind, but I can see how intrusive it might have felt for him.

As I dry my hands on a towel with dainty embroidery, I also notice the smell of lavender. I remember the floral arrangement on the entryway table, and a profound realization starts taking shape. I heard him speaking in a low tone to someone in the next room. It could be Hercules, but I have a sense that it's not.

He doesn't live alone.

How could I be so ignorant? Paige was right. I've lost myself. I would have picked up on something like this before. He has an entire life at home, potentially an entire family. There's no reason I should have expected him to share that with me. I'm rummaging through memories of all the times I mistook his kindness for flirting, and I feel like an idiot. I fix my disheveled braid and realize I'm grateful I asked to come in. I can't imagine what kind of fool I would have made out of myself eventually if I hadn't.

I walk out of the restroom and turn into the kitchen to thank him again before escaping as quickly as I can. He's standing at his stove in front of a large pot of something that smells divine.

Before I can speak, an elderly man sitting at a small corner table looks at me like I'm from another planet. I study him, too. He's wearing some kind of jersey and takes a bite of a chocolate cookie. He looks frail, but there's something undeniably strong in his eyes. His eyes are Rami's eyes, deep brown framed with dark eyebrows and thick lashes.

"Sit." He gestures in front of him. He's gentle, but I'm terrified of declining his invitation. I pause for a second and look toward Rami. He looks over his shoulder at me. I detect both amusement and concern.

I walk toward where the old man sits. "Sure. Thank you."

"Make her some tea now. You've stirred the stew too much. You look like a blender."

I can't keep myself from laughing out loud, "Let me make it. I insist."

I get up from the table and walk behind Rami as he shamefully shifts to a different task. He points toward the kettle. We make eye contact, but don't say a word. I open the canister next to the kettle and smell the most wonderful, warm spices.

"It's chai." He finally breaks his silence.

"Perfect" I smile slightly at him, and open the cabinet above. I find a collection of old tea cups and coffee mugs, most covered in wild flowers or woodland animals. Some have OneDer logos or names of medical centers.

"She loved beautiful things," the old man exclaims. "Rami's mother. She was beautiful, and she loved beautiful things."

All the vibrant colors and exquisite objects make more sense now. "She had great taste. You're surrounded by treasures." I choose a teacup covered in daisies.

Rami reaches into a different cabinet and hands me a large canister of sugar. "Don't use it all. I haven't started on dessert." There's that dimple again.

I roll my eyes and scoop a generous teaspoon. The kettle whistles. I drop a tea bag into my cup, and carefully fill it up.

"No milk?" He smirks and I remember our conversation at the office the day we went to the pub for his birthday.

"Still no milk." I take my cup and settle back at the table.

"Hazem," the old man says, "... since my son hasn't introduced me properly."

"Ollie." I don't know why that name came out of me. "Olivia, but friends call me Ollie."

He turns dramatically and looks toward Rami, who I realize is already looking at me.

"We're friends, you see?" he says to Rami.

"His name, Hazem, means something like 'firm' or 'resolute'. This man is the softest thing you'll ever meet."

"I'm as strong as I've ever been. Don't listen to him." He snaps back playfully.

"You are. You haven't needed to be helped off the floor at prayer time today."

"You have not joined. How do you know?"

He brushes off the accusatory comment. "I'm watching you, Baba." He smiles and goes back to stirring the stew. The twinkle in Hazem's eye says he knows he's taken care of.

"I like your cup." I point toward the mint green mug covered in tiny white sheep. It looks quite out of place in this modern kitchen and in this masculine old man's hand. It's chipped and well-worn.

"It's my favorite." He examines it like he knows every mark; every little crack by heart."

"Why is it your favorite?" Hercules weaves between my feet and settles on top of them.

"I don't know. We don't have to know why we love something." He says it like it isn't the most profound thing I've heard in weeks.

Nothing's said for a few moments while Hazem's attention shifts to whatever soccer - football - thing is happening on the television. He picks up a cookie from the plate in front of him and hands it to me, never breaking his focus on the TV. I take it, and look toward Rami. He's started on something that looks like pastry dough. He's focused on brushing some kind of mixture over the top, and I can't put my thoughts into words. Even if I could, I wouldn't dare say them aloud.

This isn't the afternoon I expected. I didn't think I'd be sitting in Rami Hadid's cozy, immaculate home smelling food he'd made himself and talking to his father of all people. This feels like a far cry from suits in a conference room, and the sense of warmth running through me is more than the chai tea.

He catches me zoning out as I stare toward where he's chopping something.

"You don't have a choice now." He snaps me back to reality.

"What?"

"You have to stay. Stay for dinner."

Hazem echos "Stay for dinner."

I suppose dress shopping can wait.

* * *

That meal was the most incredible thing I've eaten in years. It was kind of them to invite me to stay. It's nice that I didn't seem to interrupt their typical routine, or their father-son banter. They watched their football match, argued plenty, had seconds of the unbelievable stew Rami made, and thirds of the sticky dessert.

Walking back toward the front door, I see the shoes lined up and realize I wouldn't have spiraled in the bathroom had I noticed all of them are men's - not that it means anything at all for me. Our relationship is friendly, but it's professional.

Inviting me to stay for dinner was courteous. Loaning me his car was courteous. Inviting me for drinks on his birthday was courteous.

"I'm glad you stayed." It sounds like he means it. I bend and twist to put my shoes back on, then step toward the door he has open for me. He reaches to grab my duffle off the entryway table, and I beat him to it.

"I am, too. I am genuinely impressed with your culinary skills. Do people know this about you?'

"Ah, I don't suppose most do." He scratches the stubble on his face. I wish he'd keep it there, but he'll no doubt show up tomorrow clean-shaven. "Most don't know I look after my father. Craig does - now, you."

"I'm sorry. It wasn't polite of me to ask to come in." We walk toward the gate and stop. He looks bothered.

"Please, don't be. It's good. It's a good thing." He takes a deep breath and lets it out. "I sometimes fear people would think it takes a toll on my work. It doesn't. If anything, Baba gives me advice. He was a good business man back in the day."

"Did he get sick? Hurt?"

"Cancer. He had a transplant a few years back. He's been in remission since. His strength never fully came back. He likes to think it has."

"He seems sharp. I enjoyed his company." I realize how much I mean it as I say it out loud.

"He is sharp, yeah. He's also a pain in the ass." His perfect smile stuns me more often than it should. "He likes you. So does Hercules." He looks to his side toward the row of glowing streetlamps, then back at me "So do I."

My heart-rate picks up. "Tell them I feel the same."

"They know, I think." Something intangible shifts in the air, and I can't look at him directly anymore.

"Nine tomorrow morning?"

He doesn't respond. He looks somewhere between frustrated and eager, and I don't know what else to say.

"Stop." He looks me dead in the eye, and I'm too surprised to speak. "Stop doing that. You know what you're doing."

"I don't." I start laughing because I don't know what else to do.

"You do. You shift the conversation back to work every time... every time that... "

"I shift it back to the reason I'm here? The reason your company is paying me to live down the street?"

"OneDer's the reason you're in London, but it's not the reason you're here." He gestures to the space between us. I don't reply. He takes a step back and stares into the sky. "I'm sorry. We can keep things straight-laced if that's what you want."

"Rami, I-" There are a million things to say and nothing to say at the same time.

He interrupts, "I'm not convinced that's what you want."

"What do you mean you're not convinced? Does it seem like I've been coming on to you? I've barely known you for eight weeks."

Why am I feeling so defensive? I'd be crazy to think the way I feel isn't obvious. I can't blame him for calling it out, but I can't give in if he's asking me to act on it. I spent the entire weekend and the entire drive here lecturing myself on how important it is not to unravel right now. There's too much at stake. Finch's relationship with a massive account is on the line, and I have a laundry list of responsibilities in Chicago that are only going to pile up more before September.

I can't lose control with this magnetic man standing in front of me, towering above me and asking for something that feels dangerous and amazing. This was so much easier when I believed he wasn't interested.

"We've spent hundreds of hours together in eight weeks, and no, you haven't been coming on to me."

"Then why are you confused?" My tone is patronizing, but I can't take it back now.

"I'm not confused. I've been pretty damn clear on how I feel for weeks now." Neither of us say a word for a few long seconds. He runs a hand through his hair. He's clearly frustrated. "You're so hard to read. I can't read your mind, but I'd bet it's not always ad campaigns and press releases running through that gorgeous head when we're together, is it?" His voice shakes a little. "It's something more, I think. I can see it. I think I saw it when I was cooking earlier."

He's feeling intense, but fighting to keep calm. I'm painfully embarrassed. "I don't know what to say to you."

"Convince me. Tell me I'm reading this all wrong. I've got dishes to do and pills to organize, and I at least want to go to bed knowing how to conduct myself around you from now on." He looks exhausted. I realize in this moment that as bold as he seems, it took some courage to admit what he's said. "I won't mention it again. Just tell me."

"I can't."

"Can't what?" He looks aggravated with himself, ready to resign from the conversation."Have I made an idiot of myself?"

"No. I can't convince you that you're wrong. You're not wrong." I realize my fists have been clenched around my duffle bag strap, and I relax them again. "I'm not sure that can mean anything. I'm not sure you and I could go anywhere from here."

"That's not what I'm asking for."

"What are you asking for?"

"I needed... help." He lets out another breath he'd be holding in and thinks for a long moment before he speaks again. "I think I needed help knowing I can... be cared for by someone in this way. It's been a long time. That might not make sense. I'm not asking you for anything. I'm not sure I'd have much to give someone right now anyway."

My heart cracks open a bit because I somehow understand exactly what he means.

"You are cared for. I can't get you out of my head, even from miles away." He can probably hear how angry it makes me, but I don't feel as pathetic anymore. He relaxes his shoulders. He still looks tired, but his lips turn up at the edges and the air feels peaceful again. "I think being honest about it helps me, too." I exhale and notice the streetlamps are brighter.

"In what way?"

"You needed a reminder that someone could feel something for you. I think I needed a reminder that I could feel something for someone." I'm shocked at myself for getting this vulnerable.

He studies my face for a quick moment before folding his broad arms across his chest and sighing. "... and that's enough for both of us right now."

"More than enough." I reach and brush the Baklava crumbs off the space where his chest meets his shoulder. I'm not sure we've ever touched, so it startles us both.

He offers to walk me back and I decline.

I drag myself up the stairs to my flat, ignore the four texts I have from Paige, and sleep harder than I have since the day I arrived.

Twelve

June

OLLIE

It's the official launch day for TwoRist. The energy at the office is electric with a healthy mix of excitement and anxiety. I'm not sure I'm feeling either of those things. I'm as well-rested as I've ever been, but I woke up with that same shift in perspective people get when they come home from a long vacation. Everything looks weirdly different, like I'm seeing it with someone else's eyes. It's like the world tilted on its axis by one degree.

I grab a yogurt from the cooler and fill up my water bottle before taking a seat at a table in the corner of the break area. It's the first day of June and hot enough for a breathable dress today, which is nice. On a day when nothing else feels comfortable, at least my outfit can be.

We've prepared well. Our social media strategy is solid. Influencer marketing will play a huge part in whether this takes off or not. TV and radio promotions are scheduled to start today, and print distribution seemed to go smoothly for the most part. A few engagements are scheduled with podcasts and Youtube channels. One magazine will feature an article, but I'm not confident about the angle they want to take just yet.

Rami will be a zombie by the end of this week. Arthur isn't the best person to put behind a mic, so he'll take the lead on being the face of the brand on post platforms. Craig will join him for some, but I'm positive Rami will take most of the talking points. He knows them like the back of his hand. If there's anyone that can sell this, it's him. He cares so deeply about it.

It's just after eight in the morning. and he's already running on all cylinders in the conference room across from the break area. I can see him standing at the large monitor on the wall. He's pointing and talking through a slide I put together weeks ago detailing our first week's key dates. Lynn, Arthur, Theo and a few employees from both the marketing and digital side are learning forward and asking questions. Craig and Catherine are huddled in a small room nearby, deep in a separate conversation.

The large conference room door opens and the group begins to scatter. Theo and Rami take off down another hallway, and Lynn walks over to wear I sit.

"Good morning, Olivia."

"Morning. How are you?"

"Great! Really good. All the tough stuff's done, right? Now it's just about sharing it with the world."

"That's a comforting perspective. There's still some work left to do, but I'm confident we'll get it right."

"I know you've got it right. You've done wonderful work, Olivia. Rami sings your praises."

"Thank you. That means a lot. I'm enjoying it."

"Enjoying it?" She looks at me suspiciously. "I shared with Jim that you've been working hard. I shared that you've been challenging us. It's a good thing. I still have some... concerns on the data and security side."

"I do, too." I decide not to get into the details. I'm not sure who knows more about the situation between she and I. Rami's still going toe-to-toe with Theo on it all. "I'm here if something happens. I've got a response plan that I'm keeping close to my chest for now."

"Of course you do." She smiles. "Let's hope we never need it."

She walks toward the room where Craig and Catherine are huddled, and slips inside.

I open my calendar for the week and realize that today is the lightest day I'll have until the weekend, which isn't saying much. Beginning at nine. I'm in back-to-back meetings until five with only a few short breaks between. Then, I have to find a stupid dress for this launch party on Friday. I'm not sure how much I care about it. I could come up with a reason not to show, but I've got nothing else to do this weekend.

I emailed this morning about the prospect of long-term renting in the Cotswolds. She immediately replied to say it wouldn't be open for a few more weeks. From there, I could have it through September when I leave.

I stop dreaming about escaping long enough to eat my yogurt and prepare for my first meeting.

* * *

"Hanging in there?" Rami slips into the small meeting room where I sit, ready for our afternoon debrief. It's ironic he's asking me that question today. I don't think I've seen him sit down once.

"I'm doing fine." I stare at him with a smirk while he continues to stand right inside the door. "Sit down, would you?"

He raises his eyebrows and exhales, then sits across from me.

"Hey" I say to him calmly, attempting to slow the pace of the conversation.

"Hey" He crosses his arms across his chest and leans back.

"You're ready for your week? It's going to be wild."

"It is, and I am ready."

"I like your confidence. You've got the podcast thing in the morning. I can meet you there. I'm aiming to arrive fifteen minutes early. I think we need more time than they gave us to prep with the producers."

"I'll be there when you get there, then." He still seems high-strung, but not in a negative way.

"You're truly looking forward to this, aren't you?"

"I am." He smiles with a satisfaction that I can't resist smiling back at.

"Can I ask you a question? Please don't take this as skepticism. It's genuine curiosity."

"Fire away."

"TwoRist offers people a new way to connect with strangers, people they'd otherwise never meet when they're traveling."

"Did it take you this long to figure that out, Olivia?" His tone seeps with sarcasm.

"Let me finish! What I'm wondering is how important that truly is in the big picture. Isn't it more worthwhile to build community at home than abroad? Why does the world need another way to lose anonymity?"

"You're definitely not a skeptic." He's more amused than annoyed.

"Maybe." I'm crossing my arms now, too. "Convince me." Using the same language he used last night stirs something I'd put to sleep.

He stands up and grabs a marker before walking to the whiteboard. He draws a massive, imperfect circle and laughs at himself a little. "I never claimed to be an artist. Hear me out."

"Listening." I notice the yogurt I dropped on my pants just as I try to avoid staring at the back of his.

He starts to draw distorted continents and I can see the globe shaping up. He colors in England. "Local connection is important. You're right. That shouldn't stop being most important. When we think about the positive impact we can make on people, it can only spread so far when we're doing it locally. That's why travel's so important. That's why the internet's changed the world. Am I losing you?"

"I'm with you. Still not sold."

"When we see new places, physically be in new places, we learn enough to come back home better. When we can build relationships with people in those places, our mark on the world becomes a lot more significant than a speck in our local communities." He starts making little dots across all the continents. "It starts to look like freckles..." He looks back at me, "...like yours".

Focus, Ollie.

He goes on. "Those little freckles can start to spread, become larger. Care can be contagious." He makes the little dots bigger with his marker.

"So, you feel responsible for making more of a mark on the world."

"You don't?"

"I do, I guess. I want to be good at my job. I want to take care of the people I love. I don't think I've ever felt strongly about reaching outside of that."

He sits back down at the small table, contemplating. "I think... if people, and good companies, are doing the internal work it takes to be good... if they're committed to being humble, compassionate, educated,.. I think it's those people that should be reaching outside of their bubble. It's people like that I hope will use TwoRist. Travel more; expand their influence. I think we have a duty, I think *I* have a duty to think that way. I'm fortunate that I get to think that way."

"That's a fair challenge. I visit a lot of new places. I can't say I ever think about leaving things I touch better than I found them."

"I assure you." He hesitates for a split second. "You improve everything you touch."

"What about the power something like this gives to the people that aren't good people? What if this is another door you've unlocked for bad people to do bad things?"

"Isn't there always a risk in that when venturing out - technology aside?"

"Fair. It doesn't mean that creating technology that inflates that risk is a great idea."

"You aren't seeing the potential in it."

"I'm trying to."

"I know". He looks more empathetic than disappointed. "The unknown is supposed to feel scary."

I'm not sure we're still talking about the app.

"You know, you're the perfect person to be leading this. Everyone can see it. You question yourself much more at work than you do outside of work."

He doesn't miss a beat "You question yourself much more outside of work than you do at work."

"Hadid, you got a minute?" Craig taps on the glass door. Rami quickly erases the whiteboard, and squeezes my shoulder before exiting.

* * *

"Yellow? That's out of character for you, but I can dig it."

"I like the neckline and where the waistband sits. It's the only color they have in my size for this one". I've got Paige's video chat propped up on the ottoman in the fitting room.

"No. I changed my mind. The color washes you out. Show me that blue one hanging behind you." She's multitasking on her lunch break. "Seriously?! They gave me steak instead of chicken in my bowl again. This client I'm with today is horrific. The one thing I wanted was for my lunch order to be right."

"Is this the man who wanted you to find an abstract piece that was green but not too green, and incorporated a cat somehow?" Her job is incredible, but excruciating.

"No, this is the influencer - the one that's asking me for cream and beige everything. She let me break some of it up with wood tones, but of course she's only open to white oak."

"Tragic."

"Tragic, indeed. Your Chicago apartment isn't far from that. It's what you wanted though."

"True. I might make it a little more colorful when I'm back; a little moodier, maybe. I'm allowed to change my tastes."

"If your tastes never changed, I'd be worried. You'd still have farmhouse everything if that wasn't the case." Barn doors are timeless. I don't care what kind of expert she thinks she is. "I like that one. Where does the hem fall?"

"It's short. I hate it. I don't like any of these." My mind is not in a condition to be playing dress-up today.

"What's wrong?"

The boutique employee outside shouts through the door, "You alright? How's it all working?"

"Fine, thanks! I'll let you know." I sit on the ottoman with the blue dress half unzipped.

Paige repeats herself, "What's wrong, Ol? Missing home? You're almost halfway to September."

"No, it's not that. I'm... I don't think I can do this."

"Do what? The party?"

"I don't think I can be serious with someone. He says he doesn't have anything to give anyway, so it's not on the table even if I wanted it to be. I just-"

"Serious? What aren't you telling me?"

I don't know how to answer her. "There's nothing to tell. There's something there, but it's not just an office fling kind of thing - not that I'd know what that feels like." I laugh at myself a bit, and breathe deep. "It's something more than that. We both kind of admitted it to each other last night."

"Why are you crying?"

I realize there are tears streaming down my face. Something just snapped inside me. Tension in my chest starts to melt, apparently out of my eyeballs. I turn toward the mirror and notice the mascara smeared down my left cheek. "It's not just him. It's all of it. It's this job. It's my brain. I don't think any of the things I wanted before are the same things I want now."

"... and you're scared of that?"

"Terrified, yes. How would I support myself if I didn't have this job? Because of the split, I'm decades from retiring and not sure what I'd do with my days. I used to need my routine; my Pilates. All I want to do now is to have no schedule. I used to work my tail off for quarterly bonuses, and now I'm trying to figure out if I could survive on a quarter of my salary. I want to have the energy to do the things that make me feel alive, Paige, even if it is burning bread. I want to fill my house with antiques instead of filling up some corporation's pockets. My house costs money though, and so do antiques." I sniff and wipe my face with the dress I wore to work. "I feel stuck."

At this point, I'm sobbing so loud I know the clerks outside can hear me.

"Your midlife crisis is the most beautiful thing I've seen all day."

I can't help but laugh at her. "Shut up"

"I think you have to get more honest with yourself, ya know? You have to decide if the work you do actually fuels the life you want, or if it drains it. It's OK if it used to be what you wanted and isn't anymore."

"That feels impossible."

"I've seen you do impossible things over and over again, Ollie Kincade, but you aren't going to get any of the answers if you don't have the balls to ask yourself the hard questions." She's always had a knack for knowing went to be gentle with me and when to break me down just a little. "Those walls you put up when you signed the papers kept you upright when you felt wobbly, but now they're keeping all the good stuff from coming in."

"I'm not scared of hard questions. I'm scared of the answers. I'm scared I'll decide to blow up my life and I won't be able to put it back together if I regret it."

"Maybe not, but that's when you pick up the pieces and do something new. You've done it before, and wouldn't be doing it alone."

"I am, though. I have you. I have Judah. I am alone, though."

"That's insulting, but I get it. I am, too.." She's had a long line of awful partners, including one short-lived marriage. "Are you scared of what might happen if you open up to this guy? What's his name?"

"It's Rami." Saying his name out loud to someone feels so exposing; so risky. "I am scared of what might happen if I open up to him. I'm more scared of what might happen if I don't."

"You're scared of getting hurt, but more scared of being alone for the rest of your life?"

"I'm not scared of getting hurt, really. I'm scared of hurting him. I'm so impatient with people, Paige. I'm worried we'll find out we're too different to be compatible. If he decides he wants to take a chance on me, I'll crush him eventually. He recently lost his mom, and he's so busy with work. I can't do that to him. He also lives across the world, It'd never work."

"It seems like you're hoping for something easy. If you don't want to be single forever, you're going to need to give that up."

"How do I do that?"

"One day at a time."

"Yeah." I stare into the mirror and wonder what those tiny decisions might look like on a day-to-day basis, whether they're with Rami or anyone else.

"Is he worth it? If it didn't end in happily ever after, is he worth the leap?"

I don't think I've asked myself that question outright. The only thing I've been telling myself to do is to resist this pull I feel toward Rami Hadid altogether; to protect myself, to protect him.

Obviously giving in would be inappropriate from a professional standpoint, but how much does that really matter to me now? If it doesn't matter to me, why should I feel the right to keep my walls up just to protect his career? That's his decision to make. Careers aside, why should I feel the right to keep my walls up just to protect his heart? That's his decision, too. What I can decide is how much I'm willing to risk.

"I've never met someone more worth it."

The store attendant knocks again. I'm not going to be able to check out and pretend she hasn't heard me in hysterics, "Finishing up!"

I hang up with Paige and put my mascara-covered dress back on. I grab a velvet option I never tried on, and leave the others behind.

Thirteen

June

OLLIE

The music in here is excruciating, even on the second floor overlooking the atrium. This venue likely blew their budget, but the view of the River Thames is unreal. I haven't felt the need to go on another river cruise after the last one when Paige and I both got sunburned. It'd be magical this time of day.

Over the atrium hangs three majestic, modern light fixtures with thousands of glass prisms. Round tables below are draped with violet linens and covered with empty bottles. Orchid arrangements in the center of each one elevate the look, but the balloon pillars ruin any chance at sophistication. I guess this isn't a wedding. I should adjust my attitude, and my hair pins.

I opted for a low bun and simple pearl earrings, which meant I didn't have to wash my hair. This dress needs nothing else, really. The deep plum velvet feels right with OneDer's signature color being purple. The silhouette is fitted, and reaches just below the knee. The haltered neck is modest enough, but the back is completely open down to my waist. I should have noticed that in the fitting room on Monday. A mental breakdown can be distracting.

A waiter passes by with a tray of champagne glasses, and I decline. I don't want to be anything other than sober. There's enough to disorient me, even if I am thinking more clearly than I have all week.

I spotted Rami once. He got pulled toward the side of the stage area they've set up. I didn't play a part in planning this event, but they'll no doubt make a speech about the insane number of new users and app downloads since Monday. There are still some PR engagements to manage over the next several weeks, but it's likely I'll be out of here in ninety days.

Lynn and Arthur take the stage. Catherine and Craig follow behind, then Craig approaches the acrylic podium. The room starts to fall silent aside from the screeching music, which the DJ turns down. The rest of the C-suite sits in chairs across the front, including the CEO and CFO. I barely see either of them around.

"It is my absolute pleasure to stand in front of you and share that we have even more to celebrate than we anticipated." The room erupts, and Craig claps along. "The number of new OneDer accounts created in the past five days has exceeded projections by 20%, and the number of TwoRist activations we hoped for was exceeded by 30%."

The room erupts again, and Catherine steps forward. "Theo Bryant has played a significant role leading design and development." The room cheers and claps with Catherine as she continues, beaming at Rami where he stands to the side "Rami Hadid. You have been a pioneer of this work like no other. Your passion made all of this possible." She barely gets her last words out as the room roars with whistles and silly shouts.

My eyes migrate across the room. I don't think I noticed before how well-known he is - how well-respected he is. When my gaze lands back at him, I realize his is on me. I give him a tiny wave, not sure if he's actually looking my way. He nods with a small smile as the CMO and CTO make their closing comments.

Theo, Rami, and the project team were all gifted with bonuses. If Theo's is the same as Rami's, someone needs a kick below the belt. I'll keep my mouth shut. I'm not even supposed to be here.

Rami disappears behind the stage in a huddle of people I've never met, and my stomach rumbles with hunger. I venture down to the buffet to grab something before taking off. I made an appearance. I'll assume he's satisfied with that.

"Nice seeing you here, Olivia." Theo startles me as I'm picking through chilled shrimp. I don't know why I'm looking for the good ones like they're avocados. They're all the same.

"Hi! Glad to be here. Congratulations are in order. I hope you're feeling proud."

"I am. Thanks." He sticks his hands in his pockets, and he's holding back something he wants to say.

"How are you celebrating?" I honestly don't care, but I'd rather him talk so I can eat.

"Just keeping at it, you know. I think they want me in a bigger role here. It makes sense. I'm telling those two how to do their jobs most of the time." He nods toward Lynn and Catherine. I let it go. I pick up another shrimp instead of responding. Making him feel awkward is a sheer delight. "What brought you here? Did you pay someone to squeeze your name in at the end of the list?"

I feel a warm hand lay across the small of my back - my bare back, and it sends a shock straight up my spine.

"I think I spotted her name above yours, mate." His hand doesn't move. He smells more intoxicating than the champagne could ever be. "Olivia, can we go over something for Monday briefly?" He turns back to Theo. "Cheers".

We walk quickly toward the stairs leading to the second level and don't exchange words until we're at the top. He props his arms over the rail and looks down at the dwindling crowd. I do the same.

"How dare you." He takes a sip from a bottle of water, and doesn't look in my direction. My heart drops.

"You told me to come." Did he forget that day at the pool? Did he forget he asked me to be here?

"I did. How dare you wear that dress." He cuts his eyes back toward mine and smirks. "You're killing me."

"You're very much alive, Hadid." He's in his typical black from head to toe, but the cologne and watch change everything. Whatever product he has in his hair brightens the silver strands around his temples. He looks like someone who's earned every ounce of his success, and I hope Hazem saw him before he left home. I hope Hercules did, too."New watch?"

"From Craig. He couldn't convince Catherine that my bonus should be double what Theo's was. He gifted it to me himself.. He didn't have to."

"He shouldn't have told you that." I'm not surprised, really. ""But your bonus was still more? Don't answer that." He doesn't need me to be so protective.

His brown eyes keep shifting to my lips. I'm not close enough to be concerned about my shrimp breath, but I reach in my clutch to find something to fix it.

"It was, yeah. Don't worry on that one. I think it was too soon for them to dole anything out, anyway. There's still a lot that's up in the air."

"Up in the air isn't a bad thing. Anything could happen." I finally find a peppermint and pop it in my mouth. "I thought you were an optimist."

"I am. You aren't." He studies me closer. He probably thinks there was more to that comment than I intended. "Are you telling me you're feeling optimistic?" He grabs another bottle of water from a tray passing by, and hands it to me.

"I'm telling you I'm comfortable being up in the air." I unscrew the top and take a sip

He smiles, and raises his own bottle. "To being up in the air."

I raise mine, and lock eyes with him. "Hear, hear."

We both take another swig, and I ignore Theo looking our way from the bottom of the curved staircase.

* * *

We didn't ride to the event together for obvious reasons, but he offered to drive me back when he realized how hard it was raining. We walked out at separate times, and he pulled the car up to a side door. I'm relieved I don't have to run to the tube station in these heels.

"I can barely keep my eyes open." He undoes his cuff buttons and rolls up his sleeves. I knew he'd be exhausted. Next week shouldn't be such a circus.

"That's exactly what I like all my Uber drivers to say when I buckle in."

"I'm your Uber? It wasn't enough to drive my car yourself. Now, you expect me to drive it for you?" He pulls into the steady traffic and the glare of headlights. Right on cue, a text from Martha comes in and flashes on the screen.

Damn it. His car must remember my phone's connection.

Martha - Finch & Assoc: *What's the latest on sexy marketing boss?*

I want to crawl into the floorboard and throw up.

"Should I tell Craig you've been swooning over him? If you want to be sent home early, just say so." He's laughing at me, but definitely blushing.

"No. I don't..." He's still laughing."...but you can reply to her and make sure she knows what 'boss' means. Mine isn't on this continent."

"Who's Martha? Is that Jim Finch's assistant?"

"She's Jim's boss if you ask me." It couldn't be more true. "I'm happy for you, Rami, sincerely. It was... special to see you recognized like that. The right people rarely get the spotlight."

He doesn't reply right away. "You know why I wanted you there?"

"Because you knew I'd accidentally choose a sleazy dress?"

That catches him off guard. "Ha! No. What's it feel like to be wrong, Kincade?"

"Why, then?"

He thinks before he speaks. "Because you ground me. I'm braver when you're close." He reaches over and squeezes my knee. "And because you deserve to celebrate, too. You should have been beside me up there."

"I think you need to consider how often I'm seen beside you."

"So I'm told." He brushes it off.

He turns onto the next street. The rain is coming down hard now and he's trying to focus. We ride in silence for several more minutes. I can barely see the lamps glowing on his end of the street. In another few blocks we reach mine. The only spot open is still several steps from the entrance. He backs in, then pulls forward to parallel park.

"Thank you. This isn't as bad as walking to the train would have been." I open the door and start to step out into the downpour.

He grabs an umbrella from somewhere, and shouts after me. "Stop. I'll walk you."

"You're crazy!" This British gentleman thing is unnecessary - and ridiculous at the moment.

"He comes around with the umbrella and walks me to the entrance. He's leaning it over me and getting drenched in the process. Thunder crashes, and I jump forward several feet at once. He jogs to keep up with me.

When we reach the awning, he collapses his umbrella and leans it against the outside of the building. I realize he doesn't plan to turn back toward the car, and it sends the flutter in my stomach into a frenzy.

I look back at him for a split second, then step inside through the treacherous resolving door. When I enter the lobby, I don't turn back around until I'm standing inside the open elevator.

He pauses in front of it, facing me. He's asking for permission. He doesn't know what he's risking. He doesn't know what a damaged mess I am - how I abandon anything that gets too close.

I've already decided what I'm willing to risk. I don't get to decide that for him.

The door starts to close, forcing me to make a statement. I reach my arm out and hold it open. He steps inside, raindrops hanging from the line of his jaw, and turns forward to face the door alongside me.

Just before it closes completely, he has my back against the wall.

My hair has fallen down in the least elegant way possible. He's kissing me with a fierceness that sends my pulse through the roof of this rickety box. I can't help but run my hands up his soaked back and down again, pulling him in closer until I feel his heart racing against mine. His hands hold both sides of my spinning head with his thumbs at my cheekbones and his fingers wrapped around the back of my neck. No part of me was prepared for this.

Is zero to sixty what's happening right now? Is this the part when I'm supposed to want to pump the breaks?

He pulls away, and we both realize I never pressed the button for my floor. My arms drop to my sides and his hands drop to my waist. He's short of breath, searching for a sign of regret on my face. I pull him in once more. It's softer this time, slow enough for his hands to migrate from my waist to my hips. He pulls away for the last time and presses the button to open the elevator doors where we never left the ground.

So much for being up in the air.

"Drive safe. Rami Hadid's kind of important, you know."

He steps out of the elevator walking backward, and shakes his head. "I didn't tell you? I've changed my name." I know exactly what's going to come out of that gorgeous mouth next. "Sexy marketing boss".

I punch the button for my floor, smiling, and smooth my dress back into place before the door closes between us.

Fourteen

July

Everything about this storybook town feels exactly as magical as it did in May. The trees are greener and the sky is a perfect, clear blue. The wisteria blooms are long gone, but the rose bushes are showing off. The aroma's almost too strong.

I wish I'd been able to settle in sooner, but I'll still have a solid eight weeks of weekend bliss before I'm back on American soil. I'm growing more sad about that, but I can't wait much longer to squeeze my blonde boy's cheeks. He's sounded more confident each time we've talked. I'm hoping he'll visit before summer's end.

I've already been to the local co-op and picked up flour, milk, and bags of other essentials. A second attempt at bread and butter has been part of my plan for Cotswolds Ollie. I bought an electric hand mixer and had it shipped here. I probably could have borrowed one from this extraordinary man I know, but I wanted to travel light on the train and bus I took to get here. I have no idea what I'll do with the thing when I leave in a few months.

Rami and I haven't discussed the topic. I think we're both afraid of it. I think we're afraid of how much it matters. He doesn't travel to the states much and OneDer is our only client here. If we decide to stay connected, it'd take a heavy amount of work on both our parts. I can't imagine it feeling heavier than the thought of not spending half my days with him every week. I've been going over for dinner every Sunday evening since the launch party, so time together is shaping up to be more than that.

Things have felt like a calm companionship; simple and no pressure. Rami, Hazem, and Hercules have started to become my London home. I only visit on Sundays, but it's a new norm that's grounding me. Paired with my Monday calls with Paige and my gym routine after work, I'm getting some sense of the normalcy I keep in Chicago without the mundane emptiness. I'm far from empty here. Being in the office is the only exception.

It's Friday, and the team's working remotely. I managed to convince the property owner to choose a better WiFi plan. I dial into our morning huddle from the old oak dining table just inside the french doors leading to the courtyard.

"Morning", "Good morning", "Happy Friday", "Hiya"

We start chatting through our weekend plans, and the team is generous with their recommendations on where I should explore. It sounds like Castle Combe might be worth the bus ride. Broadway's also a prospect.

It's eight minutes after the hour and someone's missing.

Arthur comes off mute, which I'm not sure I've ever seen him do. He's sitting in a poorly lit corner. His camera angle makes him look like a walrus. "Rami's not going to make it today." He clears his throat. "I'm not sure we've got much to cover apart from the mid-year shareholder report. Finance is nearly done preparing it, but they need a few inputs from us." The shifting blue light on his face shows he's shuffling through browser windows. "Let me just... locate the email message... just a moment... I despise this thing..." He clears his throat again.

I check in with Rami while Arthur remembers how to function.

I text: *Everything ok?*

The team talks through a few other low-priority items that don't have much to do with me. The call ends early, and I close the window where I'd taken notes.

Some days I don't know why I'm still here. There are two events planned for August where I should probably be present, but it doesn't seem critical enough. I know Jim talked with Lynn and Arthur about a sooner end date, but I never heard the outcome. If Rami spoke into that, he didn't mention it.

I've checked my phone every sixty seconds. I wish he'd turn on read receipts. Part of me wishes he decided on a whim to take the day off, but I've got the sense something's wrong. Hazem did seem a little weak on Sunday.

I decide to get my mind off of it and open my bank account instead. Another task I've been looking forward to is paying off a loan I've had for two years and a car note I've had for three. With Judah contributing to bills back home, I've been able to put away some cash and whittle down my expenses.

Nothing's more fun to buy than freedom. It's nice when buying freedom means I'm less of a slave to my finances. It's also nice when it means I can escape somewhere I feel a little more like who I'm supposed to be.

I shut my laptop without actually shutting it down, which is on-brand. I slip on white sneakers that have seen better days, and head out the door to soak up more of this corner of the world that feels like it's mine.

* * *

"Those are on special, two for one." The sweet lady says to me from behind the post office counter. I turn a rotating rack of post cards, some specific to Stow-on-the-Wold, some with "The Cotswolds" splashed above a photo of winding streets or rolling hills.

"Thank you. I'll take these two." I lay a few on the counter. One's a sunset scene over a hilly landscape and the other's a quintessential Cotswolds town photo I've seen a million times. I didn't know until today that it's Bibury, which is only a short drive south.

I check my phone. Nothing.

"Are you in town for long? I've seen you out and about." I realize then that she's the lady from the church courtyard. She has her snow white hair pushed back in a headband today.

"You might see a bit more of me. I'll be spending weekends here for the next few months." She's focusing on pressing buttons on the cash register, and I'm not sure she caught any of that.

I pay, and she slips my postcards into a tiny brown sack. "I reckon whoever receives one of these will be glad to hear from you."

"My son." I take the bag from her frail hand and notice her dainty gold ring. "He might not appreciate it much." I take the receipt she hands me."I think it's nice to hold something that's traveled far to get to you, even if it's paper."

The door opens and the tiny bell tied to the handle rings. "It's true for paper and for people, dear. This one traveled from Liverpool to get to me."

The patron that wanders in is a familiar face; her beau - the man from the antiques store. "I'm Mabel. This is Billy."

"Olivia - Ollie. Lovely to meet you." I turn toward the old man with a quick wave.

"Hiya, doll. You did pop into the shop some weeks back..." I don't know why I expected his memory to be worse."... had a barney with a 19th century globe if I remember correctly."

"She might not have been the one, Billy. Your video system's older than she is."

"Oh, I remember just fine it was her, la. I don't remember if it's a 19th century or an 18th."

"Don't mind him. That thing was cracked when he bought it."

"I'm so sorry, I -"

My phone goes off with a text, and I glance down at the screen before repeating what I said before. "It's lovely to meet you both."

I move out the door into the thick July heat, and open the message.

Rami Hadid - OneDer: *Baba had some blood-work done weeks ago. The results we got this morning weren't great. They wanted to run more tests straight away.*

I reply: *Is he ok? Are you both home?*

Rami Hadid - OneDer: *He's good and we're home. Nothing to make a fuss about right now.*

I reply: *And you're ok?*

Rami Hadid - OneDer: *I'm devastated*

I'm not sure we've ever talked on the phone, but I hit the call button without thinking much of it. I can tell he answered the call, but he doesn't speak for a short moment. God, I hope he's not with someone from work.

"I hoped you'd call." The cheeky tone in his voice is laced with fatigue. He's likely sprawled across the couch.

"You sound devastated."

"I am. I missed the one chance I had to see your face today. Was the call this morning a waste of time again?"

"As a matter of fact it was productive. It ran short. You didn't miss much." The sun's beating down on my bare shoulders and I make a mental note to buy sunblock tomorrow.

"Don't you think we should go over notes before Monday? I don't like being unprepared."

"We can schedule a video call, Mr. Hadid. It's still before five o'clock on a Friday."

"You've got that spotty connection there. It's got to be in-person, I'm afraid."

"I'll be back Sunday evening. I'd planned to be over for dinner if the offer still stands."

I hear rustling and a breathy sigh, probably pulling himself up to stand. "Eh, no. Busy."

"Is that so?"

"It's so. It'll have to be sooner."

I can't stop the smile spreading across my red face. "You'd never find me here." I reach row house number six on my tiny one-way street and pull out the cast iron key.

"Do you want to be found?" He can't be serious.

"I want to be lost." I push open the door, and the cool air hits my cheeks. I lay my things down in the tiny vestibule and kick off my shoes. "...but I'd be happy to be lost with you."

"That's a poetic thing to say. Is it because I'm better with maps than you are? Be honest."

I can hear Hercules meowing. He must be in the kitchen with it echoing like that. "Guilty. It's your map skills."

"This cat will be the end of me. He's been acting like a wild animal since we got back."

"What's he aggravated about?"

"Eliza next door helped Baba into the car this morning while I packed us an overnight bag. I never know when they'll admit him." Pots or pans clang around on his end of the phone. "Usually when Hercules sees Eliza, it means I'm about to be traveling for work. She watches after things."

"So the poor guy thinks you're leaving?" I settle into the yellow wingback chair in the corner.

"You think I'm not?" I hear the stove beep, meaning he's starting dinner and not going anywhere.

"What I think is that I need a hot shower..." I don't give him time to comment on that. "...and I'd really like to wash and hang some of the clothes I brought to keep down here. I've also got dough to mix."

"Bread tonight? The saj bread I taught you?"

"A simple yeast loaf, and not tonight. I'll mix it tonight and bake it tomorrow. I'll eat in town tonight. I've been dreaming of the steak and ale pie at this restaurant I tried last time."

"It's a hot day for a dish like that."

"You don't understand. I can't be this close to it and not have it."

"I know the feeling." Hercules is still howling. "I've got garlic to crush. Talk soon?"

I start up the narrow staircase toward the hallway bath. "I'll send a picture of the pie. You're going to fall in love."

* * *

This tiny booth is just large enough for a glass of pinot noir, a heaping side of mash, and the star of the show: the glistening, steaming steak and ale pie. I snap a picture of the pie and send it, as promised.

The floors in this building are creaky and uneven. Wait staff hurriedly walking from room to room make the place sing with squeaks. Walls are painted in midnight blue with dining chairs upholstered to match. Each table is centered with bud vases and glowing candles resting in frosted votives. Lights are turned low enough to make the wildlife artwork look like a woodland fantasy. It's packed with patrons, even though it's past nine o'clock.

I make a dent in every plate of food in front of me, and I'm entirely unashamed. I take my time, and the dining rooms start thinning out. The young girl clearing the plates from in front of me has brown curls that reach to her waist and piercing blue eyes. Her nose ring suits her. I've had moments when I've wanted one, but opted for less invasive mistakes.

"All finished? Can I take this out of your way?"

"Please! It was delicious. Do you make these here?"

"My dad does, yeah."

She looks back toward the bearded man behind the bar. He gives me a quick nod as he dries glasses. "All good?" He calls over to me.

"More than good. I might be having this every Friday night."

"You're new to town?" He's drying glasses and squinting slightly to decide if he's seen me before.

"Yes, and no." I'll be staying on the weekends until September or so.

He looks intrigued. "What brings you here?"

I'm at a loss for words, and I shrug and look around. "Air."

"Air?" He raises his thick, dark brows and chuckles, still drying a stack of steins.

I decide I'm too sleepy to elaborate. "It's peaceful."

A young red-haired waiter paces toward him from the next room in large strides "Niko!" He whispers something, and Niko gives him quick direction before putting down his towel and walking out from behind the bar past me. He stalls near my table "pleasure to meet you, ah.."

"It's Ollie. Pleasure to meet you, too. You aren't from here either, I take it."

"The accent?" I nod and smile. He's got the same bright blue eyes as his daughter. It's stark against his golden skin.

"Elena! Bring our new friend a sticky toffee pudding." She nods curtly and looks annoyed with him. She's probably exhausted.

My phone vibrates.

Rami Hadid - OneDer: *The photo didn't come through.*

Horrible cell signal.

I reply: *Sorry. It's not sending.*

Elena returns with a plate of something I immediately know I'll want every day for eternity. The moment I realize I have no spoon to eat it with, Niko notices it too and holds up a finger before disappearing to the back.

Rami Hadid - OneDer: *I've no choice. I'll see it for myself.*

Niko turns out of the kitchen and stalls a few feet in front of me with a spoon raised high. He looks behind my shoulder at the relentless man that just waltzed up behind me and questions him, "Should I grab another? You know, this woman comes from a place with no air."

"I'll take a tall glass of air, then. I drove too far to find her with her heart stopped."

It is stopped, and he knows damn well the air's not to blame.

Fifteen

July

RAMI

"Tell me, are you more annoyed that I took more than my half..." I gesture down to the empty plate between us with my spoon. "...or because you didn't clear your navigation history from my car?"

There's something happening on her face, and I'm questioning whether I should have believed her when she said she didn't want to be found. Regret starts to creep into my chest.

She smirks and rolls her eyes. "I'm not annoyed."

"Hm." I'm not convinced. "You know, I didn't come with an agenda."

"But you did come with an overnight bag?" Her accusatory look is the sweetest thing I've laid eyes on today.

"Guilty."

"Good." She tips back the last sip of her red wine and reaches for the bill. I'm too fast for her, and she doesn't put up a fight. I take out my card and feel the exhaustion from the week settling in.

"Good? Do you mean that?" The corner of her mouth ticks up in a smile, and I can see she does mean it. Something loosens in my chest.

"I hoped you weren't joking about wanting to come. You did have your hands full, so I didn't let myself wish."

The restaurant manager walks back into the bar area where we're sat. He's a funny bloke. We chatted a bit when I asked what time they closed. Apparently it was a half hour ago. The young girl is making her way around blowing out candles, and the manager approaches our table again as we start standing to leave.

"Thanks for keeping the lights on a bit longer, mate. We'll get out of your hair."

"It's not a problem. We'll be closing down for a bit longer anyway. Are you staying nearby?"

I look toward Ollie, and she responds. "On Wragg's Row. I think I'll stroll around a bit before heading back - walk this meal off, you know."

"You could take a long way back down Digbeth Street to Sheep's Street. Do you know about Digbeth?" We both shake our heads. "It means 'duck's bath'".

"Huh! That's nice." She looks amused at the thought.

"It's not. A big battle happened here. I think it was the final one of the first civil war, about four centuries ago. It was a massacre. The tale is that ducks bathed in blood on that street."

We stare a glance back at each other. I turn back toward Niko, "On that note..." He laughs, and we reach the door. "Cheers. Might see you around."

"Yassas." A Greek goodbye, I assume.

We step out into the late night silence, and the streets are empty.

"Is this new?" I haven't seen her wear happy colors like this before. We wander to the center of town square where a tall pillar stands with a cross at the top.

"My cardigan?" She looks down at the peach-colored wool sweater she's got on over a white tank top. "I got it in Bourton-on-the-Water last time I was here. Feel how soft."

When she holds her arm out, I take it and pull both her arms around my waist. Her hair smells like rosemary, and I could fall asleep resting my chin on her head.

"I decided I'm going to be comfortable when I'm here." We're still standing frozen in the middle of town square, trapping each other in this position. I won't be the first to budge. "Expect to keep seeing me dressed like someone's great grandmother if you're going to make more surprise appearances."

"I'm sorry."

"I told you I'm glad you're here. I'm more than glad." She gives me a playful squeeze, and pulls away to look up at me. "It's been a weird day".

"Weird how?"

"Judah's been interviewing for this other job in Chicago. It's a tech job - the stuff he went to school for. It's looking good for him." She turns and takes my hand, pulling me toward the path to her place. "He's torn about it. They've got a reputation for working junior developers to the bone, and he's getting arrogant vibes from the hiring manager."

"Is it something he could learn from while he's there? Maybe try to find something better in a year?"

"I asked him the same thing. I think so. Nate thinks so, too. That's going to depend on his mindset, though. He writes off people in authority so fast if they're rude, or incompetent."

"Sounds like a smart fellow."

"He is. Smarter than me. That's been clear since he was a toddler."

"Nate..."

"Judah's dad." She's never brought him up before. I don't need to know the story. "We're trying to explain to him that he's got a long career ahead. He's got time to grow into better things. I'm..." She lets out a fast breath and tips her head to the sky. "...I'm not doing a great job. I'm not doing a great job trusting he'll make good decisions, or respond well to jerks at work. I can't protect him from it."

"Someone told me once that the cross in the square was meant to remind traders to make fair deals. To do honest work before God." I look back and realize we can't see it anymore.

"Apparently thousands of sheep would get sold here. Can you imagine them bombarding these streets?" She laughs at herself, and I think she's sleepy enough to be delirious. She makes a quiet "baa–a-a" sounds, and laughs harder.

Definitely delirious.

"Fleece Alley's where they were herded in. We'll pass it on the way. That's not where I was going with my point about the market cross." She looks at me confused. "Maybe Judah's got a conscience you don't give him enough credit for. Maybe you've given him a conscience you don't give yourself enough credit for." I'm probably making no sense. "Doing good work before God might be important to him... if he believes in a god."

"He is a great kid... a great man." She exhales, and we continue on a few seconds before she breaks the silence again. "Before God...." She's still holding my hand, leading me around the next corner. "... what's your stance on religion?" She's looking at me curiously now.

"I'm not sure how people get by without prayer." I've never processed my own thoughts on this out loud. "There are too many opportunities to... when we have to give up control. I don't know. For me, prayer doesn't look the way I was raised to believe it should look. It's not five times a day... unless it's a really bad day, and it's more." I recall a few of those. "I'm not sure who I'm praying to. Faith seems important, though."

"Like air." She giggles softly now at Niko's teasing earlier.

"Like air."

"I see things similarly, I guess. I don't know that it's been as important to me as it is to you."

I pick up the back of her hand and kiss it. She leads me down the row where I somehow managed to park before walking to the restaurant hours ago. She unlocks the front door, talking several minutes to get the old keys to work.

Walking in feels more like coming home than it does in my own home. She leads me through the connecting rooms I've seen through a laptop screen until we eventually land in the kitchen at the back. The cabinets are bright blue, and the off-white AGA stove has warmed the whole place. It's nearly too warm.

I didn't imagine I'd be ending my day like this given the way it started. Baba's test results scared me more than I let on. I've been running on adrenaline since. Once I knew he was fine, I couldn't fight how badly I wanted to be near her. I should call Eliza to make sure all's well, but the only thing I want to do at this hour is fall into a soft bed with this person I've become frighteningly attached to.

"I need to be clear." She grabs two bottles of water from the minifridge and hangs her cardigan on a hook. "When you and I make it to the top of those stairs, I'm going to pass out. You can sleep with me, but you can't... sleep with me." She gazes at me apologetically, likely thinking that's why I came. We haven't really gotten physical since after the launch party.

I smile in relief. "I told you. No agenda."

I take two steps to her before picking her up, and throwing her tiny body over my shoulder. The burst of energy surprises us both, and she laughs hysterically. I fail in my pitiful attempt to haul her up the staircase without bumping her head.

* * *

"You're completely depleted." We're facing each other in this creaky bed, both our legs in pajama pants and tangled together. "I wish you'd care for yourself as well as you care for your dad."

I can't keep my eyes open, but my left hand shifts to her backside in a move that can only be innocent. 'I wish you'd be honest with yourself the way you're honest with Judah."

"Honest?" I feel her tense. She probably thinks I'm referring to how she feels about me. I pull her closer, my eyes still closed.

"It seems like you keep all the little things you love separate from the person you are at work. Ollie isn't Olivia Kincade. Ollie likes bright colors and dessert. Ollie giggles, and lights up when she talks about sheep." I turn away slightly to yawn. "Olivia's a machine - amazing, but... I just think some Ollie could be blended in."

"I don't giggle." She follows her statement with a giggle. "I've known that for a while. I flip some switch when I put a blazer on. It's like I'm a little dead until the day's done. What's that quote? That one about knowing what you like and your soul?"

I'm fading away."Robert Louis Stevenson. *'To know what you prefer, instead of humbly saying Amen to what the world tells you you ought to prefer, is to have kept your soul alive'.* Something like that."

She laughs, still delirious. "How did you conjure that?" I don't reply. I'm not sure if I'm awake or asleep at this point. She kisses my forehead and rolls over to face the opposite wall.

"Do you remember the day I saw you in the pool?" I feel her head turn back toward me, and I muster the will to open my eyes. "I saw you floating. I noticed you through the glass door, and you were floating on your back. I wasn't planning to swim that day. I ran to the locker room to change. I hoped I'd be back in time." My eyes surrender and close again. " I didn't think you wanted anything to do with me."

She reaches back to grab my arm, and stretches it around her waist as she rolls back over.

We both drift off.

* * *

My chest is burning. The paved roads just outside town are nearly dead at six in the morning. It's too soon on my run for my heart-rate to be so high. I slow to a pace I'm more used to, and look over misty pastures to my right.

The sun's starting to come up, and I pass by portions of the dry stone wall that are crumbled to the ground. There's about six thousand kilometers of this stacked stone wall running throughout the Cotswolds. It must be a hassle to maintain properly.

I manage another half hour at this pace, then slow to jog onto the main street. I stop to stretch my aching calves, and decide to send a message I've been typing out and deleting for weeks. She's probably not awake yet.

I text: *I could use some help with the closet.*

It won't ever feel more ready than this.

I turn a corner, and decide to ignore the cheesy symbolism in it. I reach the door, and figure out the tricky key situation before letting myself back in.

I'm damp with sweat, hair sticking to my forehead. The stubble on my sticky face is a few days old, and I'm not sure I'll do anything about it until Monday.

Ollie's still buried beneath the white comforter, and I decide to shower in the washroom furthest from where she is. The shower stall is impossibly small, and the water instantly creates a steamy cloud. I disappear into it.

After working up too much lather and struggling to rinse off in the tiny space, I realize the floor outside the shower door is pooled with water. I quickly dry it up, dry myself, and pull on a pair of black joggers before opening up the creaky wood door.

She's in the kitchen now. I walk in as she's flipping the kettle on. The sight of her in this place completely comfortable and undone is something I could see every day without tiring of it. Her hair's braided and draped over one shoulder with a heap of strands falling out around her clean face. She's got a robe on that's too heavy for the toasty temperatures in here, but the door to the courtyard is propped open.

She motions toward the lounge chairs outside as I step barefoot over the threshold. "You could put some shoes on. I see you didn't pack any extra shirts."

I settle into one of the cushioned chairs "It's a shame. I suppose we can't leave the house." I hear the kettle whistle. Birds are waking up, and I wonder if peeping neighbors sit behind the windows to my right.

My phone goes off twice.

Mira: *Just tell me when. Maybe spot me a couple quid for the train?*
Mira: *She'll be proud of us.*

I thought she still had a working car. I slouch down further and rest my damp head back on the back of the chair.

I haven't willingly let the thought of her into my mind until recently. There was too much left unsaid; too much she'd done for me over the years that I never thanked her for. She was the most selfless person I'd ever known - the strongest.

Everyone used to claim she was indestructible. That claim crashed into the ground in an instant. Mira and I both lost the person that never stopped pushing us to be the best versions of ourselves.

My arms relax to the side of me, and I open my palms to the clouds.

I like to think she'd be happy with this version of me. I suspect that if she were here, she'd pinch my ear and point a finger in my face for not being clear about what I want with OneDer, or with Ollie.

I get back up from my chair and lean in the doorway facing the bright kitchen. She's mixing her own tea, which she'll never let me touch. She's watching a video on her phone about how to use one of the four oven types inside the stove, making little noises of understanding.

She's startled when I walk up behind her, gently spinning her hips to face me. I run a hand down the side of her neck and across her collarbone, under the edge of her robe. She drops her phone to the counter.

The only thing more pointless than this robe is our restraint. I lift her of her feet and set her on the counter, tugging at the plush belt around her waist.

Her head snaps to her left toward the window overlooking the courtyard. "Here?"

"Mhm." I confirm without words, gently kissing up her throat and around, just below her ear. My hands are flat on the wood counter top on either side of her.

The sound of birds chirping sneaks in through the open courtyard door. For a brief second, I wonder if sounds from the kitchen would escape the same way. She tilts her head and sighs, and I immediately decide not to care about shutting the door.

"You've thought this through?"

"At least two hundred times since the elevator." I kiss her on her perfect mouth. "I've thought this all the way through."

I pull away slightly, just enough to look her directly in the eyes. I won't ask for this if she doesn't want it like I do. Her smile turns mischievous, and she wraps her legs around the back of my thighs, tugging me closer by the strings at my waistband.

We don't leave the house until the sun goes down again.

Sixteen

August

OLLIE

"How many users are impacted?" Lynn's composure is astounding. I'd bet my electric hand mixer that this whole thing was avoidable, and she knows it.

"Maybe five thousand. Could be less. We're confirming now, but it's hard to tell." Theo's posture in the corner of the room is defensive. "We haven't gotten any reports of financial fraud. There's no reason to be concerned yet."

"Other than the five thousand reasons you mentioned." Lynn's patience cracks, and it's warranted. "How are we responding now?"

"Servers are shut down. We're trying to find where the breach may have happened. I'm planning to increase monitoring once we've got it sorted."

"Have you reached out to the communications team? When are we notifying users?" Arthur makes a rare contribution to the conversation.

"I've got someone in my group drafting something now. We'll require anyone impacted to change their login credentials."

Rami's been holding back his frustration, leaning back in his seat with his fist balled in front of his mouth. "Are you looking at multi-factor authentication? I suggest you don't drag your feet on that."

"I'm ahead of you on that one." Theo glares at Rami.

He grips his armrests. "I'd hope so. I also hope you run that email draft through Olivia before it goes out."

I chime in "And you might consider offering credit monitoring. I can help include that once you send it. "

"I reached out to a vendor on that yesterday morning. I've got it."

Yesterday. He knew of this yesterday, and we're just hearing about it at three on Thursday?

"When did you learn about this, Theo?" Lynn questions.

"Tuesday afternoon. I wanted to make sure things were under control before I sounded an alarm. I've been looking through our security protocols, thinking through some specialized training for the team."

"Sounds like there are some short-term things to focus on first." She's reaching the end of her rope. "Rami, would you mind stepping in and helping strategize on this? It sounds like Theo needs a hand sequencing it all."

Rami nods. He's infuriated. He picks himself up from his chair across the room from me.

We've made an unspoken point to put more distance between us when we're here. Two hours west of this place we've got a separate life.

Theo, Rami, and Arthur leave the room. I pick up my laptop and paper tea cup, and start toward the door.

"Olivia, do you have a moment?" Lynn looks exasperated. I sit back down in a chair closer to her. "I'm sorry we didn't get back to you on a sooner end date. I suspected we might need your help down the line. I'm glad you're still here for this mess."

"I had a feeling everything wouldn't be smooth sailing for long. I think I told you I put together a contingency plan."

"I'd like for you to stay a bit longer, if that's possible. I've got a feeling more might go wrong before this is resolved."

"My flight home's booked for September 14th. There's some time." It was the hardest flight I've ever had to book.

"Would the end of October be out of the question?"

I've started to come to terms with leaving next month. Rami and I have discussed what a routine could look like, video chatting a few times a week and alternating visits. I think my bread recipe will work just fine back home. The thought of six more weeks here is more of a relief than a disappointment, except for missing Judah.

"It's not. Happy to stick around a little longer."

* * *

"It's in London, near Tower Bridge. I don't think it's close to where you are." Judah just started at the company he'd been interviewing with in Chicago, and he's already looking at other prospects - across the world, no less. I think he could navigate London on his own if he wanted to, but this role sounds like a long-shot. I won't say that to him.

"Well, it's a perk that you've got a place to stay if they bring you in for a final interview. My flat has a pull-out couch."

"Aren't you in that other town most of the time?"

"Friday through Monday most weeks. I'd be in the city every second you are if you came."

I make my way through the turnstile at Paddington station. A Range Rover's a lot more comfortable than the GWR, but Rami can't come to town until tomorrow. He's got some project to do with his sister, which seems like a good use of time. He gets quiet when he talks about her. It sounds like they've got some baggage to work through.

"I could come to the Cotswolds with you for a day or two. I could see that motoring museum you told me about."

"You're not into cars, are you?"

"Kinda. Not really. There's not much else to see other than farms and tea rooms. I don't like tea."

"There's more than that, kiddo." He would like it here. If we spent time in town, someone would definitely mention the fact that my usual travel companion isn't around. I'm not ready to tell Judah about him.

"Would you fly me over, even if I didn't make it to a final interview? I don't know when I can start using vacation time at this place."

"Jude. Is that a real question? Of course I would."

"First class? I have a bad back."

"You're 23, and you're pushing it."

We wrap up our call. I settle into my seat with a caprese sandwich from my usual train station bistro. I set a reminder on my phone to see if I can extend my long-term rental agreement, and get lost in early 2000s rock music for the next ninety minutes.

* * *

"You alright?" Mabel at the post office doesn't seem to be holding a grudge about the globe. Billy might still be, but he was plenty polite when I checked out at the antiques shop with these old maps a few minutes ago.

"I'd like to send these to the states."

"Your son enjoyed the postcards?" Her memory is impressive.

"He liked them! He wants to visit soon, I think."

"He likes maps?"

"He loves maps - and history. Chances are he knows more about this place than I do."

"This was a sad, hopeless place for a time. Violent, it was." She walks behind the counter to help me pick a shipping envelope. She holds the folded maps up to the outside of each before selecting a size that works.

"It doesn't seem so sad now."

"It isn't, love. Hope lives here." She hands me a pen, and I jot down my Chicago address on the front while she rings the sale on the old cash register.

"How should I write the return address?" She helps me capture it correctly in the corner, and I seal the maps inside the padded sleeve. "I could have waited to give these to him later. He could use some happy mail. He just started a new job, and it's a tough one."

"He can handle it, mom. How old is your boy?"

"He just turned 23. I'm a little heartbroken that I wasn't there." I had a cake sent to the apartment, and it sat on the doormat for hours. He wasn't home until late.

"You were there. Our little ones always carry a piece of us, even when they become big ones. Billy and I have five ourselves."

I wonder whether Rami feels that - like he has a piece of his mother with him all the time. I only feel that way when I notice my mom's jawline becomes more evident on my face each year.

"Five is a lot!"

"We're blended. Two were his before, and three mine. They all belong to both of us just the same - their children and grandchildren, as well."

"Your life sounds full to the brim."

"Overflowing, dear." She beams and hands me a receipt before stacking my envelope in a tray of outgoing mail.

* * *

"Four miles? You've been to Bourton." Back at the cottage, Rami drops his duffle on the couch. "Why is walking that far an exciting idea?"

"I haven't been through Lower Slaughter, and I want to see it. I also ate half the loaf I baked last night. I should burn a calorie or two."

"You've got to start saving more for me." He sets the honey he brought from home on the knotty pine side table next to the wing-back chair. "That town will be mad on a Saturday."

"We won't have to park!" I make a fair point, but I can see his energy isn't high today. He looks down at the space on the couch next to his bag, and I know he wants to collapse into it.

"If I sit down, I won't get back up." He smiles in defeat. "Let's start on our way, explorer." He weaves between the furniture and back around to the door, stopping to plant a kiss on top of my head. "If you're concerned with burning calories, I could've given you some other wild ideas."

We set out on the trail from the square, and venture through a labyrinth of green meadows and gated paths. The grass is tall, waving in the breeze, and the sky is a vibrant blue.

"How's Mira?"

He groans. "Chaos, as usual. Time with her was good, though. She's kept this last job for two months. She works in a bakery. She says she's up at four each morning. I find it hard to believe."

I'm walking several yards ahead of him at this point, scanning the treeline at the other side of the field to find where the path continues. "And you two were productive?"

He's quiet for a moment, and I'm not sure he heard me. He's productive enough lately doing his job and everyone else's, so I don't repeat the question.

"We got a lot cleared. Donated it all." He pauses again for a few moments. "We worked on an old closet I've been avoiding for years. It was therapeutic, I guess." He sticks his hands in his pockets and takes a big step over a fallen log.

I slow down to let him catch up to my side. "What was she like?"

He looks toward me, surprised by the question. Hazem brings her up all the time. He should know I pick up on what he wrestles with.

He hesitates before answering. "She was quiet. People thought she was shy, but she was far from it. She didn't say things that she didn't find important to say." He laughs under his breath a little. "Money wasn't always easy. She started to collect more shoes once we were more well-off - boots, high heels, trainers that never left the box. She always wore the same pair. She had a nice collection of blankets - too many blankets."

"Was it hard to get rid of it all?"

"Not as hard as I expected it to be. She gave me this stuffed turtle when I was sixteen. It was supposed to be a joke. She was the quiet one, but she told me I needed to work on getting out of my shell. I don't think I'm in a shell anymore, but I might keep the turtle."

"Do you feel OK? How are you?" I link my arm with his. "Be honest."

He still looks hesitant to share. He's usually more transparent than this. If anyone's guarded, it's me.

"It's not completely empty - the closet. I couldn't handle much more than half. I reckon once it's completely empty, I'll feel like I'm on the other side of it all. I'll be more ready to move forward." He lets out a breath. "I'm close."

"Grief doesn't have a timeline." He doesn't reply, and we reach the turn toward the next village where streams spread under footbridges. "A collection of high heels is impressive for a woman her age. I wish I knew your mom."

He stalls on the pavement just before a narrow path suspended a few feet above the water. "I wish I knew her, too."

I walk ahead of him to the center of the stone arch and register what he said. I turn where he's still standing in front of a row of picturesque cottages topped with limestone shingles.

Things start to make far less sense than they did before.

"I didn't lose my mom, Ollie." My heart aches at what I fear he'll say next. "I lost my wife."

Seventeen

September

OLLIE

"I still don't get how it all went down." I somehow managed to navigate to the arrivals area at London Heathrow. Having Paige in the passenger's seat fills my heart in a way I couldn't begin to explain. I cried happy tears like a lunatic for five minutes before she suggested she do the driving back to Stow. I decided I'm too elated to die today, so I composed myself and declined her offer.

"He said it was a freak accident. It made local news outlets, but they never release names with that stuff."

"She just... fell all the way down a mountain? Did they find her?"

"No. It sounded pretty horrible. She hit the back of her head on the edge of a stone step." I can't imagine going out like that. I've thought several times about that moment, the split second she realized she was going down. I wonder if she felt anything, if she had a moment to look at the clouds before she fell unconscious.

Paige still has disheveled braids in her hair and pink moisture patches beneath her eyes from her flight. She looks too ridiculous for this conversation. "She just... was gone instantly?"

"Worse. She was in coma for weeks. He said there were complications. I didn't ask to know anything else."

It was like he was reliving the whole scenario when he explained it. Before I learned the truth walking through the town of Lower Slaughter, Rami went several minutes wondering who'd told me about Lana. He didn't realize I'd thought his mother was the source of his quiet pain all this time. Hazem keeps her memory alive by keeping her knick-knacks around. They lost her when Rami was tiny and Mira was a newborn.

"Jesus, Ol." She pulls down the mirror on the passenger side, and pulls off the pink patches.

"I know. I can't fathom having to make decisions for someone like that. I'm not sure if he had to make the call, you know... to take her off the ventilator." Thinking about him going through that turns my stomach. He said barely anyone at work knew. I'm not sure how he wasn't completely shattered - completely useless. All he did was take a month off and call it a holiday,

"Did she have family there? Do you think that complicated the situation?"

"All I know is that they'd known each other since they were kids, but hadn't been married long. They secretly eloped before a big ceremony they had planned. Her family was furious when they found out. It seems like they weren't in the picture at the time the accident happened."

"But she was with Rami's sister? They were close?"

"They were. Mira and Rami's aunt was there, too. Apparently Lana was reaching to catch their aunt from stumbling when she slipped. Mira didn't see any of it happen, so that's just what the aunt claimed happened. Apparently she was so traumatized by it that she moved away."

"Mira did?"

"Mira moved away, but she's just in Oxford. Their aunt moved far away. She ghosted them all. She'd basically been their mom for decades. She's his dad's sister."

"This is heavy. Way too heavy for me to be this hungry. Can we stop? Do you need gas?"

"Petrol. We say 'petrol'."

"We?" She pretends to be annoyed by my assimilation. "You think you can correct my perfectly good English because you've spent six months here and fallen madly in love with a Brit?"

"Yes! I'm not sure about the last part." I'm not flippant with that *L* word the way she can be.

She laughs and opens what looks like a flattened granola bar from the bottom of her purse, and pushes half of it into her mouth. "Oh, I am, Ollie. I am."

* * *

I'm getting better at this parking thing, even in this Range Rover that's way too big for this tiny street. I'm still convinced they made it big enough to park sheep and nothing else.

Paige pulls her massive suitcase from the trunk and looks at me like I'm the unreasonable one when my face says she over-packed .

"What? What do you want? You want me to talk around this place naked the whole time I'm here? It's starting it's cool here, and sweaters require more room."

I laugh and roll her suitcase for her to the cottage door. "OK, I'll get off your back."

"That's a great idea. Get off my back." She jokes. We're both elated she's here.

We make our way into the quiet living room where I've rearranged furniture to my liking. I'm relieved I've got a few more weeks before I have to figure out what to do with the antiques and wool cardigans I've accumulated over the last three months.

Rami won't be staying here this weekend with Paige and I taking up plenty of space. He was generous enough to loan me the car to make the luggage situation easier for her. He'll take the train into town just for dinner with us tonight, then drive the car back to London.

It's getting harder for him to ask Eliza for help with his dad every time he makes the drive here. He's starting to stay one night rather than two, or not to stay overnight at all. Work is still demanding so much with everyone on high alert after the data breech. Given Lynn's dwindling trust in Theo's judgment, Rami's taking on much more than his job description.

"I will pay you ten cold hard pounds if you can get that suitcase up the stairs without denting the wall." This will be a spectacle.

"I don't think these walls can dent. I'll take that bet. Which room is mine?"

"Up and to the right. Your bedroom actually has an en suite bathroom. You're welcome."

I make my way into the kitchen and start kneading the dough I left to rise. I let it rise too long, but it's fixable. I tie on a purple apron I found in a charity shop in Cirencester and dust the wood counter top with a generous coat of flour.

My dough sits in an over-sized yellow ceramic bowl I bought from the same shop. I like the cracks and chips in the surface. I like thinking about the life it had before me; the number of people fed from it. I remove the tea towel from the top of the bowl, and the warm yeast smell makes me eager to pop it in the oven now. I know better than that. A little attentiveness will pay off in the most satisfying way, if I can just reshape it and wait.

There's something metaphorical in there.

I haven't felt adventurous enough, or responsible enough, to experiment with my own sourdough starter. I won't put that pressure on myself right now. I'm craving more things that are simple; easy on my brain and challenging on my body - long walks outside, mixing butter, making jam. All of it calms me enough to think clearly.

Something's been rewiring in my mind since spending so much time here. My thoughts don't move as quickly. I'm starting to notice at work, and I'm not sure how I feel about that. Rami's been asking to see more of Ollie's mannerisms come through at the office, and I guess he's getting it. I don't feel as sharp anymore. I feel softer; less interested in being quick or being right.

I kneed the dough down to flatten its shape again, reducing the excess bubbles and pockets. I work methodically, folding it inward in clockwise patterns and pressing gently. This process used to take a toll on my hands. Years of typing have wreaked havoc on my fingers and wrists. It doesn't anymore.

I think I've gotten stronger in ways I never tried to, and weaker in ways I've always tried to be strong. I'm not mad about it.

"OK, America's Next Top Model." Paige wanders in. "What is this ensemble?"

"I don't like getting flour on my clothes. The laundry situation here isn't like it is in the US."

"Hence why I brought my entire closet."

"Did your closet make it up the stairs?" I set my dough ball back into the bowl and drape the tea towel across it.

"You owe me ten pounds, but I'll take dinner instead."

"Rami's running late. He told us to start without him. It's hard to get a table at this place sometimes."

"Tell me again why he's driving two hours just for a dinner that might last two hours?"

"He's really excited to meet you. I also think the driving helps clear is head."

"Fair enough. Is this a Spanish place?"

"Spanish? Where do you think you are?" She probably smacked her head on the same beam where Rami made me smack mine.

"I told you many months ago that I'd like you to find me a Spanish man because we never went to Spain. I'll take sticky toffee pudding instead, if they have that."

She settles into my favorite wing back chair, and the sight brings me pure joy. I head back up the stairs to change.

"I can handle a pud."

* * *

At my new go-to restaurant, waited on by my favorite restaurant manager, Paige and I get comfortable at a larger table than I usually occupy. The sun's been down for a long time, and the chill in the air is more uncomfortable than it was last night. I handled far worse in Chicago. I'm becoming a wimp.

Elena, Niko's daughter, walks over to pour glasses of water.

"Your nose ring is adorable!" Elena lights up when Paige compliments her. "Thank you! It didn't hurt the way I thought it would. I did it myself."

Paige's eyebrows shoot up in surprise while she takes a swig of her water. "Yourself? Brave lady!" She has to remember piercing her own bellybutton freshman year. Maybe Elena needs a little pick-me-up, and Paige detects it.

The door to the restaurant creaks open, and I realize two of the people I care about most are finally in the same room. Paige catches my gaze in that direction, and turns to see him stop to chat with Niko.

Her face whips back to me dramatically, and her jaw drops open. "You did not tell me."

I can't contain my laughter. "I did. I clearly said 'eleven out of ten'."

She repeats it to me and exaggerates every syllable. "E-le-ven!"

"Eleven what?" Rami moves in to give Paige a casual hug before he makes his way to me. "I hear your name every day. I'm glad to finally meet."

I will never, ever, get over what that silky accent does to my nerves.

"I bet her eleven quid that you'd be late, and you were." He takes the seat to the side of me opposite of Paige and gives me a quick kiss on the head before resting his hand on my thigh below the table.

"My apologies, really. I wanted to take the earlier train. Baba had some... things to sort. Eliza wasn't as confident with... new meds and such. I'm here now."

"I didn't order you a drink." He hasn't been drinking in weeks. I can't remember the last time I saw him have one, actually.

"All good. How was the flight in?" He turns to Paige, but she doesn't have time to answer before Niko approaches.

"Good evening" He directs the greeting at Paige.

"Good evening! Your place is lovely. Look at that fireplace!"

He looks back at the blazing flames. I think this is the first time it's been cool enough to light it while I've been here. "Not mine. I just look after the restaurant. This restaurant and the inn upstairs are up for sale if you're in the market." He leans one of his tattooed arms on the table and says the next part quietly. "The owner locked himself in the cooler months ago. I let him out, and he decided he was done. Still managed to eat a container of my whipped cream in there."

"Did he really lock himself? Did he get locked in?" Paige playfully asks.

Niko looks toward the kitchen and sniffs at something that doesn't exist. "Something burning? I need to check on that." He scurries back to the back.

We spend dinner talking through the latest on Paige's business. She's got a hospitality company inquiring on a partnership to design boutique hotels. It sounds like a dream deal, but Rami shares some thoughts on terms she should consider.

When the crowd dies down, Niko pulls up a chair and joins us.

"So, you're Greek? What brings you here? Is there a Greek community around?" Paige is a tad bold.

"That's a long story." Niko might be put off. "It's been a good change - for us both." He looks toward Elena tending to the only other occupied table I see.

"That's your..."

"My daughter." It's not until now that I realize how close in age they look. If I know Paige, she's going to say something about it.

"Wow! How's that possible?" She sips on her third glass of cabernet. "Looks like your sister."

He makes a face. He's not a raving fan of hers. She's not everyone's cup of tea, that's for sure. He adjusts the dark hair he has tied back in a bun at the nape of his neck. It's usually higher, but the chaos of the night probably loosened it. "She's my daughter - not biologically." He says it low enough that she can't hear.

"How? She looks like your twin." She's got to start reading energy better. Perhaps she doesn't care.

"A story for another day." His tone is kinder than I anticipated. I've seen him get a hot head plenty of times.

Rami cuts the awkwardness with more awkwardness. "My son's Greek." Everyone looks at him confused, and I register where he's going with this.

"He doesn't have a son." I roll my eyes at him and pick up my own glass of cab.

"I have. Stop lying to these people. His name is Hercules."

"God..." Paige understands now. "... the cat." Niko relaxes and laughs. These two hit it off pretty instantly. I think it's why Rami's not interested in trying many other places around here when he's in town.

"He is a god." He's oddly relaxed to be mentally preparing to drive another two hours back later. We could have had dinner in London.

"So, what's going on with your dad?" Paige can't stop with the intrusive questions. If she feels like she knows him well enough to ask, he probably feels the same about her.

"He, uh... he's been ill. Cancer. It was in remission for a long time." His eyes divert to me, and I notice he uses past tense about remission. He goes on. "It seems to be back."

He's crushed, and he's working hard to hide it. I don't know why he came all this way tonight.

Paige probes further. "What's next, then? How's he taking it?" Niko's still at the table. It'll be interesting to see how much detail he'll go into with both of them sitting here. I know Hazem's been weak lately, but this is all news to me, too.

"He's always said he wouldn't fight it if it came back. As soon as we got the news, I expected that to be the case. He seems like he's coming around to the idea, but..." He's devastated, and opening up about it in front of people that are almost strangers. "... he doesn't want treatment at the London hospital. He hates it there."

I chime in. "Where would he go? Where else could you go?"

He looks toward me and speaks in a low, gravely voice. His tone suggests he'd hoped to talk privately. "Treatment needs to start soon. It'd be a month-long process. I did some research on the train, and there's a different center about a half hour west of here." He pauses to see if I have a reaction. I don't. "If they'll take him, it could make sense to move him here for a bit. This center offers outpatient care."

"With me? My lease is up in a month." I'll help him figure this out - while I can, at least.

"No, I wouldn't ask that. We'd be next door - Hercules, too. I spoke with the owner, but didn't commit to anything. I know you'll be gone before it's over, I just... it'd be nice not to miss much of your last month. I also think Baba could benefit from the... environment here."

"The air?" Niko teases. Rami and I smile at the inside joke. Paige looks lost.

He and I exchange a look in agreement that there's much, much more to it than that. If Hazem lived here, who would be with him full time? Rami and I are both in the office three days per week. Beyond that, what happens when I go back to Chicago in a month? If Hazem's treatment here lasts until after October, how could Rami manage the logistics of it all on his own if he has to work in London?

Months ago during my fitting room midlife crisis, Paige said that taking things one day at a time is the only way I could learn to be less afraid of this risk - the risk of getting more serious with Rami. This is it. On this particular day, it looks like saying yes to something hard instead of making an excuse to run. It looks like not knowing what's around the corner, and taking his hand to walk toward it anyway - even if it's a dead end.

Paige can read the contemplation on my face, and she might be re-calling the same conversation. She reaches over and smooths the back of my hair down, smiling in a way that tells me she sees the real deci-sion in front of me.

"We're going to do anything we need to for him." I reach over to Rami's lap. and weave my fingers between his. "Move to Stow-on-the-Wold."

I grab my peach wool cardigan off the back of my chair, and start to stand. "You, sir, have driving to do, and we..." I nod at Paige. "... are going to have stale crackers for breakfast if we don't bake that dough I left rising."

Eighteen

September

RAMI

Buckingham Palace used to amaze me. Mira, Lana, and I would wander round the palace grounds poking fun at tourists trying to get the bright red guards to flinch. We taunted ducks in St. James Park. At one point, Mira tried to see how many disposable cameras she could swipe from unsuspecting victims. That might have been her lowest moment morally. If it's not, I don't want to know.

As I've gotten older, I've made sure to steer clear of this area after the sun comes up. It's a favorite running route of mine. Beating the crowd motivates me to be out the door by six. This beats a treadmill run, except on days when a better view is on the machine next to mine.

My breathing is mindless and my cadence is steady. My left calf is cramping slightly like it typically does by this point. Electrolytes haven't been top of the priority list for some time. Surprisingly enough, neither has alcohol. I forgot what it felt like to want to be present enough to remember my days rather than inebriated enough to forget them.

At mile five, I made my way from home through Soho and over Golden Jubilee Bridge. As usual, I worked my way south past the London Eye, then back across the Thames over Westminster Bridge. I stopped in the shadow of Big Ben to stretch when this calf started to nag at me.

Powering through Hyde Park back toward home, the Serpentine sprawls out to my left. I veer closer to it and stop to massage the twisting pain from the back of my leg.

The sight of sparkling water on a day like this would usually be a welcome reprieve. Watching it ripple under the rising sun, it doesn't soothe me the way it did before.

For the few weeks I spent at the hospital after the accident, I'd escape here to beg for a miracle. Everything about that time was a bloody nightmare. Signing papers and gripping this iron fence are the only clear memories I keep.

I decide to walk the rest of the way, looking up only as I pass the Peter Pan statue, recalling when I felt like a lost boy.

I don't feel lost. For the first time in ages, I don't feel lost, just misplaced.

London doesn't move me the way it did before. It doesn't pull me in the way stacked stone walls, swaying grass, and an auburn head on my shoulder do. I'm not confident that she feels the same, and that's wearing on me almost as much as all my other unspoken fears.

I am certain she means it when she says she's comfortable with Baba being based in our hideaway while he receives chemo, or infusions, or whatever they're saying this relapse requires. I'm not certain that she's open to what it could mean for she and I. It doesn't have to mean anything. I've told her that, but I can't get past this worry that moving my whole world next door to her beloved weekend escape will push her away.

Away is inevitable either way, I suppose. I have her for one more month. I've decided I'm at peace enough in Stow that I won't be in a hurry to stop renting when she returns to the states, regardless of how

Baba's treatment goes. Still, I'd like to think that she'll want something to do with me after she leaves. Everything about the way we are together makes what's coming at the end of October unimaginable for me.

The thought of loss shouldn't rattle me like this anymore.

I believed I'd developed some sense of resilience in recent years, but the potential of losing anyone else, whether it's Baba or Ollie, has me feeling more unsteady than ever. I can't take it. My career can't take it. There's too much on the line to be thrown off balance right now.

I make my way through the gate with a slight limp and a motivation to fill my car to the brim with our belongings. I can't help but wonder if my life will feel this full by the time I bring it all back.

* * *

"This boy will not allow you to put him in a box all the way to that town. He'll shout profanities so loudly your sister will hear when you pass through Oxford."

Baba's sitting in his old brown leather chair with a sleeve of chocolate biscuits and Hercules stretched across the afghan on his lap.

"I'm not bringing him until next weekend when I bring you. Would you rather try to hold him on the way? Be my guest." His arms were scratched for days when we transported him from our old place to here. He insisted that the cat carrier was cruel.

"He behaves perfectly for me. It's you he disagrees with."

"Right, which is why I won't give him a chance at destroying my leather seats. It's a good thing you've got a week to give him a pep talk about it." I'm shouting to him from the kitchen at this point, packing up the good kettle and Za'atar we're surely not to find in a Cotswolds town.

"I'll do no such thing. I'll tell him how you love your car more than you love him." He scratches the cat in the spot he prefers behind his ear, and the orange ball of fluff melts sideways.

"Or, you can tell him he'll feel safer if he's confined."

He doesn't respond for several seconds. "Like your lady."

What could he possibly know about Ollie other than me leaving nearly every weekend to visit her. "You think Ollie feels confined?"

"No." He's got to be on his eighth biscuit. "I think she tells herself she should be confined."

"What makes you think that? She came here on her own. She rents her Cotswolds place on her own. She doesn't seem afraid of getting out."

"She's unafraid of the world, yes. Is she afraid of you?"

"Why the hell would she be afraid of me?" I move to the medication cabinet and begin to organize his pill bottles and teas. "What are you saying?"

"You are my boy, Rami. I know your heart. You are anxious about the move because you are not certain she welcomes it." I walk toward him to take the almost empty package out of his hand, and Hercules jumps off his lap.

"She does welcome it. This treatment center is where you want to be. That's all that matters right now - to any of us." I make my way back over to the cabinet, toss the package inside, and shut the door a little too hard. My energy's waning and my damn calf is still sore.

"... but you are worried she does not want you so near so often."

"I know she wants my company. If she didn't, I wouldn't be there so often." I won't miss leaving him with Eliza so often. I don't like having to rely on her, and it's shortened the number of hours I spend away. "I don't sense that she wants something serious - at least not with me. I don't know about her son's dad, but I think she's done the whole 'commitment' thing."

He turns toward me and looks confused. "What then? What comes after my treatment - after her job here has ended? She is not planning to stay. Am I right?"

"I couldn't ask her to stay. She has a life; a job. She has a son." I know it'd be an impossible thing to hope for. I can't afford to let myself imagine it.

"What is life if it is not love? You must ask her." He picks up the clicker and changes the channel. "She knows what she wants with you. She knows she has it already."

"You said it. She's afraid of me. Bringing it up would be pointless." I zip the pouch holding his medications, and wonder if the thought of asking or not asking terrifies me more.

"So quiet her fears, Ibni. Love her the way I've seen you love before." He changes the channel. "It is alive again. I can see it."

I run my hands down my face. "I have been, Baba. I have been… opening up every way I know how. I didn't think I ever would again." I don't realize until now how much I've been investing without realizing it; how much I've been giving of myself knowing it may be going nowhere at all. "I don't know if I'll ever get through to her, or if it's even the right thing for me to try. Staying in England wouldn't make sense."

He's completely immersed in his TV show, and doesn't reply.

I loop the straps of two large tote bags over each of my shoulders, and walk past him toward the car. It's getting dark out, and I need to get to the cottage so that Ollie can use the car to get Paige to the airport in the morning.

As I'm about to reach the door, I can hear that Baba's made his way to the cabinet where I closed away his last few chocolate biscuits. "You young people.. you must stop searching for sense. You'll never find it."

* * *

I managed to unload every box and bag I had stacked from the floor to the ceiling in the Range Rover, and set them just inside the threshold of the row house adjacent to Ollie's. I take a quick stroll through the rooms to scope out the layout, grateful to see a bedroom area on the main floor so that Baba isn't forced to venture up the steep steps.

It's late, and I'm surprised to open the door of Ollie's cottage and discover the smell of garlic and firewood. She's got candles lit in the dim dining area and the wood burning stove lit in the sitting room.

The entire place glows like a beacon, and every second of that drive was worthwhile. It's just bright enough that I can see new treasures she's found; oil paintings and ceramics that she's determined to give a new life.

I step lightly to make my way over the creaky floors and into the heart of the place where she's doing dishes over the farmhouse sink. She's a vision standing here in her element, the way I've captured her in my mind time and time again since first shocking her with my uninvited arrival in July.

"Lasagna?"

"Ravioli." She beams with pride. "Homemade."

"I don't believe you." I close the distance between us and sleepily wander to where she stands, hands covered in suds. I wrap my arms around her waist from behind, and bury my face into her warm neck, rocking her gently. "Prove it. I'm starving."

She looks regretful now. "Sorry. Those precious raviolis didn't stand a chance."

She wiggles out of my embrace, and the thought creeps in that she might not enjoy me walking through the front door as much as she did when my own wasn't six feet to the right. She might not appreciate that I walked in tonight at all.

She sets a saute pan on the drying rack, and spins around to lean against the counter, facing me. I pick up the dish towel next to her, and dry off her hands.

"I'm capable of drying my own hands."

"Of course you are." Her fierce independence is something I admire, but I don't want to hear it tonight. "Doesn't mean you shouldn't let me do it for you every now and then." I give the back of her hand a quick kiss before releasing it back to her and tossing the towel to the side.

Her face looks happily exhausted, but something else heavy is behind her eyes. She crosses her arms across her chest, but smiles gently at me. I cross my arms in reply and smile back, giving her a few more feet of space. "Paige asleep?"

"Yeah. We were at the restaurant late. I can't decide if she and Niko hate each other. She seems to be the only person around here that Elena can tolerate."

"That makes sense." Always looking for sense...

"How's your dad?" I just registered the music she's playing on her phone in the corner. "Is he ready? Dreading the move?"

"I think he's prepared. He seems to be... accepting; going through the motions. He's more concerned about me, I think. About you... "

"Me? Why me?" If she's anything other than OK, I don't think even she would know it.

"Just... that you're good with the lot of us being in your space." I back up several steps now to lean on the counter on the opposite side from where she's doing the same.

The next song that comes on is too lively for this hour, but it's the kind that can't be ignored. She knows it, because she moves toward her phone to turn up the volume.

"I think it's against some law not to turn this up when it comes on."

The first line of *Midnight Train to Georgia* sails from her phone speakers and across the air.

"I don't disagree. It's a classic." I stride the few steps it takes to be back in front of her. I take her left hand into my right, and wrap the other around her waist. I feel her body relax into mine as we sway lazily in the center of the brick floor, stepping off-beat to the soulful sound of strings and brass.

I can't resist singing into her ear in a whisper, smiling deliriously between each phrase.

"You've never even been to Georgia." She laughs and throws her head back.

I pull away from her slightly to show the exaggerated shock in my face. "Pardon me, madam. I have twice. We've got offices in Atlanta."

I twirl her around in a silly gesture, careful to make sure her thick slippers don't snag on the old stone below us.

"I'm sorry" She laughs again, nearly asleep where she sways with me. She lays her head on my chest, and we move from dancing hand in hand to fully embracing in this very spot that makes me feel I have the whole planet in my palm.

"I'm ready to cook for your Baba" she's yawing now, arms squeezing tighter around my worn, gray cotton jumper. "I want to make him ravioli. Will he be able to eat that?"

"It depends on the treatment, I think. It might be hard for me to get him to eat anything. Last time I thought he'd whither away."

She looks up at me and twirls the hair at my ear - hair that's becoming more silver-streaked with every hour, it seems. "You're not doing this alone."

I grab her hand before she can move it away, and hold it flat against my chest. "Not yet, at least."

She's wordless. The emotion showing around her mouth makes it unclear if she thinks she'll break her own heart or mine. She rests her head on my chest again

When the song reaches the iconic last line of the chorus, she softly sings the words, beautifully off-key and invisibly tormenting.

If her only options are living in my world or living without me in hers, could they ever feel like one in the same?

Completely still now, standing with both our eyes closed, I pray to someone, anyone, that one day it'll be true.

Nineteen

September

It's overcast today, and I'm running on no sleep on the drive from Stow to London Heathrow. Paige and I have been sitting in comfortable silence most of the way.

Thankfully it's just this one way I'm driving today. I know I'll need to be in the office tomorrow, which isn't common for a Monday. I'll be at my London flat from now through the rest of the week, bracing for whatever the next few hold.

When Hazem and Hercules move down this weekend, logistics will get tricky. I'll stay in London Tuesday through Thursday like I usually do while Rami works remotely from the Cotswolds full time.

We could use the time part. He says he plans to tell his colleagues what he's tending to with his dad. I'm sure they'll understand his temporary situation, but he still seems burdened by the idea of not being in person. I've told him that If he's got to show face for something, I'll make an excuse to not be available so that I can sit with Hazem.

If the best case scenario doesn't pan out with this treatment within the next month, I have no idea what they'd choose to do. Returning to London where they've got a bit more support may be the only option.

The ache I feel when thinking about being back in Chicago is confusing. How could anyone manage a life that's split across two land masses? One half has to suffer.

"What about the sister?" Paige questions while she looks out the window at misty pastures. "He's got two kids. Shouldn't they both be stepping up?"

"I haven't gathered that she's the reliable type. He claims she's got work. He doesn't want to see her lose another job."

"Is there someone in Stow-on-the-Wold that could help? Niko said he plans to bring meals over."

"Nice guy, huh?" I look at her with a smirk. They've made sarcastic jabs at each other right from the start. Paige doesn't know how to react when her wits are matched like that.

She scoffs at the comment. "Irritating guy."

A text message flashes across the screen at the center console.

Nathan: *Got a sec to talk?*

I spoke with Judah last night. He's made it through the next series of interviews for this London job, and he's flying in next week for the final round. It's a senior developer position, and I'm honestly shocked he's made it this far in the process without much experience. Whatever Nate wants to talk about likely isn't to do with that.

"What do you think that's about?" She nods at the screen. Paige and Nate keep in touch, so it's likely she's got a better idea than I do.

"Could be taking a big next step with his new lady. He'd probably want me to hear it from him first." Her silence tells me my assumption might be spot-on.

"Would you be hurt by that?" My assumption is spot on.

"I don't know, actually." I take a deep breath. "I don't think I'd know until I heard the words come out of his mouth." She doesn't respond. "If it did bother me in some way, I think it'd be less about me and more about what I'd want for him. I'd want to know she's not going to screw him over."

"Screw him over..." Paige hasn't met her, but I know she follows her on social media and does me the favor of keeping any interesting information to herself. "How do you think she'd screw him over?"

"I don't know... by not working at things when they start to feel stale."

"Like you and Nate worked on things?" If she's consistent with anything, it's snide remarks.

"We worked on a lot of things... just not us."

"Do you ever wonder what would have happened if you did?"

I have wondered. I've wondered what kind of person I'd be if my life was still in the Chicago suburbs and I hadn't been forced to reinvent myself - to trust myself in ways no one but Paige has seen.

"Yes. I've thought about it." I've thought about it at length since being here, working all of my doubts into piles of bread dough, and baking them into something conclusive. "We never would have found the tools to work on things while inside that relationship. I think we both needed to leave it in order to see what was missing."

"And there's no chance you'd try again with him?"

I've answered this question internally before, but consider it carefully again before speaking it out loud. "No. I think we want more for each other than to have each other."

"... and what do you want for you? Why haven't you entertained the thought of staying here? You've got some tough things around the corner, but it's like you're awake now. When you go back to Chicago, how would you keep yourself from falling back asleep?"

She likes to make things sound so simple, and it drives me up a wall. "There's no way I could, Paige! Of course I've thought about it. I won't live across the world from Judah - and you - and I won't wake up wondering how I'll pay the rent. Finch would never let me be based here." I round the turn in front of the departure gate and she starts to gather her things.

"You're sick and tired of Finch & Associates. You've given them almost two decades, Ol. Your lifespan isn't getting shorter."

"Rami isn't ready." I blurt out what feels like my truest hesitation, and my eyes start to sting. I need sleep. "He thinks he is. I can't let him take a chance on someone else he could lose."

"You can't decide that for him." I could pull her blonde hair for repeating what cycles through my head constantly. "As long as you adore him the way I know you do, you can decide not to let him lose you. It's not as complicated as you're making it." She gets out of the car, and I do the same, walking toward the back and unloading her purple monster of a suitcase.

I ignore her frustration with me and attack her with a squeeze big enough to last us the months we'll go without being together again. "Love you. Mean it."

"Yeah, yeah. Go love yourself."

* * *

Parking Rami's car back at his London house before walking back to my place, I venture inside to check on Hazem. Rami won't take the train back into the city until later tonight. He's on a mission to unpack the mountain of things he unloaded into the new place last night.

"How happy am I to see you?! I reach down to stroke Hercules before slipping off my white sneakers smudged with Cotswolds dirt and grass stains.

"You've come to see if I've been left for dead, have you?"

"Stop." His humor can be so morbid. Rami hates it. "I've come to make sure you're comfortable... and eating something other than sweets and biscuits."

"My boy lies to you. There are no biscuits here."

"I take it you got rid of them carefully, didn't you?"

His rosy cheeks pucker with a guilty smile. I make my way into the kitchen to find where a few boxes sit opened, partially packed.

"Tea?" I choose the mint green mug with tiny sheep he'd used the day we met in this kitchen.

I rest the steaming, aromatic cup on the side-table next to his brown leather chair, and he picks it up to blow on the surface. We sit in silence for several minutes with occasional outbursts from him at whatever he's watching on the TV.

Hercules jumps up with wide green eyes and curls into my lap. I finally lie my head back on the sofa and close my tired lids. I try to turn off every thought I have about the commitments on my calendar for the week, and the packing I need to start within the month.

I didn't think through what it'd take to transport art and ceramics across an ocean. Ollie needs a lecture about forward-thinking in that regard. Maybe she needs a break from forward thinking in every other sense.

The space next to me on the couch cushion starts to feel more empty.

"I told you once..." Hazem spooks me back into reality. "... I told you I did not know why this mug is my favorite." Curiosity has me watching him think through his next words. "That was not the truth. I do know." He goes on. "The way it feels in my hand feels right. I cannot explain it. It could be the weight; the rough texture." He turns the mug in his thin hand, the skin stretching across his bones. He smiles softly at the whimsical creatures dotted across it. "It's got to be washed by hand if I don't want the images to fade away."

Point taken. He's saying the best things take work.

"I'm sure you'd find another just as perfect if it ever cracked - maybe one that's dishwasher safe."

"No, habibti. I've repaired this one on many occasions. Washing it is a ritual. Without it, tea may not be worth drinking."

* * *

I wander upstairs to the bedrooms as my phone vibrates.

Rami Hadid - OneDer: *How is the old man?*

It's like he knows I'm poking where I don't need to. He's a tech guy, but I can't imagine he's got security cameras hidden around.

I reply: *Just dozed off. I'm leaving in a few.*

I make my way into Rami's bedroom, which I've never seen, and run my fingertips across the king-sized bed that seems excessive compared to the tiny space we occupy in the cottage. It's flanked by two sleek nightstands and matte bronze Scandinavian lamps.

My fatigue tries to convince me to crawl under his black linen comforter and let the scent of him whisk me to sleep. Instead, I migrate to his dresser. On an onyx tray, a velvet box holds the watch Craig gifted him and a stack of classic novels with worn spines.

I step softly into the room at the end of the hall, and open the door to find a bland guest room. The air in here feels still, and the closet tucked in the corner pulls me in.

I'm not sure I'm prepared to know what occupies the dark space behind these bi-fold doors. He's said that once it's completely empty, he'll feel like he's on the "other side" of it all. I fear that anything remaining of hers today will let me know if I made a wise choice by booking a refundable flight to Chicago.

Rami Hadid - OneDer: *Get some rest. I'm washing your sheets for you, and I won't accept your disapproval.*

He knows I don't need the help. He's trying to spoil me enough that it's harder for me to leave, and I can't decide if it feels unfair.

I open the closet doors. On the upper shelf, a tiny plush turtle sits. The fabric on its shell has grayed in places, showing its age. It makes sense that he'd hold on to it.

Hanging against the wall to the right is an ivory garment bag, balled up at the bottom and so wide that it occupies half the closet floor. I unzip it slightly to find a masterpiece of satin, lace, and crystal. I know they eloped at a London town hall and never made it to a big ceremony. The exquisite thing is tragically unworn.

A wedding gown is a telling thing to hold on to.

I know now that he's keeping more than what's been folded away in this hidden nook. The stinging in my eyes returns, and I tiptoe down the hardwood steps, slip my shoes back on, and shut the front door quietly behind me.

Before reaching my building, I stop to purchase a stack of packing boxes.

After somehow making it through the revolving door and noticing the broken elevator, I lug my boxes up the stairs along with a sense of clarity I've been grasping at for months.

Twenty

October

OLLIE

"It's roast chicken and fingerling potatoes" Niko slides containers of last night's restaurant leftovers into Rami and Hazem's stainless steel refrigerator.

This space isn't the quaint cottage feel I expected it to be given it's next door to the blast from the past I stay in. It's more of an open floor plan, finished with modern appliances and stark white surfaces. Clean, but not warm in the way I hoped it'd feel for them. I do think their personal things will make the feeling more inviting once they're unpacked - more like home for the next month or so.

"How is your chicken spiced? Hazem questions, more appreciative than his assertive tone suggests.

"Rosemary, thyme, salt, pepper..." Niko's amused by his interrogation. Rami unpacks medications and other large containers into the glossy cabinets.

Hazem scoffs, likely at the lack of stronger flavors, and proceeds to scoop several serving sizes onto a plate to reheat.

I finally called Nate yesterday. My suspicions were accurate, and I'm happy for him. I haven't heard this much joy in his voice since we were teenagers, even if it was tinged with nerves. I don't know what he could have expected would go wrong. He knows better than to expect me to be anything but level-headed about it all. I'm not sure he's seen me shed a tear or raise my voice since we were kids.

I can't say it's affected me deeply. That's probably a relief to the both of us. The news of their engagement's out in the open, and the only thing that's crossed my mind is whether she's taken down the window treatments I paid a fortune for. Maybe she didn't move in. Maybe he's moved in with her or they've gotten a new place together. Judah wouldn't mention it, if so.

Hazem takes his plate out of the microwave and shuffles past where Niko and Rami chat about something sports-related I have no interest in understanding. He leans over to Niko. "I like fish." Niko raises his eyebrows, and Hazem elaborates. "Sea bream."

"Understood." Niko acknowledges, and Hazem's feet move in tiny shuffles to the cobalt blue armchair facing the TV. This ornery man has a piece of my heart.

My phone rings with a call from Martha, and I step out onto the narrow one-way street.

"We've got your next client lined up. They're a group in Manhattan, a tiny health food company - protein bars and some weird stuff. It should be a nice break from what you've got over there."

"No one else wanted it?" It seems like it'd make more sense for someone junior. I would have loved a client like this years ago.

"Jim and I were talking. We've both got a feeling you're losing some steam over there. They've kept you too long. We don't want you getting burnt out."

"I'm not burnt out, Martha, I'm just... not sure what kind of work is a good fit for me these days." I put one hand on my hip and look up at the trees turning shades of burnt orange and russet.

"You don't want to take smaller accounts anymore? I thought you wanted to slow down."

"I don't think I want to slow down. I think I might... I might want to... stop."

"Stop working?"

"Stop working in PR." I brace myself for her reaction. If I know her well enough, she'd be more sad for herself than concerned for me.

"I hear you." She takes a deep breath into the phone. "What would you do instead?"

"I'd regroup back in Chicago - maybe look into something related to interior design. I wouldn't want to build another career from the ground up. I'd just want something mildly fulfilling to keep me busy until I retire."

"Well, that sounds riveting. You've got a decade or two before retirement, I'd assume." I can hear her sarcasm over her dogs barking in the background. "Do you see yourself in London? I know you're downplaying the new friend you've made in that marketing man. What's his name again?"

"Rami, and I haven't even mentioned it to him. I probably won't. I don't want him to expect that I would stay if I'm not with Finch anymore."

Two realizations hit her at once, "You're thinking about resigning soon. You're also more serious with this hunk than you've said."

I don't deny it. I wander to the edge of the street where it collides with the main road. "Don't tell Jim - not yet. Please?"

"I'm offended that you feel you have to say that. Of course my lips are buttoned up." She will always, always be my favorite.

I bring my arm to rest across the top of my head and sign a deep breath of relief. "Thank you. You know you're the best, Martha."

"I know it. Olivia, don't waste time doing things that suck the happiness right out of you. I can't tell you the amount of things I wish I'd let go sooner so I could grab hold of something else."

In hindsight, letting go is something I'm getting good at. It's the "grabbing hold of something else" I can't do.

* * *

On Wednesday, Rami and I both have to make an appearance in the city. Hazem doesn't start his treatment until tomorrow, so it worked out that Niko could check in on him after lunch rush.

The senior leadership team and their direct reports decided an off-site planning day would be a good idea. Myself and a few other vendor partners were invited to speak into next year's strategy, which I suppose is a good way to stretch the money they're still spending on me during these last weeks. I'm not doing much else.

After spending the morning in a penthouse conference room across the river, someone had the wild idea of scheduling an axe-throwing activity to break up the brain work. Keeping a healthy distance from OneDer's Director of Brand & Marketing, I make my way with the caravan to the barely-marked building down the street..

I don't know how moving my arms like this is going to work. My clothes are far tighter across my torso than when I arrived. I'm not sure if happiness or stress is to blame - likely both.

Craig, Rami, Theo, and the other vendor partners take the first lane, tossing the weight of heavy axes from hand to hand. They transform into teenage grown men, arguing about aim and wrist positions. I'm less excited, but up for a challenge that doesn't have to do with sponsoring podcasts or sporting events.

Lynn, Arthur, Catherine and myself take the next lane. Arthur takes the first practice throws, and surprisingly hits just outside the center ring of the target both times. I'll be glad if my axe even sticks to the wall.

The lane beside me erupts into laughter as Craig's axe hits the wall and slides to the ground. Rami follows. His pummels into the wall, just above the center of the target.

Theo focuses hard, maybe too hard, and flings his axe toward the wall next. It hits the dead center of the target, and his ego explodes louder than the claps that follow.

Rami rolls his eyes at Theo, but seems unbothered by the stiff competition. This change of pace is well-timed for him today.

I can't say that watching the way his body moves is well-timed for me right now. The man can wear the hell out of business attire, but they haven't seen him dressed in nothing but skin. I'd hope they haven't, at least.

I snap my thoughts back in line, and focus back toward where Arthur's taking this task more seriously than I've seen him take anything.

Lynn migrates toward where Rami squares up for another throw. She asks quietly, "When do your father's appointments start?" He filled the group in on the situation before we began this morning. As expected, he was met only with empathy about needing to be remote more often.

"Tomorrow." He sighs, picks up his axe, and flings it - hitting closer to the center this time. Lynn says something else I can't make out. He turns to make eye contact with her and nods. I imagine she's said something encouraging, which he could use.

I toss my axe for the first time, and it smacks sideways before dragging to the ground.

Theo steps up to take his next shot, and blurts toward Rami and Lynn. "Olivia's a helpful hand to have around, I imagine." He hits far left of the center this time, and walks away aggravated.

Conniving prick. If anyone heard him, they're acting like they didn't.

Rami and I don't dare make eye contact. He walks up to the spot where Theo just was, rubbing at his mid-day stubble. His axe pummels into the center of the target with a violent thud that jolts everyone. Craig initiates the next round of applause.

Lynn scrolls through her phone, and looks up searching. "Theo. A moment?"

Theo wanders toward a corner with Lynn, and the rest of the group continues on with a few more rounds. Theo, shockingly, walks out of the building without saying a word.

Lynn wanders back over to the group. "Theo's got some pressing things to respond to. He'll be taking the rest of the day to get it under control."

Craig glances between Lynn, Catherine, and Rami. "Everything alright."

"I'm expecting an update by three o'clock. I'll share more then."

The team's still silent, quietly rejecting Lynn's attempt at being vague.

She decides to go on. "The data breach from August has started to make waves. We're getting messages from financial institutions. It sounds like there were some loose ends we didn't tie up when we addressed it - supposedly addressed it."

Rami curses with a rare slip of composure. "Dodgy bastard!"

Craig's look toward him is piercing. He knows good and well the outburst was warranted. Craig directs his attention to both Rami and I, standing calm amidst the thick tension. "You two might want to prepare a statement when we know more. It'd be good to have it in hand by Monday at the latest."

We both nod, and look at each other briefly, still standing awkwardly far apart relative to where the rest of the group hovers.

I mentally take inventory of all the other things we need focus on back in Stow before Monday, and buckle up in hopes that this is the hardest problem I'll have to solve before boarding a plane.

Twenty One

October

RAMI

I'm trying my hardest. I'm trying not to let my short temper get in the way of these expiring days.

Baba's weak after his first round of treatment, but in good spirits. I've been able to be here since Wednesday evening despite the madness at work. Ollie was able to return this morning, though I haven't walked over to see her in-person. She got off the bus, and immediately dialed into a call we both joined from the opposite side of the same wall.

I hope to get at least a few moments away from this wretched computer before she leaves tomorrow to stay with Judah in the city.

I can see the green dot indicating she's online. I open a chat window and send her a message. It's completely unnecessary, and hopefully more amusing than annoying.

Rami Hadid: *Fancy a stroll?*

I can see she's seen the message, and starts typing.

Olivia Kincade: *A professional stroll?*

She's considering the company's ability to monitor these conversations, but my concerns about that are virtually zero today - even if Theo does have viscous motives. Chances are he wouldn't know how to go about monitoring a chat window anyhow.

I lift myself out of my chair in the top floor bedroom, and make the long journey next door. I knock, which I never do, and hope I'm a welcome distraction.

This is exactly what I've been telling myself not to do.

She opens the door, standing in a pair of loose jeans and an oversized sweater. Her hair's tied in a knot on top of her head, just the way I like it.

"I'm here on strictly professional business."

She looks at me suspiciously, and glances back toward the dining area. She was definitely in the middle of something. A smile creeps across her face, and she steps out of the way to let me in. "Let me get my shoes." I step in behind her and shut the door.

"I've almost got that draft statement done. I'd feel better if you look over it before it goes to Craig and Catherine. The second line reads weird for me... "

"I'm not worried."

"You sure seemed worried at the axe place yesterday." We haven't had a chance to talk about it since then. I acted like a child in front of my leadership team, and I want to put it out of my mind.

"I'm not focused on those things when I'm here."

"I don't believe that for a second, Hadid." She never calls me that anymore. "I felt your frustration through my laptop screen on the call earlier. I think it was seeping through the wall, too." She sits at the seasoned wood dining table, and laces up her trainers.

"Sure. I'm livid with the idiot. I can't see how he keeps getting away with not doing his job."

"Do you get the feeling that Craig and Catherine are winding down? How close are they to retiring?"

"No time soon." I hope I'm right on this one. I can't imagine Arthur stepping into his place.

"I don't know. I'd bet Lynn wants to address it, but can't get Catherine's buy-in to fire him."

"It's not easy to terminate based on performance with someone like him. They'd have to have solid documentation."

"I know. Nate's company got sued a few years back for wrongful termination. It's a muddy process." She stands up, and we weave back through the maze of furniture and collected antiques before taking off out the door.

"So, Nate... " I'm not sure yet what I want to ask.

"What about him?"

"What's the story? Not details, just... curious."

"We're on good terms - friends, really."

"Good. That's good. I imagine... parenting still takes two."

"True... and we grew up together in a lot of ways. We had to grow up really fast." She looks at her moving feet and curls her hands up into her sleeves to warm them. "That kind of creates a... bond no one can touch, you know? Unless he was a jerk. He wasn't. He isn't."

I don't know how to craft my next question, or even if I should. "Why didn't it work?"

"We didn't know how. I don't have a better answer than that." She pauses for a long moment before we wind down the alley toward the square. I don't press for more. She eventually starts sharing her stream of thought again. "I don't think anything was ever broken. I just think parts of us didn't match. Judah went off on his own, and we realized our parenthood pieces fit perfectly for a long time. Our... partner pieces didn't click. We didn't know how to change that."

"Too different?"

"Too similar." She laughs softly. "Like when you hold the same sides of two magnets together. They push apart."

We walk for a few minutes in silence, pointing out autumn displays at the storefronts in town. There's a crisp chill in the air, and we both should be wearing something heavier.

"What if we were magnets?" I ask reluctantly.

She doesn't reply, and instead laces her fingers between mine.

* * *

If it weren't this slow this early on a Saturday, Niko would have a problem with me taking up space at his bar just to order club soda with bitters.

"Where is she?" He lifts bottles down from the top shelf, taking the opportunity to dust while he can. It looks like it's been a while.

"London. Her son's here for an interview, so she'll spend the weekend with him."

"Is he moving here?"

"I imagine he would if he gets the gig."

"And if he doesn't? Would Ollie stay?"

"Your guess is as good as mine, mate." I take a swig of my drink, and fiddle with my coaster.

"You don't think she cares enough for you to stay if he doesn't get the job?" He looks at me like I'm a fool for questioning it.

"That's what's mind-boggling. I think she does. I think she knows Judah's quite alright on his own, though she'd miss him." That's the piece I couldn't ever argue with.

"Hm." He gets it better than I do, having a kid. "The missing is the hard thing."

"I think there's something else keeping her from the thought of it. If by some miracle she stayed because Judah got this role and she figured out something with Finch, I'd still question if she would have stuck around for me, for us, or only because it became convenient. She's got some wall up. I'm starting to wonder if I'm wasting my damn energy chipping away at it."

"You think she's got trust issues?"

"No... that's not it. I think she's afraid of losing her independence. It's important to her. She might even be afraid of hurting me. I don't know."

He makes his way to the next row and starts wiping down a bottle of bourbon with a label that's barely there.

"Sounds like space is what she wants."

"Yeah. I could do a better job there."

"And maybe some reassurance?"

"Reassurance that I care for her? She's not a moron. She knows."

He laughs. "I think everyone knows. I mean reassurance that you can handle her. You said she might be afraid of hurting you. Show her that she doesn't need to coddle you."

"You think I should tell her that I'd be fine without her? Seems counterproductive."

"That's not what I said. You want her. You don't need her, kollitós. There's something more powerful in that."

I've made no secret of wanting her. Needing her isn't something that's crossed my mind. She knows what I've been through at this point. She knows well that I can stand on my own two feet. I won't be an obligation to her, and I know Baba would feel the same.

He goes on. "Does she know you want her to stay?"

I told him she's not a moron. "She has to."

He looks at me with a healthy amount of skepticism. "... but have you said it? Have you asked her?"

"I can't ask her to make that decision. It'd be unfair. She's got too many reasons to say no."

"It's her decision to make. Making it for her isn't fair. If you don't ask her outright, she'd have one less reason to say yes." He walks to the kitchen and back to the bar, then slides two containers of dessert over to me. "Bring your father these. Chances are he won't like one of them. The man needs options." I reach over to squeeze him on the shoulder, and turn toward the door.

"Ask her!" He shouts. "Not because you need her." I chuckle to my-self and shake my head.

Because I want her.

* * *

Back at the cottage, I squeeze into the love seat next to where Baba's sprawled with his feet propped up on the cheap coffee table. It might be made out of something like cardboard, but it's sturdy enough to hold two pieces of cake.

"The chairs are not comfortable. They've ruined my back." His back has been ruined for far longer than those chairs have existed.

"Cake. From Niko." I open one container without checking the other, and dive in.

"Nice boy." He opens his, and is less than enthusiastic. "You have chocolate. Mine is carrot." He hates carrots.

"That's unfortunate." I shove a bigger bite of the chocolate into the empathetic face I'm making. "I'm truly sorry."

He laughs, still managing to eat a few small bites of his cream cheese icing before closing the lid. I hand him my chocolate slice, most of it, and it's gone in a matter of seconds.

He rests his head on my shoulder the way he rarely does - always when no one's around. This time, I tilt to rest mine on top of his. Her-cules is curled up on the couch cushion behind where we sit.

I could manage. I could manage not needing anything but this.

* * *

Before sunrise I set out on a new route I mapped when I couldn't get to sleep last night. I still prefer to wake up before dawn on week-ends. It makes Mondays less jarring. I can't imagine not having the time to clear my head before I have to focus it on a marathon of meet-ings.

Ollie sent me a text to say goodnight. I assume she hasn't told Ju-dah about me, so a phone call wasn't on the table. I read it, but didn't reply until this morning. If space is what she needs, that's what I want to give her.

I plan to ask her to stay, just to make my wants clear, when the dust settles on this data nightmare at work.

I never did question Niko on what qualifies him to give relationship advice.

My calves aren't bothering me today. I wish I were as well-rested as I am well-hydrated. I pick up speed until I reach my usual pace, turning onto a narrow street leading west. Roads are sleepy, save for the occasional lorry heading east into town.

My mind is tired, but my thoughts are clear. I'm growing more at peace with whatever's around the bend for any of us.

Part of why I choose to hit the pavement, to train my body, is because I need a constant reminder that I'm stronger than I think I am.

I wish I didn't.

I seem to need that reminder more often than most, so I protect my routine with reverence. If I stopped, I'd rely on everyone around me for validation. I'm responsible for too much, and disappointed too much, for that to be sustainable.

My heart beats hard against my chest, and sweat tickles the small of my back. The narrow bridge several meters ahead of me is dark, making it harder to anticipate uneven stones or cracks.

I decide to keep my pace and trust my footing, easing over the dark bridge and circling around the corner between two old buildings at full speed. The sun's beginning to come up, partially blocked by headlights moving toward me - quickly.

In the same moment I realize there's no shoulder to step to, the horn blares.

Twenty Two

October

OLLIE

"How did you do in the technical sessions?" Judah insisted on fish and chips. I've been ecstatic about him being here, and couldn't say anything but yes - even if it is barely lunch time.

"Good... " He chews on a floppy fry, apparently thrilled with it. "... obviously. I wouldn't be here otherwise."

"Smart-ass" I don't filter myself around him these days. "Are you feeling prepared? They'll probably ask about culture stuff... team chemistry and all. You should be ready to ask good questions, too."

"I've got until Tuesday. I'll look over some stuff before I go."

"You brought a good belt?"

"Jesus, Mom!" He laughs, and I back off. "Can we do that Tower of London tour thing today?"

"If that's what you really want, sure." I work through a piece of battered cod, counting my regrets in advance. "We can. There are other things you might like more - museums that aren't so touristy."

"I don't care if the big ones are touristy. I haven't seen them."

"We did Tower of London when you were ten." His strawberry blonde hair is darker now. I remember the day we realized he was taller than me, and it was the weirdest feeling. This patchy beard situation he's working on tops it by far.

"What do you do when you're not working? I mean, aside from the cottage place you go to? Do you have friends?"

"I have Paige. I told you she came."

"I know. She told me, too." He finishes off his basket alarmingly fast. "You haven't made any British friends? I guess it's not like you have Chicago friends..." He laughs at himself, but peers up to check my reaction. He's more sensitive than he lets on about my feelings.

"Ouch!" I reach across the table and gently shove his shoulder, probably getting grease on his gray hoodie. "I've been kinda busy, Jude. Not much time for friends."

There's no sense in sharing about anything I've left to the west of here - not until, or unless, it lasts after I return home.

My phone rings with a number I don't recognize. Judah looks down at it before I answer.

Sorry. Probably spam.

"Hello?"

"Ms. Kincade?" I hear machines and voices in the background. It's a hospital. I stand to my feet, shuffling closer to the shop door.

"Yes?" Hazem. I brace myself to hear whatever he's been admitted for. I know it's part of the process, and nothing Rami isn't used to.

Why aren't they calling Rami?

"This is Dr. Richardson calling from North Cotswolds Hospital. I'm reaching out about erm.. Hadid."

"Yes."

"Rami Hadid."

My mind goes blank, and I immediately feel sick. "Yes."

"Mr. Hadid's been in an accident." My knees go weak, and I reach to steady myself with the door handle just before two men yank it out of reach from the other side. The caller goes on. "He's stable" are the only two words I register from the rest of the call.

The line disconnects, and I return to the table to sit across from Judah. "I lied about friends, kiddo."

The concern on his face is genuine. "I know."

"Paige." He shrugs at my conclusion.

"What happened? Where are we going?" He questions, ready to be my sidekick however I respond.

"A nasty fall. He's in the hospital. ... and *you're* going to an interview on Wednesday."

"I'm going wherever you're going until then."

I know at this moment that I can choose to stay with Judah. I should choose to stay here with Judah.

"I don't have to go. There's someone else that could pick him up. I can call him."

"I'm telling you that you do need to go..." Judah stands up to carry his trash to the bin. "... and I'm coming."

He walks back to the table where I'm still sitting. "Get your priorities in line, Mom. You want to be there right now, don't you?"

I'm stunned by his bold demand. I can't lie to him. "I want to be with you both."

"So, let's go. When's the next train?"

I check the time on my phone. "Not for another hour. The last one just left." I drove Rami's car here, but parked it at his apartment before meeting Judah at the train station. I didn't plan to have Judah near it for obvious reasons."I do have a vehicle we could use."

"A busted up rental car? Is it a manual?"

"It's a Range Rover. Automatic."

"I'm driving. You owe it to me for lying. Get up." He playfully lifts my arm.

I finally get up from my seat. "Absolutely not. You're out of your mind."

I reach up, grab my boy's sweet face, and plant a greasy fish kiss on his cheek before we dash out the door.

* * *

We spent all of Sunday evening after Rami was discharged, getting him comfortable on the tiny love seat in his sitting room. Niko had Elena drop off food.

There's not enough space for Rami to sit comfortably, let alone for his dad to sit with him. It'd make more sense for him to post up on the larger couch at my place, but he won't accept the idea of relying on me to check on Hazem. I don't have the heart to argue with him while he's strung out on pain killers.

Rami did muster up the energy to text Arthur and Craig last night before passing out on the love seat. He sent a short, disorganized message explaining he'd torn his ACL trying to jump out of the way of a truck. He hasn't explained much else to me, but the medical team said he was spotted by another driver after struggling part of the way back to town.

Physical therapy is in question. Stairs are out of the question. He won't let Hazem give up the first floor bedroom for him, so his short-term sleeping situation is still unclear.

Now that it's Monday morning, Rami's more alert, but not in a mood to talk much. "Did you leave Judah in the city?"

I sit cross-legged in one of the rock-hard blue chairs with my computer in my lap. "No. He's here. He didn't want to intrude. These are weird terms to meet you on."

He doesn't respond right away. "Please tell me he didn't miss the interview."

"It's Wednesday. I told him he should stay there and prepare. He wanted to come here instead."

"Did you want to come?"

He's not thinking clearly on these meds. "Of course I did."

"I'm sorry for giving them your number. Your name was the first that came to mind."

"Were you in a lot of pain? Did you think to call instead of dragging yourself home?"

"You were two hours away. You were with your child."

"I mean you could have called someone closer when it happened - an ambulance... or Niko... or Mira."

He stretches and winces. "It was too early to bother either of them, and an ambulance didn't cross my mind." I realize his ice pack is melting. "I could've given Niko or Mira's number to the hospital instead of yours, if that's what you're implying."

I steal the ice pack from his hand and walk toward the kitchen to replace it. "I'm not implying anything. I said I wanted to come." I don't know what's gotten into him. I put the melted ice pack back into the freezer, and take him a fresh one. The creases in his forehead tell me this is worse than he's letting on. "Did you take your eight o'clock pills?"

"No." He picks his head up and looks around to see if they're in reach. I grab the bottle from his side table, tip one into his hand, and hand him his water bottle.

We sit for a while longer before he breaks the silence. "Could Judah come over?"

"You want to meet him?"

"I do." He's caught off guard by my surprise. I'm glad he's up for talking with someone, even if it's not me. "If you're alright with it."

* * *

Forty-five minutes later, the energy in the room's done a complete turn. Judah's got Rami laughing at an irritating British talk show he watches back in the states. Judah sits in one chair while Hazem has the second. All three men giggle like schoolgirls, and my heart swells despite the circumstances.

I take the opportunity to get some work done in the kitchen. I haven't had to confront the in-office obstacle yet with it being Monday and everyone's remote. I don't have any calls scheduled for today, so this email draft's top priority. I sent it to the leadership team to review, and haven't heard back.

As late afternoon sets in, Judah heads back next door to search for whatever snacks I have on hand. He's out of luck being that I hadn't planned to be here all week.

With Baba taking a nap in the side bedroom, I settle back into one of the chairs near Rami's love seat.

"He likes you. I wouldn't say that if he didn't." His soft smile suggests he likes him, too. "Paige had told him about you... about us. When I got the call, he knew it was about you."

"You hadn't told him before Paige did?"

"No. I'd planned to. It wasn't time."

"Was it ever going to be time? Before he found out on his own, would you ever have told him?"

"Probably. Does it matter now?"

"It's the only thing that matters." He winces, and I see the sharp pain shoot across his face. His scruff is nearly a full-blown beard at this point.

My phone rings. Lynn - probably questioning the draft I sent.

"Nice weekend?"

I choose my words carefully. It's supposed to be what I do best. "Eventful. Yours?"

"I can relate. A long bike ride... shopping for a fancy dress party for Halloween. It was a nice reprieve from the past week."

The line goes quiet. Rami knows who's on the other end, and tries to appear disinterested.

"How is he?"

My heart drops a little. I can't pretend not to be with him. Who knows if I'll make it in tomorrow, and any other excuse would be a joke. "He's... in good spirits." My eyes dart toward him, and his are wide with concern. "It's only partially torn, but still a bad tear. He's pretty stationary."

"Would you mind putting me on speaker if he's up to it? I have an update for you both."

I take the phone down from my ear, and press the speaker button.

"It's good to hear you're on the mend, Rami." He's still stunned at us being out in the open now, likely struggling to sort his thoughts under the haze of medication.

"Thanks. It'll get sorted soon enough, I hope." He sounds more apologetic than he should.

"Rest. We'll talk through how best to support you later." She goes on. "Listen... a PR statement's been put out. It was published about twenty minutes ago. It's not the statement Olivia had drafted, but what's done is done."

He uses his arms to lift himself to sit straighter. "What's done? Who's statement was it?"

"Theo had a communication drafted and sent directly to the communications team over the weekend. He felt responsible for the mess, and wanted to act quickly. He only ran it through one layer of leadership. He did get input from the Brand & Marketing side."

"From Arthur." Rami concludes, burying his face in his hand.

"Correct." Her sigh says she knows he circumvented everyone else on purpose.

The line's quiet for a few seconds. I can't suppress my curiosity "What were the key points?"

"That we know what caused the gap in security and take full responsibility." Good start. "He mentioned the number of users impacted, though I think what he quoted is lower than what's true." Questionable, but OK. "He pointed to one of our vendor partners for not detecting the risk sooner. It doesn't change the fact it was our fault... ." Irresponsible. "He committed to cutting ties with that vendor, who has a track record of solid work for us, if I'm honest."

"He discussed ending their contract with you before making that claim?" Rami questions with dwindling patience.

"He doesn't need to. He has full autonomy over that."

"None of this concerns you, Lynn? This could come back to haunt us on several fronts." His face twists slightly in pain as he adjusts again on the couch.

"Not yet - not in terms of brand risk. It obviously concerns me on the topic of Theo's judgement. That stays between us."

"And you've called Olivia to warn her?"

"Sadly, Olivia's time with us is coming to a close. I called to thank her." I've got one more week working for OneDer. This sounds surprisingly finite. "Olivia, we've been more than pleased with your work. I'll continue to sing your praises to Jim. We'd welcome you back on a future project if you wished to return."

Rami locks eyes with mine before I respond. "Thank you. It's been a pleasure."

"You can ship your badge and other assets back to headquarters, if that's easiest." I realize at this moment her letting me go early has nothing to do with not needing me anymore given Theo's audacity. It has everything to do with how I'm needed here. She's doing us a favor.

Rami gestures to the cushion next to him, waving me over to join.

"Thank you... thanks. I'll drop it off at soon as possible." I nestle in under his left arm, careful not to bounce where his leg is stretched. He wraps his arm tighter around my shoulders.

For months, I'd been both dreading and dreaming of the moment that my engagement with OneDer ended. Turning in my badge would mean I had an impossible decision to make.

I don't feel that tension anymore.

I've called a cease-fire on all the inner conflict I've cultivated since an unplanned round of birthday drinks in April. I called it the moment I walked into Rami's hospital room after driving and praying my way back here from London. God, I prayed, and I didn't even realize I remembered how. I don't think there is a right way.

I could have told Judah we'd both stay in London rather than coming here, but I would have hurt a part of myself as a result. That wonderful boy knew that, even when I didn't.

Today, the only decision I want to make is whether to refund my flight to my credit card or as an e-credit. I'm exactly where I'm supposed to be, exactly where I want to be - for now, at least.

Twenty Three

November

I won't miss the horrible revolving door. I won't miss the lobby with a weird smell. I might miss the elevator.

I needed to get the London flat cleared out by today. The lease ran through the first week of November, which gave me a nice window of time to get back to London. Finch & Associates could have canceled it sooner given they received my letter of resignation last week.

When I used to fantasize about quitting, I saw myself being anxious about what came next; anxious about bills. I wondered what my identity would be if I wasn't in the corporate world or a helicopter mom. I'm not thinking about any of those things.

My mind's quiet, actually. It's oddly quiet. I'm just existing in Stow with the tiny circle of people that's formed around me. I don't find myself thinking far beyond the present day. In some ways it feels like breathing for the first time. In some ways it's like holding my breath.

I fold the three blazers I brought along with four pairs of shoes into my suitcase, and sit on top of it to zip it up. The extra ten pounds I've accumulated makes it easier to force the two sides to meet - so would donating all these useless suits, I guess.

I asked Paige to ship a winter coat to me. She stopped by the Chicago apartment to visit Judah when she came to town to visit family for the holidays. I could've bought another, but I need to start thinking about my spending now that I've moved from building my bank account to depleting it. We've still been chatting every Monday, and she's calmed down with her lecturing. When I told her I'd resigned, she squealed so loud with pride that all of Utah had to hear her.

Rami Hadid: *How's it coming along?*

He's working, but hasn't been to the office since the accident. Cabin fever's coming in waves, but he pretends it's not.

I reply: *Finishing up. Baba's prescriptions are ready. I'll get them on the way.*

I take the elevator down the stairs with my suitcase and one box under my arm, then set out to toward the car.

He asked me to check in on his place while I'm here. He wants me to grab a few extra sets of winter clothes for him and Hazem. I plan to bring it all, since neither of them seem to have interest in coming back when treatment's done.

The closet in the extra bedroom still pokes at the back of my mind, and I intend to steer clear of that whole corner of the house.

Starting the car, I veer onto the icy street to make the short drive to Rami's place.

Something has been nagging at me when my brain doesn't have a choice but to wander - usually when in the car. Rami never did say that he wanted me to stay. I'm afraid I assumed it all along. When I think about what's tucked away in the closet, I wonder if some part of him hoped I'd go back to Chicago, even if just for a while - just long enough for him to let go a little more.

When he got hurt, choice was stripped from both of us. I knew he'd have a hard time getting by without help. He knew he needed someone, even if needing someone pisses him off.

I do think we both were relieved, but it's difficult not knowing if we both would have taken a shot at a future outside of him needing me right now. He questions me about whether I would have stayed, but I haven't dared question him about if he wanted me to.

Perhaps it doesn't matter if a feeling of necessity brought us together. Maybe that's a gift, in a way. Still, what happens when that necessity is gone and coexisting is optional? Will he start thinking about commitment? Will I? Is thinking that way good for anyone when it comes to relationships?

I'm not sure I've been more content with someone that I am now - now that I'm just sitting in the moment instead of fixating on what's next. I can't picture a future without him in it, but there was also a time I couldn't picture one without a career.

I park in front of Rami's house and decide to do all of us a favor and stop picturing anything at all.

* * *

"Are you trying to starve your father?" Hazem complains from the love seat.

Rami's sitting at the small rectangular table against the kitchen wall, still absorbed with work after seven in the evening. "It's on its way. You'll survive." He stands carefully from his chair and grabs a sleeve of biscuits, taking small steps toward the living area where Hazem and I sit. He tosses the package to Hazem.

"I could have gotten that." I reprimand him. He bends to kiss the top of my head, and returns to the table.

He's moving around better this past week. Through gritted teeth, he's made it up the stairs once at his place, but severely underestimated how painful it'd be to come back down. He still won't let Hazem give up the first floor bedroom, so I've convinced him to crash on the couch at my place until he's more healed.

A knock sounds at the door, and I hop up to let my favorite post office employee, Mabel, inside. She quickly removes her heavy lilac coat and storms into the kitchen area like a tiny, white-haired tornado.

Hazem pops up, more slowly than he used to, and shuffles to the kitchen to hover.

"Just a bit of bread, some carrots with thyme, and roast gammon."

"Gammon?" Hazem looks toward Rami, questioning.

"Pork." Rami says to him quietly while Mabel situates her dishes. "Lahem khanzir."

Sweet Mabel struck out with two out of three items she brought. Hazem's made no secret of loathing carrots, and Muslims generally avoid pork.

Rami gives Hazem a sharp look, daring him to vocalize the fire in his eyes.

"Thank you." Rami makes sure to give Mabel his full attention. "We appreciate it."

"It's no trouble." She makes her way back through toward the sitting room, taking the blue chair next to mine where I sit with Hercules sprawled across my lap. "Billy's pup, Charlie, enjoyed some pig scraps." I remember the sweet brown dog from the antiques shop.

"How is it all going - the treatment?" She speaks quietly while Hazem rummages through the cabinets for other options, mumbling something to Rami.

I whisper, leaning toward her, "The infusions he's gone in for aren't improving his numbers the way they want." Her face droops with empathy. "They plan to start a round of chemotherapy next week."

"Oh." Her hand moves over her mouth for a brief second. "I imagine that'll be a challenge. He must be a fighter." She looks back toward the kitchen where he's filled a plate with bread.

"He is. It did take some convincing from Rami to go through it again. They've agreed to let him come home after - while his immune system is weak. There's risk in that, but I'm glad he'll be more comfortable." She reaches over and pats my knee without responding. There isn't much to say in response, anyhow. "Thank you, Mabel, for the food. You're a kind soul." I smile at her, still scratching Hercules' stomach to distract him from the ham.

She zips her coat back up and heads out the door. Rami looks up from his computer at me, and we share a silent laugh at Hazem's lingering anger.

* * *

"So, he'll make it work at the Chicago company? Are things getting better there?" Rami shifts the pillow on the coach at my place, stacking two where he plans to lie his head.

"For now. I guess he has to. He said he doesn't have any regrets about how the final interview went. The other guy was just a better fit - had more experience." I sort through clean laundry at the dining room table, hanging cable-knit sweaters to air dry. I don't know when I started wearing so many colors again.

He picks up one of the many classic books he brought from his shelf in London, and slips on a pair of thick reading glasses that make me weak in the knees. He makes a concerned noise in response to Judah's rejection for the London job. "He seem to be doing alright with it? Upset?"

"Maybe he'd appreciate a call from you. He doesn't listen to me. Nate can't quite relate to him. He'd probably take your advice on how to make the best of it. I don't think he's got it in him to interview anywhere else for a while."

He turns toward me where he sits on the couch with a spark of enthusiasm. "Sure! You think he'd want to hear from me?"

"Are you kidding? He never wants to know what I'm up to when we talk. He's always asking if you watched the last soccer... football match thing."

"And you tell him how you watch them all with Baba and I - how you're on the edge of your seat?" His sarcasm is palpable from a room away. I peer toward the living room and I'm not sure how I know he's smiling by the back of his head.

"Always." I hang up my last sweater. "Want to try to make it up the stairs tonight? That couch is probably a decade old. The bed's got to be a tempting thought."

He considers it seriously. "You're a tempting thought." He waves me over to sit next to him. I stroll into the sitting room and nestle next to him as he sighs and continues. "I've got to stop pushing it. I want to try a long walk tomorrow. I'm feeling a bit more squishy." He pokes at his stomach.

"It's freezing outside. There's snow and ice on the ground. If you slipped, that'd mess you up more than walking down the stairs."

"We'll be alright." He smirks at me, rubbing my shoulder furthest from him while his arm rests on the back of the couch behind us.

"We? Speak for yourself." I laugh at him. "If I'm going anywhere, it's on four wheels. Speaking of four wheels, how was driving into the office on Thursday?"

"It was bearable. I'll be back to three days in the office next week - as long as Baba's stable."

"Three days?" It seems like a lot so soon.

"Yes. I'm feeling good. I'll come back each evening. I don't want you to feel responsible for checking on things."

"That's ridiculous. Stay in London. You can't get up the stairs in the London house, but your couch there is a huge upgrade from this one."

"I might." He doesn't like the idea of accepting my help. "I've got to stop and bring something to Mira on the way back."

"Is she alright? Does she know about the treatment changg - the chemo?"

"She does. She's concerned, but not eager to get involved."

Her lack of involvement frustrates me for his sake. I know it frustrates him, too. "I hate it - how you've let her abandon both of you."

"She's still working through some things. I don't think she's really processed what happened." He's everything a patient big brother should be, but that doesn't make it less annoying. "I've been holding on to a dress for her. She doesn't have a place for it - asked me to keep it." My focus jumps to attention as he goes on. "It's enough that I'm her father's caretaker. I don't need to be her storage locker." He smiles, proud of his new boundary and changes the TV channel.

* * *

It's too cold to go to bed with wet hair. I finish blow drying the mountain of dark red and wonder if it's time for a cut. It's gotten far longer than I usually like to keep it.

He wasn't keeping the dress for his own reasons. It didn't sound like he was attached to it at all.

I'm annoyed at the assumptions I make. I did the same when I first visited his London place and spiraled in the bathroom because I thought he was hiding a wife. I wasn't wrong on that one, I guess. It doesn't change the fact that I should start asking more questions instead of searching for what could go wrong. That's not my job description anymore.

After slipping on the flannel pajamas Paige included when she shipped my coat, I skip back down the L-shaped staircase and tend to the small wood-burning stove to the right of where Rami lays. I shift a stack of frames and a heavy marble bust out of the way.

He reaches his long arm over to where I stand, stretching it across half the room. I'm not sure what he finds *squishy* about himself. Every inch is still pure strength.

He tugs at my soft pants, and I step over to where he's sprawled longways, sitting on the edge of the sofa in front of him.

"I'm happy." He says simply.

"Because you have a personal fire-tender, Lord Hadid?" I run a hand through his hair.

"Oh!" He makes a pleased face. "I could get used to that one."

"You also insisted on *sexy marketing boss* at one point, and it didn't stick."

"That was Martha's doing. I only agreed." I miss Martha.

I kiss his forehead, and walk back toward the stairs.

I pass through the heavy wood door to my bedroom, and the hinges squeak as it closes itself back into place. I sit on the edge of the bed, realizing we've barely touched in six weeks. He's been too uncomfortable, and I've been too hesitant. I'm not sure either of those things are true tonight.

I tiptoe back toward the top of the stairs, and turn the corner to find him standing at the base with his hand on the rail. We've both been caught with our intentions on display.

"Decided to risk your winter walk tomorrow?" He shrugs. I continue "Go sit down."

"I feel fine." The sparkle in his eye makes his begging tone more irresistible. He doesn't realize I've already made up my mind.

"I told you to sit down." I demand, taking two steps down. He turns around and sits back down on the couch, still warm from where he's occupied it all evening. I walk over to face him.

The room is completely quiet apart from the crackling of the stove and the occasional car passing by the front window. The curtains are drawn shut. Headlights creep through the cracks, splashing across his eager face in brief flashes.

His long-sleeved thermal shirt is a shade of olive that he never wears. It looks perfect on him, but it'd be more perfect on the floor.

I lift his arms, and slip it over his head.

I climb over him, resting one knee on either side of his broad thighs. He winces briefly, and I hesitate before he holds me in place and orders me. "Don't you dare move."

I dive in to kiss him in a way that makes all the others we've shared since his accident feel like handshakes. This one's hungry; submissive.

Any inhibitions that crept into this house before aren't in this dim, warm room now. I'm not concerned with anything but keeping him still and taking my time.

If this is what it feels like to be a working woman now, I'll show up every day.

Twenty Four

November

OLLIE

Cornbread dressing trumps stuffing. That's a hill I'll die on, and I can't keep my mouth from watering as I think about replicating Thanksgiving dinner with the AGA stove. We're familiar with each other now, so I might get her to cooperate with a sweet potato souffle. I'll need to make a stop at the supermarket when I'm back. There's no chance the co-op will have all I need.

I flip through a pile of heavy oriental rugs, making audible gasps at the hand-woven fibers and naturally-dyed colors. I'd be balked at for dragging these back. I couldn't bring it onto the bus anyway. I take up enough space in this massive black coat.

Hunting for treasures in Cirencester, I'm relieved to be out of the house. Rami's been in London not just on the weekdays he's obligated to be. He's been spending some weekend hours there doing some youth mentorship work that Lynn convinced him to get involved with. I'm not confident he's been up-front about Hazem's situation. Rami knows better than anyone what his treatment progress and prognosis look like, so I'm certain he'd be here if he was concerned.

If I wasn't confident that Hazem was OK in Stow for the morning, I wouldn't be here spending more money I don't have on things I don't have a place for. Rami thinks I should start a business selling antique finds online - not because he wants me to be making money, but because picking is an outlet I enjoy. The problem with this hobby is that I love everything I find too much to part with it.

I've been wanting to visit Chatsworth House. Apparently the photos don't do the architecture and design much justice. I don't think I'd want to go on my own, which is odd for me. It's quite a drive from here, and probably too close to the place in the Peak District where his world fell apart years ago.

I wonder if he feels like it's back together now. There are obviously some scary things at stake, but he seems joyful in this particular England AONB. He seems fulfilled, even if he's spending hours in the car lately.

I don't know if *fulfilled* is the word I'd use for myself. I'm content - there's no question about that. Eventually, I'm going to have to consider my dwindling savings account and my ambitious, struggling boy. He's making waves at his job. He claims he's suggesting improvements to broken processes, but I'd bet it's coming off a tad abrasive. If he loses this gig, it'd help if I was there. If he couldn't contribute to rent at the Chicago place, I suppose it wouldn't be smart for me to pay for a living situation in both places.

I walk past a shelf full of textured and hand-painted planters, and calculate how much my England rent and Chicago rent would be. It'd make too much of a dent in my account to justify keeping the Chicago place, but I can't see Judah wanting to live with newlyweds Nate and Nat.

Rami hasn't been pressing the topic of me leaving. He hasn't been bringing it up at all, actually. He may be coming around to the idea of something long-distance. He's immersed in work right now, and solely focused on Hazem outside of that. He also might be growing tired of my messy habits and cluttered environment. I don't let him touch anything, and it drives him crazy.

I step out of the building into the freezing wind, and tuck my hands into my fleece-lined pockets. This short trip was a trek for me to be leaving empty-handed. I give myself a mental pat on the back for not buying something for the sake of buying something.

The idea that Rami might be perfectly happy with just Hazem and Hercules makes me glad for him, I suppose. It also makes me wonder why I'd stay if it gets too costly - or if he doesn't need the help.

We could also find we're too different. We're wildly different. He's exudes good vibes and gratitude. He does most the taking socially. I make a conscious effort to be kind, but I'm well aware of my chronic RBF and cynicism.

I've seen how being too similar also doesn't work, so I don't know what compatible would even look like.

Maybe I'm not compatible with anything.

* * *

"That one smells of vinegar." The tall brunette sniffs. "That stench!"

The couple looking at laundry detergents next to me have Scottish accents - hers thicker than his. "Then, put it down, Maisie. Christ." His voice is like low thunder. The mountain of a man is clearly annoyed.

I pick up what I need from the shelf and venture to the dairy section to grab the last item I need before heading toward the front.

I'm smart enough not to attempt a turkey in my oven, and obviously can't opt for ham. I decided that sides are the star of the show for Thanksgiving anyway, so I'll do all the prep work I can tonight for dressing, sweet potato souffle, and green bean casserole.

I fully expect Hazem to take issue with all three, but southern cuisine isn't something someone should have to give up just because they gave up on the south.

"That's brilliant! You reckon you're going to shut the inn down while ya do the updates?" The cashier at the checkout next to mine questions the couple from the laundry aisle. They must be the ones that just purchased the inn - and restaurant Niko runs.

"We think we'll do it room by room, yeah?" She glances up at her partner. She's tall, taller than me, but he's a full head above her. "Slow an' sure, if I keep my head."

The cashier hands her change, and the brunette studies it. "You counted it wrong." She holds the bills and coins out toward the lady in her hand. "You owe me ten pence."

I make cheerful conversation with my own cashier, chatting through my dinner plan and her own friends that live in the states.

When our shopping carts merge in the same direction toward the door, I step out of character and introduce myself. This town is tiny, and we're bound to cross paths soon.

"Hi! I'm Olivia - Ollie. I just wanted to welcome you. I'm a regular customer at the place you bought - the restaurant part, I mean."

"Halo. Thank ye." She doesn't seem to understand why I'd stop them.

"You did just buy the inn, right?"

"Aye. Well... he bought it." She looks toward the man. His hair is a rusty red and cropped short like his well-groomed beard. "He's the money, I'm the boss." She's amused with herself. "You're American?"

"I am. I've been here since March. Well, not here... I've been in England."

"Happy to escape the circus over there, I suppose." I vowed not to talk about US politics when I came over here, and I won't budge. "Hard to escape it. Is the deal done already? Officially the new owners?"

"Official today! The last lad left the place a total guddle." The man looks toward her with impatience. " The restaurant's good enough. The rooms upstairs need a serious do-over."

"I really enjoy the restaurant. Don't change much there, especially not the steak and ale pie - or the sticky toffee pudding!"

"The mingin' animal decorations gotta go. I've got a nice plan. This town'll learn good taste." The man's down to his last ounce of restraint as we all head into the sharp winter air. "What'd you say your name is?"

"Ollie." I hold both grocery bags firmly in each hand.

"I'm Maisie. This is Lachlan." He nods toward me politely, but at his wit's end. "See ye!" She takes off.

I've been sending up little prayers more often recently, and I have a feeling Niko could use a few.

* * *

Back at the cottage, I change clothes, unload my dairy products into the tiny refrigerator, and line the dry goods and vegetables across the counter.

Rami Hadid: *On my way. Any chance you could get bell pepper when you're at the supermarket?*

I don't know how he thinks he's going to ruin my Thanksgiving dinner with anything that has a bell pepper in it, even if he is a better cook than I am.

I reply: *Already picked it up. I saw it on your list.*

I open the package of cornbread mix, and assemble the ingredients into a gritty batter, spreading it evenly into a baking dish. It already smells divine. Once the oven brings it to life, I'm afraid none of it will make it into a pan of dressing.

After popping the baking dish into the heat and closing the door, I stroll next door to check on Hazem. I don't go through the trouble of tucking into my coat, and instead scamper the few feet to their door in my lounge clothes and slippers.

Hazem sits on the love seat watching something on the news that's surely not good for his nerves at this stage. He's weak and nauseated, but it's nothing he hasn't been through before.

"Baba?" He wakes to attention when he realizes someone's in the room. He calls Rami that, too.

"Not Rami" I walk past him to the kitchen, and put Rami's pepper on the counter. "Did you eat your lunch today?" I open the refrigerator and notice he hasn't touched it. He's had no appetite these fast few days.

"Bring my cup, Ollie." I notice it sitting in the drying rack where Rami must have washed it before he left.

"You want ceylon? Chai?" He doesn't respond. "Hazem."

"Bring... the cup."

I bring the cup over, certain that he's going to look at me like I'm an idiot. He reaches his hand out, and I pass it to him. His fingers are so slender; his olive skin translucent.

"Sit." I do what the man says, and we sit in silence for a few full minutes while the news broadcasts horrific happenings in Lebanon, detailing an official that was killed by Israeli forces.

Rami wasn't born in Lebanon and Hazem hasn't been back in decades, but I imagine what's happening in Beirut weighs heavy enough to drain the life out of him.

I'm not sure how much of that he's got to spare.

He goes on. "I'm not in need of this thing anymore." He continues to study it, running his fingers over the cracks

"Don't be morbid, Hazem." He doesn't seem to hear me, or at least doesn't feel like making a face like he normally would.

"You know why I care for it. It feels right. It endures through time." He breathes in a deep breath, and lets it out again. "The repairs... they make it stronger than it was at the start."

"Hazem."

"No. It is yours. Take it." He musters up enough strength to hand it back toward me - a tad aggressively.

I pause before grabbing hold of it, stand up, and walk back toward the kitchen. "At least let me make you a cup of tea in it. Which kind?"

I start the kettle.

"No... no, I am too warm."

It's cool in here - far colder outside. I venture back to the sitting area to take the blanket and Hercules off of his lap. Hercules protests with an aggravated meow and claws the afghan as I pull him away.

How didn't I notice how pink his cheeks are before? "Hazem, may I touch your forehead?"

He grunts. He's burning up. Fever is the one symptom we're not supposed to ignore.

As I dart toward the front door to get my phone from my place, the forgotten kettle whistles at the same moment I smell scorched corn-bread..

Twenty Five

December

RAMI

"**W**ould you rather I have a ciggy?" Mira snaps back at me as I'm organizing stacks of dishes and plastic containers crowding every shelf in the refrigerator.. I'd prefer it if she wasn't vaping on the love seat. I don't have the patience to quarrel, especially with people shuffling in and out constantly.

In the sitting room where Mira and Ollie sit in silence, lost inside their phones, bouquets of flowers overpower the cheap coffee table. Arthur and Craig were both kind enough to have their spouses, or their admins, send a nice arrangement here rather than the London place.

I tend to forget how tiny Mira is. She's still wearing the dress she wore to the mosque - a dress that must've also fit her when she was twelve. She removed her hijab, which she hasn't chosen to wear regularly in over a decade. Her jet black hair is cut to her chin. I can't tell if the dark circles under her eyes are from crying, age, or other bad habits I wouldn't want to hear about today.

She is beautiful, I'll give her that. Baba would tell her she had our mother's full lips and bump on the bridge of her nose.

I'm not sure if the two women in the sitting room are fond of each other. I reckon they both have reason not to be.. When our collective shock wears off, it'll be easier to tell if the tense energy in the air is only solemn after the prayer service this morning, or if there's some animosity there.

Mira didn't know about Ollie. There was no need to share yet, really. When the sepsis was discovered, I had to make quick work of notifying her and introducing the two. I spent the following hours next to a barely conscious Baba, quietly arranging a burial plan if things went bad.

It turns out we'd need it.

I shut the refrigerator door and return to the table in the corner.

Mira stands. "I've gotta go. You need me for anything else?" She says it like she's contributed anything since coming here, save for tossing out prescription bottles we haven't a need for. She's also consoled a devastated Hercules, which I'll give her some credit for.

"No. Thanks for staying for a bit. You sure you don't want a ride back? Niko's supposed to be coming by in a sec, but I could tell him to hold off..."

"I could drive you.' Ollie offers, surprisingly.

Mira looks toward her with unmistakable disdain. "The bus is good. Thanks." She steps into the kitchen, and I see her off with a long hug and quick kiss on the cheek.

As the door shuts behind her, Ollie gets up next and makes her way toward the kitchen where I'm still standing. She pauses, crossing her arms and leaning a hip on the edge of the counter. She's trying to read my expression.

The past several days have been a lightning storm of shock and adrenaline. My fatigue is setting in, and I'm not well-rested enough to process any part of the hurt that's bound to hit at any moment. I've been mentally prepared for this for months - years, really. It's another thing for it to have actually happened.

If I hadn't insisted on being at the office so much when I knew he was in a delicate state, maybe we could have caught it sooner. Maybe we wouldn't have needed the charity meals people brought by when he came home from treatment, likely bringing the sickness that stole him away.

Ollie steps closer to me, reluctantly, I pull her in and wrap her under my arms.

"I'm going to go back next door and take a shower - maybe do some cleaning. Do you need anything?"

I sigh, and let her go. "I'm alright. If you have another refrigerator hiding somewhere, I'll take it."

"Niko's not bringing food. He's just bringing his company."

"I'll be poor company. I've no brain cells working at this present moment."

"Promise me you'll take a nap when he's gone."

I reach out and twirl the hair falling from her low bun to the side of her face. "Promise." She wraps herself in a knee-length gray sweater, and disappears into the cold.

If Niko ever arrived, he must have found me passed out on the love seat because I don't wake up until eleven o'clock the next day.

* * *

"That shade of red - look at it! Do you know how tough it is to find a *good* red?" Ollie points to the velvet ribbon on the massive wreaths hanging outside this jaw-dropping estate.

"I can't say I do, no." I can't help but smile at her giddiness, burying one hand into my pocket and loosely holding her gloved hand in my other. Her bright energy is a welcome change from the gloom that's shadowed us back in Stow over the past few weeks.

I pull a hand out of my pocket to adjust my woolly hat over my ears, and step into the entrance of Chatsworth House.

Black and white marble floors sprawl across the echoing grand hall with tiles laid in a diamond pattern from wall to wall. A burgundy oriental carpet lines the center staircase to the second floor. Framing the staircase and catwalk above are gilded iron railings forged into ornate curves.

Intricate murals depicting Julius Caesar cover every inch of the upper half of the two-story room, and painted images of clouds and celestial beings stretch across the ceiling.

"This is called 'The Painted Hall'." Ollie looks up at me with pure wonder in her eyes.

I can't contain my own surprise. "Can you imagine? Can you imagine what it took to get up there - to paint that?"

"In the late 1600s, no less..." She's been doing some reading, I take it. "... over three hundred years old." She lets go of my hand and turns in a circle to see the full effect of the well-preserved masterpiece. "Incredible. We're supposed to find a little figure with wings on his hat. It's supposed to be Mercury, the messenger to the gods. He's in other rooms around the house, too. You're gonna help me find him."

We start making our way to the stairs, and she climbs up before me as I take off my woolly hat and gloves. I'm still taking stairs more slowly than before. The pain's there sometimes, but manageable.

I pick my phone out of my pocket, press the side button, and speak into it.

"Where can I find Mercury in Chatsworth House?"

When she realizes my cheating antics, she turns to slap my arm. "So sly! You're ruining the fun."

The voice coming through my phone answers my question with a disrespectfully loud echo, and I fumble to silence it. "I'm having loads of fun."

I glance at my email and see a message I've been waiting on for days, and slide my phone back into my pocket.

We reach the top of the steps and take a silent moment to look back down at the room over the gilded rails, taking it in from a dif-

ferent vantage point. Towering Christmas trees with glowing ornaments on the first floor reach up past the floor where we stand one
level above. Long garland is draped across the balconies with sparkling
lights.

If I'd seen a picture of this before seeing with my own eyes, I'd
swear it was AI generated. It's a perfect mix of historical character and
seasonal magic, and I think it might actually be taking Ollie's breath
away.

She's stunned by the spirit in it all, and I'm stunned by her.

She looks like she belongs here, maybe not as much as in her cottage kitchen, but the richness matches how I experience her. She's
depth and color; assertive and reverent.

Ollie's been by my side every moment since she found Baba with a
fever - well, nearly every moment. She seems to have a sense for when
I'd like space, even if I don't realize it.

Our days haven't ever felt normal, but whatever time we spend together has felt like a comfortable dance for a long time. Recent events
have kept me from focusing too hard on how long that dance will last.

I don't panic over the idea of her leaving the way I used to. Happiness is what I want for her. If happiness is closer to her child, I couldn't
begin to question that.

I do think she's happy here. I can sense it. She's transformed since
I met straight-laced Olivia Kincade in a stuffy conference room nine
months ago. Maybe this side of her, this vibrant and adventurous side,
has always existed and I'm only now getting to see it. I have a feeling
that England's awakened it in her. I do wonder if I've played a hand in
it.

If she chooses to go, I could be at peace with it. I'd be shattered,
sure, but shattered is nothing I haven't been before. Part of me is a little shattered at the moment, in fact.

For the first time since March, she has no obligation - no practical
reason to stay here. I'm healed. Baba's gone. Her career isn't a factor.

She's just... existing with me, and I'm curious when that will stop feeling like it's enough.

To add to her shrinking list of reasons to stay, her cottage is on the market. I don't see her being interested in buying property here, and certainly don't see her being interested in moving into my place next door - or in London.

"Are those tears?" She looks back at me as we walk into the music room. Her overwhelm has grown with every new room we've explored, whether it was a bedchamber, library, or drawing room. Each of them were decorated with glistening trees and branches, and scented with aromas of orange, cinnamon, and spruce.

They're all starting to run together for me, but I loop her arm through mine, and acknowledge her emotion nonetheless.

By the time we get to the dining room, there's a cascading display of a holiday feast across the table, complete with artificial turkey legs and plastic slices of cake.

We walk in a crowded parade of visitors, taking opposite sides of the wide table.

"Mm. Hungry." I jest - too loudly - and lean over to pretend to grab a shiny fake dinner roll before a guide announces to the room "Welcome! Welcome! Please refrain from touching the display." Obviously directed toward me.

Ollie peers at me with disapproval and shakes her head.

By the time we make it to the sculpture gallery, Ollie's in a state of exasperated joy, like she's just seen the end of a heartbreaking movie. I'm having a hard time making it between these carved, naked figures without cracking a priceless piece of art - or a vulgar joke.

Ollie can read the juvenile expression on my face. "It's time to get you out of here.'

* * *

Sleigh bells ring through the car speakers on the winding drive back from Chatworth House to Bakewell where we're staying the night.

"Turn it down. Please..." She giggles as my shoulders bounce to the beat of 1960s holiday classics. "These turns are nauseating."

I slow to a relaxed speed, and reach over to rub her thigh. The rolling green landscape up here is unbelievable, especially as the sun does down over the sheep-filled pastures. "So, no shepherd's pie? The plan was to get dinner, right?"

"We can..." She sits up straighter and adjusts the heat setting down. "... as long as I can lie down after. That was amazing - don't you think it was amazing? Thank you for coming. I know the timing wasn't the best."

"I think he timing was perfect. This has been good for my head." Speaking of timing... there's no better time than the present. "I've been meaning to say something... for a long time I have, actually." She looks forward out the windshield. Her expression is blank. "I want you to know that if you decide you don't want to stay, if you decide to go back to the states, it's OK." She looks toward me now, and I can't make out her thoughts. "I'm OK, I mean."

"You think I've only been here since I stopped working because I didn't think you were OK?"

"No, that's not what I think. I think Stow has started to feel like home for both of us. I just know it's... not easy being away from everything else."

She hesitates. "No. It's not." She lets out a breath that she seems to have been keeping inside for months. "So, that's it? You're telling me it's time to go?"

"No - no, not at all." I cannot leave this conversation feeling misunderstood. "I want to be perfectly clear." I pause for several seconds while I park in the narrow spot next to our rental overlooking the town.

"Yes, please be clear." She's annoyed.

I put my car in park and turn toward her. "I was planning to tell you outright before I... got hurt, then everything got messy." Now it's my turn to let out a breath. "I want you to stay here, Ollie. I don't want you to go." She looks back out the front windshield where the car is stopped, staring out over the towering bell tower. "Please... don't go... but if you want to, I'd understand."

"What if I stayed? What are we, Rami?" Her voice is raised now, which I'm not sure I've ever heard.

"You need a label for us? We can do that." I'm genuinely surprised that matters to her.

"No, that's not what I'm saying. I'm spending my days baking bread and buying piles of old treasures, and I love it. I do. My bank account's only getting smaller and my waist is only getting bigger, and... " She's got tears welling up again. She's so tired. "... and you work constantly. You come back to Stow, and it's amazing when you do, but you're going back to the office - when?"

"Tuesday."

She scoffs at me "*This* Tuesday." It's a statement, not a question.

I can think of a million things I should probably say to address the first part of her response, but I only manage to reply "I know.".

Several long seconds pass, and the car's starting to feel cool now that the engine's been shut off.

"I don't have plans to leave immediately. I mean, I have thought about it. I want to feel a little less... reckless, you know?"

"You find being here reckless? Or do you find being with me reckless?"

"I don't know. Both?" She's got tears coming down her face now. I've never seen this side of her. "I'm not planning to go yet. I'm not, but... where do you see us in the next few months if I'm still here?"

I might give her a reason to book a flight right now with what will come out of my mouth next.

"I'd love to know how you'd answer that. I'd love to hear what would need to be true for you to still be here then. I'd do it, whatever it is... but one thing's already been done."

"What the hell did you do, Hadid?"

"I put an offer in on the cottage - your cottage. It was accepted." She's floored, and I can't make out if it's in a positive way. "You've got complete freedom to decide that this place you love isn't your home. That doesn't keep me from deciding that it's mine."

"So... you're telling me you'd stay in Stow indefinitely after I leave?"

"With the exception of midweek when I'm in London, yes."

She wipes at her tears."...and you're saying that if I didn't want to leave, you'd have the power to kick me out." She laughs now, because she knows there's no chance of that.

"...or you could let me move in with you, and you'd no longer pay rent." She looks out the window and shakes her head. "What do you want, Ollie?"

Long, silent seconds pass.

"I still want to pay the utility bills..." She exhales. "... and I want shepherd's pie." She grabs the handle and steps into the frigid December air.

Twenty Six

December

OLLIE

"Vanilla cardamom or cranberry orange?" Rami assesses each boule on the counter. "I like how the scoring turned out on the vanilla cardamom. Look - it's like a wreath!" He makes a semi-impressed face. "...but the smell of the cranberry orange is just..." He bends down to smell the lop-sided loaf.

"Insane." His eyes roll into the back of his head.

"Right?! I think they'll like this one." I place it back on the wood surface and gently squeeze to see if the crust's crunch satisfies me. "Perfect", I whisper to myself.

"Let me smell!" I have my phone propped up with Paige on a video chat. I jokingly hold the bread up to the camera and she sniffs obnoxiously.

"They strike you as cranberry orange people?" Rami asks.

"They don't strike me as vanilla cardamom people."

"Really?" Sarcasm pours out of him. "Lachlan doesn't come across as a vanilla kind of guy?"

"I don't think that man has a flavor. She's got all of it. What's her name? Milly?'

"Maisie." He corrects me.

"Who are Lachlan and Maisie?" Paige questions.

"The couple that bought the inn and restaurant. So far, it seems like he left his personality in Scotland. She should have left hers."

"Maybe they are vanilla cardamon people if he's basic and she's spice. You sure sound fond enough of them to be making them bread..." Now it's her sarcasm seeping through the phone.

"I'm not un-fond of them. Is that a word? They don't know anyone here. I am going to bring them the cranberry orange, mostly because I worked hard on the wreath for the vanilla cardamon. Mabel and Billy deserve it more."

"What if Billy hates cardamom - or doesn't even know what it is? What if he hates you for damaging his globe?" Rami's trying to get under my skin for the fun of it, and I turn to scowl at him.

He walks over to grab my waist from behind and plants a kiss on my cheek. "If this is the hardest decision you have to make today, this is a fine Christmas Eve." He flips on the kettle. We've been drinking an excessive amount of tea since Hazem passed, always choosing his favorite blends without ever acknowledging it out loud.

"Last Christmas Eve we were on your couch in Chicago deciding between pad thai, green curry, and tom yum soup." I'd be lying if I said a part of my heart didn't ache to be on the couch with her again. Judah chose to spend last Christmas with his dad, and she's never booked a faster flight from Salt Lake City.

"We ordered all three." We both laugh. "Impossible decision."

"Impossible," she echos.

Rami locks eyes with mine for a split second, and I look away. I can't hide the pang of missing them from him. When the kettle whistles, he pours hot water into our cups and starts to open the sugar container for mine. I swat his hand away to do it myself.

"I'd bet Judah's keeping that couch warm for you even more now. You'll be coming back to a cozy spot - if you ever come back."

I don't know which part of her statement to address first, so I decide to go in order while Rami respectfully steps out of the kitchen. "Judah doesn't get much holiday leave. If he's there, he'll be at his desk working." The call is silent, and I divert my attention away from where I'm wrapping bread loaves and back to the phone screen. Paige says nothing. "Paige! Did he get fired? Quit? Tell me right now."

"He said he'd call you after he texted me about it! I'm just the messenger. He hated it there, Ollie."

"So, he quit? Damn it..." I tuck my two carefully-wrapped loaves into a canvas bag.

"He'll deliver food again or something. He'll figure it out. He's still a kid, Ol."

"That kid's been paying half of my Chicago rent."

"Yes, and it makes it easier for you to stay unemployed. I get it." I could smack her through the phone.

"Stop. It's not about that, and you know it. He can't keep quitting jobs just because he knows he has a safety net... and I'm perfectly capable of covering the rent myself."

She laughs "You mean you're capable now that you have a hot live-in landlord covering your England bills? I'm not trying to be a pain. I think you're exactly where you're supposed to be. I just don't want you worried about Judah. He's only quit a job once, right? This doesn't mean it's going to be a trend."

I take a deep breath. "It'd better not be." He is a pretty responsible guy... and he was so unhappy with that company.

"I take it you won't bring this up with him today. Have you talked to him?"

"He's on a ski trip with Nate and Nat. He hasn't answered."

"Oh, yeah. He said he told you not to bother coming home for Christmas because he wouldn't be there."

I pick up the phone and walk back toward the living room with my bag of baked goodness. Hercules is curled up in one of the two wing back chairs facing the television. Rami's pacing with his phone to his ear, and he's clearly not happy. "I'm going to get these scrumptious little bundles delivered before it gets dark."

"Leave some cookies out for Santa! Digestive biscuits do not qualify."

"Santa's on the phone and pissed off at the moment. I'm going to go."

I tuck my phone into my pocket just as Rami takes his own away from his ear and ends the call. He lifts his hands to the back of his head, and tilts his head upward with his eyes closed.

"Ugh! She's a disaster!"

"Mira? Is she coming tomorrow?"

"She is. That's not why she called." He lets out a brief laugh, frustrated. "It seems like she's also joined the unemployed club."

"By choice?"

"They fired her."

"Did she say why?"

"Didn't ask. I told her we'd celebrate."

"What the hell?"

"It's the longest job she's held since... for years."

"She's what? 36?"

"35."

"And how long ago was... the accident?"

"Four years... but that's not fair. It takes time. She just lost her father, too." His frustration's directed toward me now.

"Did you not just hang up the phone and say she's a disaster?"

"She is, and it's justified. Some people just need more... help... to stay on their feet."

"I know. I'm sorry." I mean it.

He still looks aggravated. He's been making a valiant effort to stay positive - to enjoy this season. I have a feeling it's for my sake. He's grieving more than he's letting on, but that's not the turmoil I see in his golden face now.

"You're giving her money, aren't you?"

He exhales, standing with his hands on his hips, and stares blankly toward the dining area. "She'd do the same for me."

My look back at him says I don't believe an ounce of that.

"Ok." I give him a small smile, but don't cross the room to kiss him goodbye like I normally would. Instead, I shrug my coat on, pick my bag back up, and take off out the creaky front door.

* * *

Stepping over the threshold of the restaurant, the warmth hits my stinging cheeks instantly. I don't bother wandering toward the bar with Niko and Elena being in Greece for a few days. The restaurant is closed, lights are off, and there doesn't seem to be any guests staying at the inn.

The garland and ribbon draped outside are perfectly timeless. When Niko's got a hearty stew on the stove and the hearths inside are blazing, this place feels like the heart of the town - maybe the heart of the Cotswolds. I can't say I feel the same warm and fuzzy way about the artificial white trees Maisie has in each corner inside sparking with hot pink and lime green ornaments.

"Hello?" I call up from the foot of the stairs. There's one dim light lit at the bottom and one at the top.

Silence.

I knock on the wall. "Hello?"

A door slams, and a deep voice booms like an explosion over the screeching female voice I recognize. What he's shouting is inaudible. He must be at the end of the hall. She's closer to the top of the stairs now, but I can't understand a word she's screaming apart from a few expletives.

"Naebody forced ye to come here, ye arsehole! Yer maw was right glad I did, though. She's taken a scunner to ye!" She turns the corner at the top of the staircase, and seems to have expected me to be at the bottom. She must not mind an audience. "Halo, Ollie. Ye got somethin' there?"

"I do." I start rummaging through my bag, not able to move especially well in my tight wool coat. This bread habit might need to take a break. I hand her the loaf. "It's cranberry and orange, if I grabbed the right one. It's really good if you toast it a little and spread on some soft honey butter."

"Ahm no a fan o' cranberries. Did ye bring honey butter?" I shake my head. She shouts back down the hall. "The American lass brought some bread!" She turns back toward me. "Sorry. He's fumin' at me. Ah bought all new mattresses for the rooms. They're nice anes! Wasn't in the budget, but it was needed, so it was. He's nae wise with money."

"Ah, I see. Good mattresses are important." I smile at her and realize I don't need to add fuel to her side of the argument. She makes her way down the stairs, and I hand her the bread. I realize in this light that her face is quite young. She can't be older than 28.

"He wouldnae be this angry if I hadnae gotten the karaoke machine, too." She points at the flyer taped to the wall. "Yer comin', eh? Hogmanay Karaoke? Hogmanay is how Scots celebrate New Year's Eve."

"Wow! I, uh… I'll be the best audience member you could hope for. I won't be doing any singing."

"Suit yerself." She takes off back up the stairs. "Am stuck between three Taylor Swift tunes. Ah'll likely end up sangin' the lot of me."

I smile at her, more amused than anything. "Suit yourself. Merry Christmas, Maisie."

"Aye - Happy Christmas!" She shouts it down the steps without turning around.

I take off back into the icy air and start on the long trek toward Mabel and Billy's.

The only thing I wish I had more than honey butter and a thicker scarf is that cranberry orange loaf back in my damn bag.

* * *

"Why are you dumping salt into the water? I need some of that for tomorrow."

I toss my empty tote bag onto the counter top and rub my hands together rigorously near the stove. That walk back was the most physically challenging thing I've done in weeks. My body is aching and numb all at once.

"You don't salt your pasta water? It's the only correct way to boil pasta." He shakes the salt container slightly to see how much he managed to save.

"I've had no problem making pasta for decades without you." I don't look him in the face, but he can hear my patience is thin.

"Easy. You ok?"

"Why are you just now starting dinner? It's after eight o'clock. We never eat this late."

"*You* never eat this late... and I had to hop on a call with the IT team."

"Work, Rami? You're serious?" I don't wait around to hear his reply. Instead, I make my way toward the front of the house and turn up the staircase. Hercules follows after me, hauling his fluffy body quickly up each step.

Near the top, my toes miss the landing and I slam my knee on the step with a loud thud.

I get back up quietly, and hope Rami didn't hear a sound.

That's going to leave a lovely bruise.

When I reach the bedroom, I hear Rami's footsteps in the stairwell and he halts in the doorway. "I'm sorry. I should have known you'd be hungry. It was stupid of me."

"Actually... I'm not even hungry." I take my hair down and turn my back. I'm too on-edge to be anywhere near him.

"Did it hurt?"

My cheeks are hot with frustrated now - definitely not embarrassment. "Yes."

"Good." He smiles to himself and walks out.

I hear him running a bath.

"Stop." I dart into the hallway bathroom. "Just... stop. I didn't ask you to do that. You never get the water hot enough."

"...and I don't know how to put enough sugar in your tea. I'm not capable of carrying your luggage. I can't pay the bloody internet bill."

"I don't need any of that from you!" This man has got to learn to give me space.

"Then I suppose you also didn't *need* me to start dinner an hour ago, did you?" I don't know how to respond to that. "I know you're a grown woman. I don't do anything for you because you *need* it, but you do need to calm the hell down and sit in this tub for at least twenty minutes." Instead of turning the water off, he turns it to the hottest setting. He storms out of the bathroom past me. "Your dinner will be on the table when you're done."

He pummels down the steps loudly, and I shout after him. "Will it be as salty as you are?"

"You bet your sweet arse it will be." He shouts up the staircase. "If you aren't out in half an hour, I'm getting in with you."

* * *

It's a miracle that I iced these cinnamon rolls without ruining this burgundy cashmere sweater. It's like wearing a cloud.

I told Rami not to gift any clothing to me. I'm too picky. I should've trusted his taste more, because the color and quality are unmatched. He can't walk by without touching my arm or my back, even if we are still annoyed at each other's presence.

"It's probably not bakery quality, but the recipe online has a ton of good reviews." Foot in mouth. Maybe "bakery" is the last word Mira wants to hear given she was just fired by one.

"They're not bad." I'll accept that as the best compliment I'll get from her.

The three of us sit quietly in the toasty sitting room, each with a massive cinnamon roll sitting on a plate in one hand, and a fork in another. I've got the tiniest tree propped in the corner by the wood burning stove, topped with a gold star. Hanging on the sparse branches are vintage mercury glass ornaments and dried citrus garland.

"Do you like Oxford? You have a good community there?"

She doesn't respond immediately. "It's alright. I've got a few good... acquaintances. My flat's decent. The last one was a dump."

"Good location? Easy to get around?"

"Easy enough. I've got a roommate. He lets me borrow his car. We've got a good situation worked out... when I'm not late on rent." Her eyes cut to Rami.

"Well... you shouldn't be worrying on that one for a while. More, anyone?" He gets up and walks back toward the kitchen.

He finished his entire roll in seconds while we're still picking at ours. He's nervous.

Mira and I sit silently and continue eating before I try to cut the awkwardness.

"It's hard." I make a pitiful attempt at relating. "I'm still paying for a place in Chicago where I don't even live. My bank account's shrinking. My son just quit his job back home." Something tells me that every part of that was the worst thing I could've possibly said.

"You know, you don't have to stick around." Her voice is low. My eyes jump up to hers. "I'd check on him. I'll be around more. I know you have... stuff back home."

I choose my next words more carefully. "I'm not here because I'm worried about him."

Rami shouts from the kitchen. "Another cuppa, Mira?"

"One more. Thanks. I'll be going soon." She calls back to him, then speaks to me again. "Then, why are you here?"

"Because it feels... right. Right now, it feels right - for me."

"If you're not sure if it'll feel right later, then it's probably best you go. He's too fragile to be toyed with."

He's the furthest thing from fragile. If she was ever around, she'd know that. "Trust me. I don't consider him a toy."

She smiles in the most unsettling way. She's gorgeous. Her features are delicate, but assertive. "Then you'd better make sure you aren't playing." She pokes the last bite of her cinnamon roll with her fork, and Hercules twirls between her feet on the floor. "... and no, I don't trust you."

"Generous splash of milk, just like you like it." Rami walks in with a mug - my sheep mug that was Hazem's - and hands it to Mira. My blood's hotter than the tea.

Mira and Rami talk through holiday memories growing up, none of which were centered around Christmas for obvious reasons. Eventually, my blood pressure regulates. I start to see Mira more as a hurt girl, sitting with her big brother, having just lost her only parent. I can't blame her for being so protective. I also can't relate to her on any of it.

When I lost touch with my parents, it was a slow detachment. I suppose I mourn them in moments - small, fleeting moments. I mourn the grandparents Judah could have had. I question if they could have played a healthy part in our lives if I'd made an effort to keep them in it. Usually, move on from that thought when I remind myself that if I had made an effort, it would never have been returned. They faded away with no contest.

When Mira makes it out the door after a "thank you" for the cinnamon rolls that sounded somewhat genuine, Rami crashes onto the couch like he'd just run a marathon.

"That was good. Right?" I walk back toward the sitting room after bringing the plates and mugs back to the kitchen.

"Good. Yeah." He replies. I walk over and curl up next to him. "Always draining with her, but this was good."

"I did a good job with this one, didn't I?" I pull the throw blanket I got for Rami off the back of the couch. It's made of soft alpaca wool and chocolate brown.

He takes it from me and opens it wide, draping it over both of it. "It's smashing. Absolutely brilliant."

"We're even, then. Perfect sweater. Perfect blanket."

"Maybe not." He makes a cringe face, apologetic. "I have another for you." He stands up and walks toward my mini tree glistening in the corner. I didn't notice a wrapped rectangle leaning against my stack of collected paintings.

"You got it for yourself, actually. I just had it framed."

He hands it to me, and I feel a speck of guilt as I carefully rip into his wrapping. I remove the paper, and turn the frame upward toward me.

It's the very first purchase I made in the antiques shop during my first trip to Stow-in-the-Wold. I've never told him that. He had it matted in a gorgeous deep green and framed in rich walnut.

I run my fingers across the glass. "I love it. It's all exactly what I would've picked." I look toward his face, noticing how the fire light dances over it. "It looks good on you."

"What does? The blanket?"

"No. Unwinding does. Peace looks good on you."

He's different. He's so different from when I first met him. His hair is messy, tousled on top of his head like it always is now. His beard is full, covering the lower part of his face in black with subtle flecks of silver.

I never expected to ever adore a pair of crows feet the way I do the fine lines reaching from the corners of his deep brown eyes. All I want is to reach up and touch them. Sometimes I can't believe that if I wanted to, I could.

He's not the same Rami Hadid that commands a conference room. He's not the man that provokes a roaring round of applause from a room full of people that should be envious of him, but instead wants to follow anywhere he'd lead.

At the same time, he's exactly that person. He's OneDer's Rami Hadid, and somehow my Rami, too. That thought doesn't just feel conflicting. It feels like a dangerous thing to decide.

He points toward the three animals in the drawing. "I liked the sheep in this one. I thought you might, too, because of the ones on Baba's cup."

"I bought this print here before I ever met your Baba - the first time I borrowed your car."

He chuckles and thinks back to that time. "I was so worried."

"Hey! I brought it back without a scratch."

"No, I was worried you'd never let your walls down. I was worried I was crazy for hoping you would." He takes a deep breath and runs his hand down my thigh. "Baba made sure I didn't give up."

I look back down toward the drawing. "Is it you, me, and Hercules?" Hercules is curled up on the old couch blanket that's been demoted to the floor in front of the hearth.

"If you say it is, then it is." He leans over and kisses my temple. "Happy Christmas."

I whisper back, "Happy Christmas".

Twenty Seven

December

OLLIE

This is too soon.

Lynn clearly had no problem picking up on whatever Rami and I are. She basically called us out on it when she called to check on Rami after he got hurt. I'm sure the rest of the office is well aware of us now. That doesn't mean that showing up as his plus one at OneDer's holiday dinner is an idea that excites me. My contract ended just eight months ago, and my patience with this company is dangerously thin.

"Why are you looking at me like that?" He's smirking at me like he just made a dirty joke in gym class. The childish glint in his eye is one I haven't seen in a while.

"I like this one. That's all." He nods down toward the black sequined mini-dress that's definitely more snug that I wanted it to be when I ordered it.

"Thanks." I can't help but blush, cracking the annoyed attitude I maintained the whole drive up here. "Where are those pants from?" They're on the snug side, too. I'm not mad about it.

He opens the door to The Victoria, the same pub we went to for drinks on his birthday in April. That feels like a lifetime ago.

"Your dreams." He winks, and guides me into the warmth of the host stand.

"The OneDer event?" He asks the young hostess.

"Just upstairs and to your right. Happy to take your coats."

We make our way up the curved staircase, and I pray just as hard not to face-plant in these heels as I do to be seated as far away from Theo as possible.

Rami enters the room first, and I realize I underestimated how odd it'd feel to be with this group on these terms.

Lynn's the first to greet me, as expected. "Olivia! So nice to see you." She leans in with a light hug and an air-kiss. "Are you well?"

"I am - yes. Please call me Ollie. How are you?"

"Ollie! Alright then." She responds with a wide smile. "I cannot complain." Her radiant warmth hasn't faded a bit since the day I met her outside OneDer's headquarters. "Rami" she turns toward him with a light hug now, despite the fact they were just together days ago.

We make our way to the long table, and a wave of relief washes over me as Rami guides us to two chairs across from Arthur and his wife, opposite from the end where Theo sits solo.

I make an effort to make eye contact with him and nod. He does the same. I'm glad that's out of the way.

"How's the countryside treating you, Olivia?" Arthur asks politely when there's a break in conversation. He obviously feels more awkward in my presence than anyone else has.

"It's good. It's... far from the city. I'm grateful Rami still has a place in London to stay during the week."

Craig walks through the door now with his dapper husband on his arm. He's about a foot shorter than he is with deep brown skin and a sharp jaw. His navy sport coat's perfectly tailored. Everything about him exudes quiet class.

They make a direct line to where we sit.

"Olivia, lovely to see you." Craig puts a hand on my shoulder and shakes Rami's hand. He mumbles something into his ear, and they both snicker. "May I introduce my partner, Sam?"

"Lovely to meet you, Olivia." Sam nods at me kindly. "It's nice to see you, Rami. I hear you've made yourself more of an asset than you've ever been. Craig raves about you."

He actually seems caught off-guard for once. "Oh. He's being generous. Thank you. That's too kind."

Typically that comment would make me swoon with pride. Tonight, it only makes me wonder if he'll ever decide that his reputation can afford him spending fewer hours with these people - even if they aren't with me. No one can truly love their job enough to let it drain them the way OneDer drains him.

The rest of the evening is filled with nothing but harmless small-talk. The only stimulating conversation was when someone didn't realize I'd left Finch & Associates after I left OneDer. That admission was met with a mixture of reactions ranging from enthused to concerned.

I didn't let on that I had reacted the same way after turning in my resignation letter.

"So, what's next for you, Olivia?" Craig's counterpart, CTO Catherine Neely, leans forward and asks from the other side of Craig's husband.

I look toward Rami, unsure what kind of clarity I'm seeking in him, and look back toward Catherine. "You know, I'm really happy with this in-between season I'm in. I'm enjoying new hobbies. I'm not feeling rushed to decide what's next."

He looks back down toward his plate, and focuses intently on slicing his beef wellington. He didn't like that answer.

"That's brilliant." Catherine replies. "Just brilliant - the in-between."

* * *

Back at Rami's London home, the air is still and quiet as I shimmy out of my dress and into my button-down silk pajamas.

He's taking his time getting ready for bed, pacing back and forth between the bathroom and bedroom and quietly cursing at himself for forgetting things he needed to bring over from Stow.

As I climb under the gray covers of this big, modern bed, I realize I've never felt more like I was getting in bed with a client.

This world in London is different. He's the same in every sense. He's just as genuine everywhere he goes. He's just as kind everywhere he goes. It's the way I think of him that's different. It might be the way I think of myself that's different.

I ease my tired head back into the stack of down pillows, and look blankly at the ceiling.

In the past nine months, I was given an international assignment in England, fell for my suave client, quit my job, and I'm still here. I'm lingering like a desperate housewife, except without the deep pockets and bad lip filler.

Great question, Catherine. What is next for Olivia?

Does Olivia exist anymore? Do I want her to?

"It seemed like you felt tense toward the end of dinner." Rami stands across the room taking his watch off at his dresser, still in his crinkled, untucked shirt with his pants unbuttoned.

"Tense?" I roll over to face him, but close my eyes as we talk.

"Yes. I asked you a question on the way home and you didn't hear me at all. Distracted, perhaps?"

"What was your question?"

He doesn't reply for a few seconds, and instead walks into the bathroom where he changes in front of the long onyx vanity. "I asked you what you meant by *in-between.*"

I knew he wouldn't let it slide before it ever finished escaping my mouth at dinner. "I'm not going to be unemployed forever. I'm not going to be Stow-in-the-Wold's American bread delivery lady for the rest of my existence."

"I think you're the best American bread delivery lady they'll ever have. I also think it's good that you're not rushing into the next thing."

"I'm not. I am getting restless though. I need something. I don't know what."

He walks back toward the bathroom and comes back out in those irresistible glasses and a pair of boxer briefs. "I agree." He climbs into bed and pulls his covers up over his shoulders as he rolls toward me. "I'd like to see you have an outlet. You could try your hand at curating and selling antiques. There are plenty of shops you've never visited. I could even build you a website. It'd be proper good, I assure you. Then you could -"

"Rami, stop. You always do this." He looks toward me with confusion on his face. "You always go out of your way to..."

"To help you? To make you happy?" He slaps his palms down on the top of the blanket, and jerks his head to face me. "You are impossible sometimes."

"You're trying to make me need you - to make the idea of ever leaving England feel outrageous."

"Bloody hell, Ollie." I've set him off. "You've caught me! You've finally got it right. Every nice thing I try to do for you is just to trap you here. Heathrow's closer to you now than it's been in weeks. Maybe you can make the eleven o'clock flight before I have you cuffed to something."

We both seem to stumble mentally at the thought of that. "I don't feel trapped. I'm not saying that. I just think I've found pieces of myself I didn't know existed here... but I'm starting to wonder if I lost some of myself, too. It's like I'm your shadow."

"I don't want anything about you to fade with me. It's the opposite. You light up when you're in Stow living by your own rules - designing your own schedule. Nothing I do for you is to take your independence away. It's to feed it." He's still fuming, exaggerating every word. "I want more of your energy to go to the things you love - things that make you more yourself than you ever were in a pencil skirt. Does that not make sense to you?"

"It does, I just... it does." I turn off the nightstand lamp and roll over to face the wall away from him.

"Good. Start getting used to the thought of being taken care of." He takes off his glasses and turns his lamp off, too.

"During the four days a week you're around, you mean?" I mumble. The bed shifts. He turns his lamp back on.

"I have a career. I like my career. I feel a sense of purpose in it. It's not my fault you didn't feel that in yours."

I turn back toward him now. "Your career is your entire life."

He sits up straight. "You want me to tell you it's not? You want me to tell you that my entire life is you now, Ollie? I'd bloody love it if that were true, but it isn't. You know why it's not true? Because every day you say something that makes me think you'll pack your bags at any moment."

"I didn't say I should be your entire life. I'm saying your job shouldn't be - and my bags aren't packed."

"Should they be packed?" He has tears in his eyes now, and I know it's anger. "As long as you've got one foot out the door, I'll be making sure I'd be fine if you were gone."

"I can't fault you for that. I'd want you to be fine if I wasn't here. I'd want to be fine, too, but I don't think I would be. That's why I have this sickening fear of us becoming too attached."

"If it's sickening, does it mean we already are?"

"Probably." I chuckle lightly through tears. "I'm attached."

He smiles and shakes his head now, still frustrated. He looks back at me from where he still sits up, head in his hands. "Put some roots down with me here. Call this your home." He whispers. "I want you to want that."

I sit up with him and run my hand up his arm and around his neck until my fingers weave through the wavy black hair on the back of his head.

He grabs my forearm, and his eyes burn into mine. I pull him in, giving him whatever permission he's asking for.

In one movement, he wraps his other arm around my waist, and pulls me onto my back under him. His large hand is still wrapped around one of my forearms, pinning it above my head.

Nothing about his scrunched brow or his firm grip makes me expect anything that comes after to be gentle.

I don't want it to be.

In an instant change of energy, the storm inside us both is quieted by soft pecks across my throat. We breathe each other in as if it's the first time - or the last time.

With my free hand, I lightly scratch up from the gentle dips in the small of his back and between his shoulder blades. He growls against the side of my neck, and lifts back up to hover over me, studying my expression.

I rest my wrist above my head next to where he holds the other, and return the fire in his eyes. "Turn the lamp back off" I demand without a drop of humor.

"Not a chance" he dismisses before his fingers cling to my collar and my pajama buttons take flight.

Twenty Eight

December

OLLIE

If Lachlan had an issue with new mattresses and a karaoke machine, I'd imagine a disco ball hanging from this four hundred year old ceiling also wasn't in the plan. I might be a little annoyed at it, too, but it's lighting up Mabel's husband, Billy, singing in the corner. That's not something I could possibly complain about.

"Well done! Crackin' job!" Rami claps enthusiastically for Billy as he lays the mic back down on the wooden stool and exits the makeshift stage in a corner of the restaurant.

It's just past eleven on New Year's Eve, and I'm running on pure adrenaline and pretzels. Huddled around a cluster of small tables are Rami, myself, Niko, Lachlan, Mabel, Billy, and a few other familiar townsfolk that couldn't pass up the chance to ring in the new year with karaoke regrets.

"You'll have to leave before the bells, ye know." I've learned Lachlan's a bit more talkative when he's three whiskeys deep.

"You're closing?" Rami questions him, confused, while Niko stumbles toward the stage and I fear for what's next.

"Nae. First footing. You'll leave out the back door to take the year's bad luck with ye, then come 'round again through the front door after midnight. It's said that the first person to cross the threshold brings luck for the next year."

"Why's it have to be me?"

"It's got to be a tall dark haired man. The only other I see might not be able to walk anywhere soon enough."

We look toward Niko. "Lach!" He shouts from the corner. "Would your lady have a problem with me if I did a Taylor Swift tune?"

"Suit yerself! She's up there doin' her hair for the next one." His cheeks are rosy and his eyes are a grayish-green. I can't imagine what else would make sense with his dark red hair.

Rami's cheerfully intent on gathering more instruction. "I just walk out the back before midnight, then walk into the front door, and I'm a symbol of good luck?"

"Naw, you'll need to have something. A coin's for prosperity. Whisky's for good cheer. Coal for warmth. There's others. Look it up." He points toward his phone. "Just can't be a lady. Women are a bad omen."

We watch the train-wreck that is Niko in full-blown performance mode, singing an early 2000s country ballad. He flings his head around and waves his tattooed arms, belting the lyrics until his dark locks start to fall free. I'm certain this will be burned into my brain for many New Year's Eves to come.

Just before twelve, Rami embarks on his mission and leans toward me before getting up. "Join me- to take the old year out?"

It's freezing outside, but I'm light-headed and could use the air. I put on my coat and we leave out the back door and into the alleyway, stepping into the blustery night wind.

We walk down the alley and back around toward the front of the building. I notice he still has a drink in his hand, which I don't see him with much these days. The red in his eyes tells me he's probably a few more in that I realize.

"How did it feel to usher out the old year?"

"I don't think I could describe this past year if I tried. It was... wild."

"It was." He laughs softly. "It was wonderful..." He puts his arm around my shoulders, rubbing my arm up and down to warm me up. "... and it was difficult. I'm ready for it to be over. I'm ready for whatever's next for us."

He's well aware I'm not interested in circling this topic again.

As we get closer to the entrance of the restaurant, Niko bursts out the front door cackling and lights a cigarette. "Don't bring her in with you! Lachlan says it's bad luck. You might want to wait a bit anyway. Maisie's on now, and it's..." He makes a sour face.

"I'll wait a minute after he goes in. You've got a coin?" I question Rami. He digs his hand in a pocket while still holding his drink in his other hand.

"Don't worry, kolitós. I'll keep her warm while you bring in your luck." Niko puts his arm around me - definitely wasted. "You'd better have a coin. You've got gin in your glass, not whisky. Don't know what type of luck that would bring."

Elena walks out. Niko lets go of me and calls to her "Matia mou, what did you think?" He does a little dance like the one he did on stage. "You used to like that song!"

"It was painful." Her light blue eyes roll at her dad's drunkenness. I still wish I knew why she looks like the spitting image of him, but isn't biologically his. "Why is she here?" She nods toward where Mira steps out of a beat-up car. I'm confused about how Elena knows her.

"Pathetically late." Rami must not have picked up on Elena's question. "Nice of you to show up!" He shouts toward his sister.

The crowd inside counts down.

5, 4, 3, 2, 1.

Mira approaches the four of us as Rami leans in to ring in the new year with a gin-flavored peck. He rests his cheek against mine and whispers "there's nowhere else I'd rather be."

My teeth chatter, "not even a beach in the Caribbean?"

"Fine. If you're there, I'm there."

"Happy New Year!" Mira directs toward Rami and I, then walks straight past Niko and Elena and through the door. The realization hits that when she stepped over the threshold, she brought ill fortune in with her.

"Cold shoulder?" Elena directs the question at Niko. His gaze burns into her. "I take it she won't be sneaking past my bedroom door later. You need to call it quits tonight anyway." She takes both Niko and Rami's empty glasses out of their hands and walks inside.

"Niko, why would my sister be sneaking past your daughter's bedroom door?"

"I didn't know she was your sister!" Niko panics, throwing his hands up in the air.

"When did you meet her? When she came for Christmas? You were in Greece!"

"No, weeks before that. I don't know - a month ago? She sat at the bar."

"The day of Baba's service?! You were supposed to come over that day. She left my house, then you didn't show." His voice booms through the town square now.

"I *did* show! You were asleep on the couch. I came back to the bar, and she was sitting there. I didn't know she was your sister." Niko yells back in defense.

Rami's shouting at full volume now, raising three fingers in front of the burly Greek man. "There are three brown people in this town, Niko! You knew my father's service was that day. Are you too daft to put those things together?"

"It was one time!" Niko's sobered up plenty now. "Two times."

"Sleep with who you want to sleep with. Trust me, she always has." He scoffs. "Just don't bloody lie to me about it."

Lachlan opens the door and calls after Rami now. "Lad, what was that? You had a job to do!"

"Sorry, mate! I couldn't stop her." His voice drops low and he directs his next line back toward Niko. "She'd be bad luck either way."

"Rami." I chime in now. He didn't mean that about her. If anyone has a shred of faith in Mira, it's him.

I take hold of his arm, and he pulls it away before starting toward the cottage on his own.

* * *

"Christ, that's a lot of people." I sit cross-legged in the armchair watching a parade of people walk past my video doorbell in Chicago last night. "I think the gas money he asked for was liquor money." Rami snickers on the loveseat with his laptop, but doesn't have much else to say. "Explain to me what work could possibly need from you on New Year's Day."

"Not work," he peers at me over the top of his computer. "I'm looking at website templates... domain names."

He's relentless.

I stand up and take my empty teacup to the kitchen, and set it next to the sink. I rest my palms on the smooth wood counter top, and notice the icy branches stretched above the tiny courtyard outside.

Am I going to end this year the same way I'm starting it? Would I be happy enough if I did?

"I am sorry..." Rami startles me, leaning against the door frame leading into the warm, blue kitchen. "... for storming off last night."

I turn back toward the window, flipping the kettle on again - for the second time since noon. "Who are you worried about? Niko or Mira?"

"Both. They'd be terrible for each other. They both have baggage. I don't know what his is, but I know it's there. He's not stable."

"You don't think it occurred to her that sneaking around with him would bother you?"

"She had no way of knowing he's a friend. He's just a random bloke to her. Honestly, I wouldn't expect her to care even if she did know."

"Are you planning to say something to her?"

"No. I expect more consideration from him than I would from her."

"There's something we agree on." I pour hot water into my cup, and he watches - contemplative.

"Would you let me pour that into a travel mug? Take a walk with me."

I sigh in protest.

"Please" he pleads.

* * *

I zip on my boots while he pours my tea into an insulated cup and makes his own. We head out the door without a word, blocking Hercules from bolting outside.

Our feet scuff against the salted, icy stones below. The quiet alleyways and dark storefronts are dormant. The silence is more chilling than the air.

We walk past the towering church where I sat alone under lush green trees many months ago. It was summer, and everything was alive and vibrant. I rested on a bench facing the ethereal sight of the church doors. Mabel and Billy passed through, and I mulled over the thought of how important having a companion truly is.

The seasons have changed twice since then, and I'm still mulling over the same thought. This time, there's snow crunching under my feet and a hot cup between my mittens. The footprints next to mine belong to the man I was trying my best to keep at a distance back then. My weak attempts failed. Now, he's fighting to stay close and I'm secretly fighting the urge to pull him closer.

"Is Judah angry with you?" Rami asks.

"If he is, he's too afraid to show it. I'd bet he wants to stay on my good side as long as he needs a place to crash." I wasn't easy on him when I called him about quitting. I didn't wait for him to get home from his ski trip with Nate, and my timing wasn't great.

"Are you angry with me?"

His question surprises me. "Angry?"

"You're quiet. You have been since the night of the company dinner. What is it?"

We turn past the locked gate to the church courtyard, and back toward the town's center. "I'm tired." I'm too exhausted to be anything but honest. "I'm physically tired... and I'm tired of feeling like I have to decide between you... and my real life. It's impossible." Saying it out loud brings a cascade of relief, even though I know it cuts him like a knife.

He buries one hand deeper into his pocket, and grasps his tea with the other. "Is this place too difficult to feel like it's your real life? Am I too difficult?"

"It's all too easy." I admit. I see now that being with Rami is as easy as breathing, and I need more than that.

"Was nothing we've been through... nothing we've endured together *real* enough for you? You pulled me through the biggest project in my career, through a god-awful injury, and through losing my father. You ended almost two decades of tenure with Finch here, and I was by your side. What else could feel more *real*?"

"You're right... but we're past those things now and being here feels... indulgent sometimes."

"Reckless?" He uses the word I've used before.

"Yes."

"You don't know how to be happy." He chuckles and takes a sip of his tea. His steamy breath billows in the cold air. "You'll never stop counting reasons to leave. I'll always be outnumbered by them."

"I'm not *counting* reasons to leave."

"You aren't? First, working with me was the issue. Then, you were afraid I wasn't ready after losing Lana. After that, Baba was in treatment and I was hurt. You had a purpose here for a while after you quit working. When that went away, you were in flight mode again. Am I wrong?" He isn't accusatory. He's calm; conversational.

"I wasn't in flight mode. I'm not in flight mode."

"Judah's had some tough moments. You miss Paige. You miss having a project to focus on. They're all good reasons, Ollie. I'm not calling them excuses."

"If I didn't want to be here, I wouldn't be."

"I know." He looks down and kicks at a row of pebbles resting on top of the icy pavement. "I think you want to be here more than you realize. I also think it's getting harder for you to see a future here. Actually, I think you're trying not to see a future here."

"That makes no sense. Why would I avoid the thought of that?"

"You hate my career. You hate... being loved."

He's never used that heavy word before.

Our stroll comes to a halt near the market cross in the square. "I don't know what to say to you."

"Say nothing. I'm tired, too." He turns toward me, and tucks a lock of my stray hair behind an ear, then adjusts my woolly hat over it. "I hope you let someone in one day, Ollie. Some bloke out there deserves the privilege. You're too astonishing not to share yourself."

I lift my hand to his, and he strokes his thumb across my cheek. His are weathered pink by the cold, and a new snow flurry lands on his eyelash.

A video call rings in my pocket with the worst timing.

Rami's hand drops to his side, and we continue walking the loop back toward our street.

"Happy New Year!" Paige's energy feels horribly out of place right now.

"Happy New Year," I echo.

"Where are you?" She can see naked branches coated with ice crystals above my head. "Narnia?"

"Just a walk into town."

"You look exhausted. Hung over much?"

I smile at her. "I am entirely sober, I assure you. I didn't sleep much."

"Rang in the new year spicy style, I take it. Listen, I have news." She sounds way too wired for nine in the morning on New Year's day.

"Listening." Rami walks ahead of me. I'm not sure if he can hear her.

"I just signed a contract with a new client - the hospitality brand I've been talking to about the boutique hotels."

"What?! That's incredible!"

"Right, and they're your vibe - not mine. They've got locations in old buildings and historic homes in places like Boston, Savannah, and New Orleans. You've got a house full of European antiques over there. You could make a killing on them with these people."

"You want me to ship it all to you?"

"I want you to work with me - to help me style it. I need a partner on this one."

Rami's still walking ahead as we turn right onto Sheep Street. "Like... remotely?"

"Whatever. I mean, obviously it'd be more fun if you were in the states, but I won't push you if you're dead-set on staying there. If you're planning to come home anyway, I could bring you along on more site visits - we could spend weeks in a new city."

"Sure sounds a little pushy, Paigey."

"... and it sounds amazing."

"It does." I agree. Rami turns left down the walkway toward the front door, and fumbles around with the keys. "I'll call you later."

My nose is numb and my cup is empty. I step over cracks in the pavement and turn toward the door Rami holds open for me, into the thick heat of the sitting room.

He walks back toward the kitchen while I remove my heavy coat and hang it on my usual hook. I light the wood-burning stove under the stairs, and nestle down into the couch next to Hercules. I massage between his fluffy orange ears until he's a puddle in my lap.

Rami steps back into the sitting room and stops at the base of the stairs.

"Don't drag it out."

"Rami." The most painful mix of pity and longing hits my stomach.

"Pack what you need. I'll ship the rest."

"That's ridiculous."

"Let me do this last thing for you. I won't ask for anything again."

"You're being irrational."

"Pretending I can compete with everything pulling you away is irrational." His expression drops in surrender. "It's ok, Ollie. I'm ok."

Tears well up in my eyes so quickly that I can't catch the drops that fall from my quivering chin before they splash onto Hercules. "Ok." I wipe at my wind-chapped face. "I'll go. Tomorrow."

He turns up the stairs just before my heart shatters in my chest.

* * *

London Heathrow's pure madness, and the only place I can see to sit through swollen eyes is a corner chair in an American diner.

The smell of seared beef and mustard is awful.

I refused to let Rami drive me to the airport. I couldn't bear it. Every step I took with my suitcase to the bus and to both trains was an excruciating feat - physically and emotionally. I broke a wheel on an escalator at Paddington, and took a full three minutes to compose myself.

I snap a picture of my boarding pass and text it to Paige with the caption *"Is there a new employee orientation?"*

Everything happened so fast. I haven't told her - or anyone.

I'm here. I made the hardest decision I've had to make in years, maybe even my whole life. If I'm being honest, Rami made the decision for me. I'm not sure if it was selfish or selfless on his part. Either way, he was right for it.

I know the hurt will subside soon enough.

I try to imagine my Chicago home; my magnificent bed, my glorious coffee maker. I can't picture it without longing for scratchy sheets, perfectly steeped earl grey, and an orange cat curled up at my feet.

I can replicate those things, I guess. It's less easy to replicate a strong body cradling mine and the deep rumble of "good morning" in a silky British accent.

It'll get easier. It'll get easier. I'll play that on repeat for weeks - months, if I have to.

My phone rings.

"Hey, Nate."

"Where the hell are you? It's so loud."

"The airport. You can tell Judah I'm headed back. Is he still pissed at me?"

"Nah, not pissed. He said you weren't happy with him."

"I'm annoyed. He's got more reason to be annoyed, I guess. In about seven hours he'll be a young bachelor living with his mom again."

"You're coming back for good? He's doing fine, Ol. I was worried he wouldn't come around much after the engagement, but he stays here quite a bit."

"It's not just one thing. He probably told you I quit Finch. I'm not working over here."

"He did. He said you're a different person over there... baking and all kinds of crazy stuff. He said you have friends." He says the last part enthusiastically enough to be insulting. He isn't wrong for it.

"... and he mentioned a stupid British fling?"

"He said you're weirdly happy. He said some British-Lebanese dude there makes you happy." I bury my face in my hand as he questions me. "Why are you leaving? Did he turn out to be a loser?"

"No. He's a pretty good one, actually. It's the smart thing to do - leaving. Paige wants a partner to work with on a big new client she landed."

"I happen to know Paige thinks you should stay in London."

"I haven't been in London for months."

"Ok, the Causewalls. Whatever."

"Cotswolds. She did tell me I could do it remotely, I just..."

"You just love running away?"

"Ouch. Why did you call me?"

"I'll get to that." I can tell he's driving, probably to lunch. "I'm sorry. I didn't mean to imply that you ran... from us, or anything."

We haven't talked about *us* in years. "We both did."

The line is quiet. "You did."

"You served up the bloody papers, Nate." I let British slang slip and I feel like an idiot.

"After years - *years* of trying to wake you up. I didn't know what I was doing, but I tried. Do you not remember that?"

"No. I don't."

"You don't remember practically falling off the other side of the bed because you couldn't get far enough from me? Complaining through every date night I set up, desperate to reconnect with eighteen year-old you?"

"I'm sorry. We were kids."

"I know. I know." He exhales into the phone. "We did our best. I'm just... saying you shouldn't bail on this guy if he's worth a shot. I couldn't make you feel anything. If he can. even if it means he pisses you off, don't chicken out."

"I'm draining my bank accounts over here, Nate."

"Gah..." He laughs. "Shut up, would you? I got the house. You got the investment accounts - and there are a lot of zeros in there. You stopped working for survival over a decade ago. You could also give up that bougie city apartment. Judah wouldn't be homeless."

"I'd grow bored out of my mind if I stayed here."

"So find other work to do. It doesn't have to pull in six figures. Your career's never been who you are."

"Why are you pushing this? My boarding pass is literally in my hand."

"No one prints paper boarding passes anymore." He's ordering something at a drive-thru window now.

"Are you shaming my airport habits? Airport habits are deeply personal."

"You're right. Let's get back to talking about things that aren't deeply personal. For example, if you don't learn how to let someone care about you, you'll regret it. You aren't getting younger." He's getting under my skin in the way only he could. All of this is so jarring coming from him. "Geez, that poor guy. Jude likes him. He's probably sick and tired of chasing your ass."

"He is. He told me to leave."

"You're smarter than that."

"Why did you call me?"

"To tell you Judah has a court date. I'll go with him. My buddy thinks the charges will get reduced."

"Court date? For what?!"

"That kid... the super-speeding thing. He didn't tell you?"

"I'm going to lose my mind when I get there.."

"So don't come here."

I let out an exasperated noise. "I've got to. I'll be perfectly happy the second the wheels touch the ground."

"You've already lost your mind. Bye, Ol."

I hang up without responding, and feel sick to my stomach. I can't see the screen clearly when Paige replies - at least not without feeling dizzy. Boarding still isn't for another hour.

Across the crowded terminal, I spot Maisie's doppelganger walking away from a snack stand and rub my aching eyes before lying my head down on the cold tabletop.

After thirty more minutes of sitting in this metal diner chair, my phone goes off again. This time it's an image from Nate.

Nathan: *She deserves more than Chicago.*

He attached a photo of teenage me in our old church gymnasium, purple color streaked through my frizzy hair and braces with lime green bands. Paige smiles in french braided pigtails under my left arm, and Nate's in a torn ball cap under my right.

All I've ever wanted is connection. I wasn't born this afraid of it.

Twenty Nine

January

RAMI

My head's clear. It's like I've done this before...

I've insulated myself over the last several months enough that the sting is bearable, but sharp. It's not constant. With every cardboard box I fold and tape, a fresh pang of pain shoots through the new hole in my chest.

In a way, I'm relieved. I'm breathing deeper than I did before. The paranoia is gone, just like it was when Baba took his last breath. There's nothing to dread.

I suppose I do have the emptiness of this cottage to dread once every piece of her is packed up.

I have done this before. I'm an expert at loss now. It's a new, morbid qualification on my resume. Realizing that doesn't feel like self-pity. If anything, it's reassurance that I could get through anything if I had to.

I'm not through this. It's going to take a long while, but I am proud in a pitiful way. I'm proud of risking another chance at forever with someone. I don't regret any of it. I knew all along it could be fleeting.

I prayed so hard that it wasn't, even after she booked the flight last night. I prayed that she'd feel certain about her decision, no matter what she decided. I hated seeing her so torn. I hated imagining that she was afraid of hurting me, so I made the choice for her.

In the dining area, my packing workstation is sprawled across the same knotty table she sat at the first time she dialed into a conference call when she visited on her own. I remember the sunlight through the window behind her casting shadows across her face.

I wonder how long it'll take me to forget it.

I wrap each piece of art carefully in bubble wrap. It's fascinating - the images that spoke to her; wild animals, overgrown pastures. There's a freedom in them - a lack of restraint. I'll never know if what she felt here was the same or the opposite. I'm not sure she'll know either.

I tuck each wrapped rectangle methodically into a larger box. It's like a game. It lifts my mood in a tiny way along with the upbeat music blaring out of my phone in the corner.

I make my way to the kitchen and start on dishes. I have no idea if she'd want these. We didn't go over much of a plan. I won't dare ask her. I'd rather send something she doesn't want than vice-versa.

I'm hoping we'll be in touch regularly when the dust settles. I'm not sure if that'd be too painful now - too pointless.

I start wrapping her beloved mixing bowl, and the fresh pangs start again. My sight grows blurry, and I swipe at my eyes so that I don't drop this thing and cause some new devastation.

How can I stand in this kitchen without feeling her? How did I think I'd be able to do that when I decided to buy this place whether she stayed or not?

The next song that plays has me spiraling from nostalgia to anger.

I white-knuckle the mixing bowl before tucking it into a sturdy box, and find my sight growing cloudy again as *Midnight Train to Georgia* reaches the chorus.

We danced over these crooked bricks more than once, even when I couldn't stand straight on both legs. She held me.

I can hold myself.

I pick up coffee mugs she's collected one by one. When ceramic crashes against the floor, I curse loud enough that Hercules darts down from the counter.

I can't hold a mug, apparently.

I bend down and collect the three pieces that make up Baba's sheep cup.

Any amount of unexpected peace I feel today is because I know she must feel some relief. She'll be where her heart is, and that's all I truly want for her. I used to think it was here. It was too much for me to hope for - too much to ask for.

The final line of the chorus fills every room on the first floor.

I remember standing close to this same spot with her wrapped under my arms, wishing that one day she'd decide to relate with the lyrics - to live in my world, rather than living without me in hers.

A thought that hasn't crossed my mind before is being in her world instead. It might be too crazy an idea to entertain. If she's happy in the states, and could be happy with me, why couldn't I see myself based in OneDer's Atlanta office? Why'd we assume she'd have to be the one to turn her life inside out?

It is too crazy to think about.

Arthur and Craig would never allow it. Ollie will forget me soon enough. The funny thing is that if either of those things weren't true, I'd waste no time packing my own bags. Six months ago, the only move I wanted to make was into a VP position.

I tape a box up and climb the staircase to address my wrecked hair and face before my four o'clock call with Craig. I slept on the couch last night, and everything about the disheveled man in the mirror shows it. Craig'll know something's up.

I sit in a wooden chair in the corner of the second bedroom and dial in. I can't hide my puffy eyes, and also can't hide the confusion on my face when Catherine Neely joins Craig on screen.

"Our weekly check-in? Did I miss something?"

"You didn't." Craig replies. He looks well-rested.

Catherine's image is choppy. Her connection must be weak. "Rami, how was your holiday? Did you ring in the New Year properly?"

"In some ways, I reckon. You?"

"In bed by nine. At least I'm consistent!" She jokes.

Craig kicks off the conversation. "Right then. New year, new chapter. Catherine and I want to connect on some news. There'll be some changes in leadership. It means new opportunity - new *responsibility* for you, if you'll have it."

I clear my throat and let a few seconds pass. "Alright. I'm listening."

"I'll be retiring before the end of Q1."

There's Arthur's CMO promotion - maybe the VP role I've dreamed of. I don't know how to react.

"Mate." I muster up the excitement he deserves. "Congratulations!"

"Arthur's will follow in Q2."

"Arthur's?"

"Yes." Catherine chimes in. "Craig and I took a recommendation to the executive board. They agreed. We'd like you to move into the role of CMO."

For the first time today, my mind's blank. "Chief Marketing Officer."

"Correct. It's... unconventional - skipping over the VP level." Craig explains. "Your work warrants it. Your leadership warrants it."

Their faces suggest they expect me to be ecstatic. I should be. I take a few seconds to get my thoughts together.

"Do you need a moment?" Catherine looks more curious than concerned.

"No, I am honored. I'm grateful you'd consider me - that you'd *recommend* me." I'm having trouble organizing what I want to say in my head.

"It's well-deserved." Craig assures. "We have full faith in you."

"Would you be open to considering another option?"

They're taken aback. "Alright. What's on your mind?"

"Lynn is the best fit for CMO. She's the most well-respected leader here. She knows this brand from the inside out - protects it."

"The same can be said of you, Rami. You're ready for the next thing - you have been for years."

"I am. It's not this. I'd be thrilled to take Lynn's role as VP of Digital Innovation."

Craig is dumbfounded. "You've been offered my position as CMO of a multi-billion dollar business, and you're asking to take a VP role instead? Is this you being humble, Rami?"

"It's not. This is me asking for what I want." My thoughts are sorted now, and I'm crystal clear on what I'd need in return for committing more to OneDer. "I do have requests, if you'd hear them."

Craig throws his hands up and smiles, welcoming my thoughts. "Please."

"Yes. Please." Catherine realizes it'd be her call if I reported to her as CTO.

"Two new positions to focus on security and data protection."

"That's not out of the question. We can look at the budget." She responds.

"I'll take that. I'd also like complete control over hiring and terminations in my business area. Innovation and integrity are paramount for me. I'll build a team in service of those things."

Craig squints at me as if he knows what I'm thinking.

Catherine doesn't miss a beat. "That, I trust you with entirely."

"Thank you. If you want to help me with a head-start, you can have HR prepare a generous severance package for Theo Bryant."

She raises her eyebrows at me and hesitates a moment. "Understood. I expect Lynn won't object."

"I want OneDer to do a better job of honoring the hybrid workweek we've agreed to. My department will be in the office only Tuesday to Thursday - myself included."

"That's reasonable - and wise. We should all be doing the same."

Craig attempts to move the conversation forward. "If there's nothing else, then -"

"There is one more. It is a future consideration; however, I do want it seriously considered." They're both focusing closely on me through the screen now. "We should be thinking about expanding our satellite offices. We need a stronger presence in east Asia... in North America. Standing up an IT function in the states would make a lot of sense."

Craig smirks at me, and I ignore him as Catherine chooses her words. "It's worth exploring. I don't disagree."

"You're ready to switch gears, Rami? First of March? The announcement will go out in a few weeks." Craig questions.

"I'm ready. I appreciate this - truly."

Before I get the entire phrase out, the wall in front of me rattles as I hear the front door close with a thud..

"Thanks - thanks so much. So sorry - I've got to step away." I smash the Leave button on the video call and run downstairs faster than my knee can take it.

A pale, stunning Ollie stands just inside the threshold. She left her key behind. I might have left the door unlocked

"Did you miss your flight?" I'm trying to read her face, and all I see is exhaustion.

She's barely audible. "I need to lie down."

"I'll get your luggage." She doesn't protest, and I know she's not feeling like herself. I take the handle of her suitcase - her broken suitcase - and lift it up the curved stairs.

She strips off her sweat pants and over-sized sweater and crawls under the thick covers like she'd never left.

This morning, I stared at that subtle indention in the mattress expecting never to see her fill it again.

"Are you ill? What can I get you?" I walk over and sit on the edge of the bed in front of her out of instinct.

"Sleep. Just... I need to sleep for a bit."

I walk downstairs in a haze and sit on the couch next to a trio of three open boxes. I realize Hercules is curled up snoring - or purring inside one of them. Whatever he's doing, he's not conscious.

I'm not sure I am either.

* * *

When the sun goes down, I make my way back upstairs to put new sheets on the bed in the second room. I'm plenty used to the couch by now, but I'd like to be close if she needs something.

As quietly as I can, I step lightly into the hallway bathroom to get my shower supplies and take them to the en suite off the second bedroom.

I can't get the water scalding enough for my preference.

Every muscle in my body is a bundle of tension. The sight of her walking back through the door made me seize up all over again. I don't know if she's sick. I don't know if her flight's moved to tomorrow. I don't know if she's mixed about leaving again.

I won't watch her sit on the fence anymore. How can I tell her I need her entirely here, or not here at all?

I dry off, get dressed, and venture back downstairs. Her tote bag still sits on the floor beneath the row of hooks on the wall. I walk over to it, and pull out her folded boarding pass.

Sitting on the edge of an armchair, I use my phone and look up her flight number. It was on time and departed four hours ago.

"Booking me on the next one?" She stands at the bottom of the stairs in one of my t-shirts. "Sorry." She notices me looking at it and tugs on the hem. "All mine are packed."

Too much hangs on my next question. "Do you need to re-book?"

"I don't want to." She looks at me now, assessing.

"I don't want that either, but... we can't keep doing this. I'm done with being up in the air."

"I know. I am, too."

"You made it to the luggage counter, and decided you're still undecided?"

"No. I made it to the gate. Can I go get a glass of water? I didn't come down here to argue." She rounds the counter through the dining area and into the kitchen, weaving between the boxes I've been packing for her all day.

I walk after her "Let me. It's a right mess in here."

She leans against the counter next to the sink as I pull a tall glass from the cupboard and fill it for her. She takes it, and doesn't look me in the face while she guzzles it down. "Can we talk in the morning? I do have things to say. I'm just too..."

"Too torn?" I'm being too assertive - too eager.

Her wavy, tangled hair has grown long enough to cascade past her chest. My t-shirt reaches just to the top of her smooth thighs, and her cozy socks make me wish our dancing days weren't over. How could I tell this perfect creature to leave again?

She slams her glass to the counter, nearly shattering the second dish of the day.

"No, Rami." She exhales and closes her eyes before walking back through the sitting room toward the stairs. "I'm too pregnant."

Thirty

January

OLLIE

The winter sun darts diagonally across the crinkled bed sheets. It's got to be well past ten. My phone's been dead since I stepped off the train in Moreton-in-Marsh yesterday.

I've fallen asleep and woken back up three times since I got back, and this all still feels like a dream.

I drag my aching body out of bed, and step into the hallway bathroom. I start the bath, a little less hot than I usually like it, and pick up the glass bottle of eucalyptus-scented bubble bath at the corner.

After sitting on the edge for fifteen minutes, staring at the shiny tiles stacked to the low ceiling, I slip slowly into the soft, warm suds.

The house is silent. Rami's likely on a walk. I hope he's not trying to run yet.

I've made him angry. He doesn't want me here. I've put him through hell for months. I can't blame him for being tired of all this. He's never been anything but certain about me, and he deserves that same certainty.

I lightly run my fingertips over my lower belly under the surface of the water. I need to make an appointment, but don't know yet if that'd need to be in Chicago or here.

How does it make sense that I'm overflowing with joy - and fear? I'm not afraid of going through with this. I'm afraid of losing this. It's risky at my age. I wish I knew why I'm wired this way - to not know how much I want something unless keeping it isn't in my control.

I lie back and let my arms float to the top, starting with my hands, my elbows, and finally relaxing my shoulders enough that my whole torso rises. I bend my knees and slide my unruly hair into the steamy water.

The last time I floated like this, I was staring up at the glass ceiling of an echoing indoor pool at a gym in London. While Rami glanced through the door, I was drowning in thoughts of how I quietly, willingly gave up on Nate. I didn't know how to fight. Abandonment was easier. I didn't realize until my boarding zone was called yesterday that everything about this place has changed that. It's changed me.

I did the work to change me, too. I gave up fabricated parts of me when I gave up my career, and it left me as bare as the wood beams across the ceiling. It left me less afraid of being seen - less interested in control. Now, I just have to figure out how to keep those walls down now that they've crumbled.

If learning to trust is what I'd have to commit to, no one's more worthy of that than Rami.

I lift one hand into the steamy air, and bubbles slip between my fingers. Unfortunately for me - for all three of us, it could be too late.

* * *

In the wingback chair next to the wood burning stove in the sitting room, Hercules stands to stretch and arch his back while I tend to the fire and pick him up. I wrap myself in the blanket I gave Rami for Christmas, and reposition him into my lap. As I run a brush through my damp hair, he claws at the expensive fabric and I lightly tap at him to stop.

This space feels so empty. Stacks of boxes and objects wrapped in brown paper are scattered around every room.

He didn't waste any time moving on.

However our conversation might go when he returns - whenever he returns - I'll respect what he wants.

I can't get over how much I regret blurting out what I said last night before storming off to bed. The last thing I want to be to him is an obligation. I know what kind of man he is, but this doesn't have to rob him of the choice he has in me staying.

I hear the lock at the front door shift, and my heart drops to my empty stomach. He walks in and kicks snow off his shoes, holding two grocery bags in his right hand.

He stops, and we make eye contact for a long moment.

He pulls off his hat and rubs his head. "Scrambled or over easy?" I don't react for a moment before he starts to read my face. "Can't do eggs?"

I shake my head. "Pancakes?"

He smiles slightly. "I forgot his food anyway." He nods to Hercules. "I'll go back."

"I'll come with you. I think he's glad I'm here."

"Interesting." He tugs his hat back on. "He and I agree on something."

Something about his rigid stance keeps me from believing him.

* * *

Turning out of the aisle with pet supplies, the mountainous red-haired figure across the store is one I could recognize from a mile away. Holding a bundle of balloons makes him impossible to overlook.

Rami's got a bag of cat food tossed over his shoulder as we walk toward Lachlan. "Your lady's birthday? I'm surprised she didn't mention it a few nights ago."

"Nae, one of the kitchen staff. It's her sixty-sixth. I reckon she'll retire soon enough. Ye know anyone looking for a line cook position? I could use a baker, as well."

I look at Rami and wonder if he'll respond with the same thought I'm having. "I might know of one... I know she could start straight away." I'm stunned by his suggestion.

"Send me their details." He nods at Rami in appreciation. "Ye wouldn't happen to know of someone that could run the inn, would ye? Maisie took off."

"She took off? Why?" I refrain from mentioning I saw her. I wouldn't want to explain why I was there.

"I cut off her renovation budget - was draining money on rubbish, she was."

"I'm sorry, Lachlan." He doesn't seem particularly upset.

"Dunna fash. She goes and does this once a year or so. She won't be given the chance again."

"Isn't she the one that wanted to come here?" Rami questions.

"Aye. I reckon I'll try to leave it better than I found it - sell it in a year's time. Maybe turn a bit of a profit. I've done well on some others."

It occurs to me I've never asked what kind of business they were in before coming here. I don't even know what part of Scotland he's from.

"You'll do a fine job. You've got no shortage of support." Rami assures him, and adjusts the heavy bag of food over his shoulder. "Cheers."

* * *

After a stack of perfect sloppy lunchtime pancakes, the early afternoon feels normal enough to be unsettling.

Rami and I don't exchange many words. He insists on doing dishes, and I step into the courtyard in lounge clothes and a thick coat. I knock some of the melting snow off of a cushioned chair and onto the stone pavers below. It's cold enough out here to be stimulating, but not shocking.

He pokes his head out the door. "You really should bundle up more if you want to be out there."

"So should you." I brush the snow off the chair next to me and pat on the cushion. The invite doesn't reveal how anxious I feel. He steps back inside.

When he sits beside me bundled in his own coat, I realize I've never felt so vulnerable with him - so fragile.

He tilts his head back toward the sky the way he always does in this chair, closes his eyes, and opens his palms to the winter air.

When did this human become so deeply important to me? What exactly did he do over the past ten months to make himself so vital? I study his hands; his pursed lips. I think about the brilliant mind in his gorgeous head. The thought of carrying his child, Rami Hadid's child, is overwhelming to say the least.

"You aren't happy." I state. His face shifts quickly in my direction.

"Ollie, seriously? Not happy?"

"You're not."

"You're wrong." He laughs in surprise. "I am overjoyed. I'm... trying to let my head catch up."

"You're convincing yourself you want this."

"Stop. I've never wanted anything more. I just... didn't see this coming. How long have you known?'

"Yesterday. I wouldn't have kept this from you."

"I know. I'm happy you're here - truly. I'm happy for me. I'm sad for you."

"I'm not upset about this, Rami. I want this." I'm urging him to listen now. I can't find the words.

"If you hadn't learned you were..." He chokes up now "...we were having a baby. If you hadn't found out, you'd be on the other side of the world right now. You didn't choose what you wanted. You didn't even choose me. You came back because you felt like you had to."

I get up from my chair and pull my coat tighter as the cold wind above the courtyard walls sends a shiver through me. Stepping through the toasty kitchen and into the sitting room, I step over boxes and rolls of bubble wrap on the way to my tote bag. I pick it up off the hook and return to the chill.

Back in the bright courtyard, Rami's leaned over with his head in his hands now.

I hand him a crumpled receipt. "Look at it."

He looks up and takes it from me. "I can barely read this."

"Read the location at the top - the timestamp."

"Here in town... just before you arrived yesterday."

"Right." I cross my arms and sit back down into my seat as the realization hits him. "It didn't occur to me to buy a test until I almost got sick on the bus."

"You'd already decided to come back."

I nod. "Decided. No doubt in my mind."

He meets my eyes now, challenging me. "You're here? Both feet here - and you're sure?"

"I knew at the boarding gate that I wasn't so devastated because I was going home. I was leaving home."

He reaches over and grabs my hand out of my lap now. "Why'd you have to make it that far before you knew?"

"I spent so much time being... undecided. I dragged you along while I fought the urge to open up. I'm sorry." These hormones are making emotions impossible to manage. I swipe at my eyes. "I have a list of reasons to go. You're the only reason I need to stay."

He lays his palm across my belly and holds it there. "Two reasons now, I reckon."

"Two." I chuckle. Hercules steps out the door leading into the kitchen. "Three."

We sit listening to the soft rustle of the breeze across the hedges, occasionally interrupted by the rumble of a car going by across the wall.

He breaks the silence. "I'd like your assurance on a few things. If we're going to do this, we're going to give it all we've got. I know I will." He pulls his hand back to himself and leans back in the chair, staring forward into ice-coated branches and the frosted roofs beyond. "Will you hear me out?"

"Listening."

"I have three. First, you find a new project. Do something that energizes you. Give those paintings a place on the walls, or start an online business. Work for Paige.. anything. I'll only be as involved as you want me to be."

"I can do that."

"I know." He gives me a small smile before moving to the next one. "You let me do small things for you. I won't do it all the way you like. I'll try. I don't do it because you need it. I do it because I do."

"Be patient with me on that one."

"I've got a lifetime of patience stored up for you."

"You'll need it."

"Oh, I'm aware." He laughs now, and both of us start to relax into this feeling of settling. "Are you ready for my last one?" He reaches over and rests his hand on my knee now, stroking his hand back and forth.

"Can I handle it?"

"Oh, you can. I might not be able to handle it." That childish smirk is back. "You'll wear my t-shirts more often - even when your perfect belly is round enough to hang out the bottom."

I roll my eyes, "Are you ready for mine?"

"I'm ready to get you inside where it's warm. Can we do that first?"

We move into the toasty kitchen, remove our coats, and he flips on the kettle before resting his hands on the counter behind him.

He leans and waits. "Ready."

I lean in the same pose on the one across from him. "I also have three."

"You're going easy on me?" He teases.

"You haven't heard them yet."

"Fair. Go on..."

"Please think about better boundaries with OneDer. You love it too much to ever give it up. You're incredible at what you do. I want your work to energize you, too. Don't let it drain you."

He raises his eyebrows. His expression tells me there's more to say on this topic. "You won't need to worry about that anymore."

"Good." I turn and start unwrapping my mixing bowl. He taped it up so carefully. "Read more. You told me once you used to love it. I don't see you with a book in your hand often enough."

"Audio books?" He negotiates.

"No. I'm not counting those." I stand firm, and he laughs in disagreement.

"My glasses do something for you, huh? I suspected so. That's why I wear them."

"Do you even need them?"

"That's not important. Go on... "

I shake my head at the thought of forever with this charmer. "The stew you made the first time I stayed for dinner with you and your Baba. I want it every Sunday."

He tips his head back. His bright white smile glints between under golden cheeks and dark beard, now warm from the AGA's radiating heat. "I can manage that. I'll teach you."

"No. I'm putting my foot down." I playfully pick up my slippered right foot and tap it back to the floor. "It has to be you every time."

He takes two large steps across the kitchen. He threads one arm under mine and around my waist, picking up my opposite hand into his own. We sway back and forth, dancing to the sound of nothing but a steaming kettle and one bird outside the window.

"You're a tough one. Are those your only terms, Olivia Kincade?"

"Do we have a deal?" I pause our swaying and squeeze my arms around his waist now, leaning back to look up at him. "I'm expensive."

"You're worth it." It's the third time he's said those words since I've known him, and it's meant something different each time.

He holds my face in his hands, just like he did when we were drenched with rain in a London elevator. He kisses me softly, letting it linger even after the kettle whistles.

When he pulls away, he sets two cups side by side followed by tea sachets in each. I don't protest as he pours my cup, mixes in an unreasonable amount of sugar, and hands it to me.

He returns to the sink to finish the dishes he'd started long ago, and I get to work unpacking my kitchen treasures while the tea steeps.

My phone's charged enough on the counter now that several texts and voicemail messages come through at once.

Judah: *You aren't going to believe this.*

Judah: *Just got sent a junior developer job offer from across the pond. Same company from before.*

Judah: *Wanna gift me that first class ticket now?*

I'm too astounded to relay any of this to Rami yet. I've got to process one thing at a time.

"How'd I do?" Rami questions over his shoulder as I take the first sip of tea and lay my phone back down.

"It's perfect... except for one detail. Where's Baba's mug?"

He makes an apologetic face and sighs while drying his hands. He nods toward the far corner to the right of the stove. "Finally bit the dust, I'm afraid."

I walk over and lift the three delicate, mint green pieces while Hazem's voice rings in my mind.

"*The repairs... they make it stronger than it was at the start.*"

I turn back toward Rami with sheep-covered remnants in my hands. "I've decided on my next high-stakes project. It's the most important one I've had yet."

He crosses his arms and beams at me with the same reckless love I have for him - the same I'll use to glue us together time and time again.

Epilogue

MIRA

Four years is a long time for rolling green hills and a horrifying cracking sound to riddle my nightmares. Sometimes the images flash under my eyelids when I'm not sleeping at all.

I can go days without thinking about Lana. Other days, the hum of the hospital ventilator buzzes in my ear for hours at a time. I've never asked Rami if he's haunted the same way. If he is, he doesn't let it show.

I turn 36 this month. I'm a grown woman, and old enough to learn to be happy for him. I've no reason to be so harsh on the American woman apart from her bad sweaters.

It seems she isn't going anywhere.

It's nearly half eleven, and I'm pulling the sheets back over my cold shoulder.

My recent days haven't needed to feel hurried apart from an interview I have today with a restaurant west of here. I'd be a fool not to agree to it. Rami set it up. He doesn't know I'll be missing rent again. I was told the last time would be the last time before I'm kicked out.

If I can scrape up enough someday to buy a half decent car, I could sleep and work anywhere. It could be green. I could have the tiny plush turtle Rami gave me sitting in the windshield, balking at nosy onlookers. My new niece or nephew could name it something clever.

Niece or nephew.

I'm not positive I would ever let me be an involved auntie if I were Ollie. I'd want to be one. I'd want to take a little tot to the park, or to a pond to feed ducks. I'd want to teach them to make buttercream icing or laminate dough for croissants.

I'm not sure how I got to this useless state of existence. I completed most of a culinary programme years ago, and wasn't half bad at it. I'm not sure Baba ever knew how much Rami lent me so that I could get by before I decided to quit. I couldn't imagine asking him to fund me going back to finish. He was so angry at me for un-enrolling without telling him.

I can learn to be plenty happy with bakeshop gigs until the end of my days - if I can ever find someone to work for that doesn't fuss over small mistakes.

To be fair, being late each morning for a week and ruining an industrial mixer aren't small mistakes. I'll own that.

Living on cigarettes and crisps might also fall in the category of mistakes. I can't think clearly enough to consider eating a vegetable or finding some sunlight. Maybe I'll start asking strange men for a hearty meal rather than a vodka soda for a change.

Something has to change.

If someone asked me how I was doing, which no one does, I don't know whether I'd say I'm empty or I'm exploding. The only desire I have in the world is to sleep enough to escape my mind's screaming, and work enough to pay for whatever it takes to stay numb.

The radiator is making the buzzing sound it makes just before it decides to shut off.

Freezing to death is an option. It'd be a slow way to go.

Instead, I decide to kick the dying beast back to life and continue altering Lana's wedding dress before the hour-long ride to Stow-on-the-Wold. I haven't thought much about how I'd get there.

Before stretching my arms to the headboard and my blue-polished toes to the wall, I reach out to the only lifeline I have - at least the only one with money.

I text: *Spot me a couple quid for the bus?*

I lift the tattooed arm draped across my waist, and rouse his dark head awake.

He needs to make it there before I do unless I want a scary, stunning Scotsman interrogating us both.

ABOUT THE AUTHOR - By day, L. Elyse Kinyoun is a clumsy adventurer and decent therapy-baker. Her home in the quiet suburbs of Atlanta, GA is her sanctuary, but she schemes to be transported, whether by plane or by pages. It's best with her teenage boys and anglophile husband by her side. By night - and by her snoring dog - she writes moving stories about imperfect people learning to hope in inspiring places.